Sleeping Dogs Lie

Media Mysteries
Book Three

SLEEPING DOGS LIE

Sleeping Dogs Lie

GAIL HULNICK

from Sirocco Press, an Imprint of
The WindWord Group Publishing & Media
#324, 1083 N. Collier Boulevard
Marco Island, Florida, 34145
USA

http://www.windwordgroup.com

ISBN: 978-1-947527-13-3

Cover Photograph by Gail Hulnick
Cover Design by David Stone

Printed in the United States of America

DEDICATION

For Casey

CHAPTER 1

THERE WAS NOTHING SO GOLDEN as an October morning, with the entire park to herself. Just silence, empty spaces, and solitude.

She wasn't completely alone. Carl was there, of course. The chocolate Labrador retriever walked over toward a palm tree and seemed to stop to examine something in the shrub beside it. Lillian watched while he strolled toward it, backed up a few steps, and then turned to look at her.

She didn't react, even though she could sense that he was trying to entice her to come over to his side. She had things of her own on her mind, and exploring trees wasn't a high priority.

Carl abandoned his silent call to Lillian, then put his head down to sniff. Lillian couldn't see anything unusual about the tree from this distance, but her eyesight wasn't what it once was. Carl certainly seemed intent on investigating.

She turned her head to the west, toward the shore about half a mile away, where she could see the waters of the Gulf of Mexico shimmering in the moonshine. She could hear the waves if she concentrated, and one more time, she appreciated that she didn't have to have a conversation with Carl. He expected nothing more than the opportunity to get out in the fresh air, and once he was in the park, he entertained himself, silently and energetically, giving no impression that he had any sense of time passing. He was always 'in the moment'.

Time with a good dog is just as wonderful as time by yourself, Lillian thought. *And so much better than time with another person whose company or conversation you didn't care for.*

For a few minutes, she watched her chocolate Lab dash back and forth from the base of the palm tree to the sidewalk. Then, across the lawn, she saw an ocean-gray luxury car pull slowly through the parking lot. This tiny island in southwest Florida was packed with expensive cars; you couldn't drive three blocks without seeing half a dozen Bentleys, Rolls Royces, and Jaguars. Most of them had out-of-state license plates but very few were driven all the way south from Michigan, Wisconsin or New York. Every year about this time, huge tractor-trailer trucks started to show up on the streets of this little beach town, as the winter residents had their vehicles shipped down. Some people warehoused their cars in Tampa or Fort Myers while they were up north for the summer, but some wouldn't be separated from them, even for a few months, and so they sent them back and forth, like a box of favorite clothes or books that you wanted with you, no matter where you were.

Lillian squinted to get a good look at the car, then walked slowly toward it. As it moved under the streetlight near the entrance, she could see the plate. Orange and black, New York. A Bentley. It would not be unusual to see that car here on Alamos Island, but at six a.m. it was unusual to see anything or anyone at the park. That was why Lillian did Carl's morning walk at that time every day.

"Carl!" she called in her no-nonsense voice. Something made her feel that she wanted him, his sixty pounds, and his protective nature beside her.

The dog instantly ran to her and dropped into a sit. Then, as they both stared across the park at the car, its headlights came on.

Lillian felt blinded and frozen for a moment, but it did not startle Carl. She heard him give a low growl that escalated into excited barking and before she had a chance to snap his leash back on, he was off at a run toward the Bentley.

"Carl!"

But it was no use. He'd taken over, and to his doggie mind, those bright lights were a challenge to be met.

Now what? The car swung to the right and was heading for the parking lot entrance. Was the dog going to try to catch it, run it down? Retrieve it? It was a lot bigger than a duck. Herd it somewhere? Not usual Labrador behavior. Jump up on it? Lillian could just imagine an angry Bentley owner berating her about a scratch on his paint job.

"Carl! Come!"

It was no use. He was ignoring her. She jogged along as quickly as she could, but her seventy-one-year-old legs hadn't been given much recent running practice. Carl was barking like a crazy thing; they'd probably wake up the whole neighborhood.

The big car stopped, then the headlights swung around again in Lillian's direction. Dear God, were they coming at her? Was he driving up onto the lawn, cutting across the grass toward her? Why? If he wanted to talk to her about her dog's behavior, why wouldn't he park the car and walk over to her?

It amazed Lillian that she was thinking so much, so early in the morning and in such a situation. What did it matter *why* this car was coming at her and why the driver was sending it that way? It was happening!

Carl seemed to be surprised by the direction change of the car, too, and Lillian took advantage of the moment to snap the leash onto his collar. She pulled his head toward her and re-asserted her authority.

She waved. "Hey! Stop your car! My dog is under control," she called. Maybe his window was down and the driver could hear her?

If he did, he gave no sign. The car seemed to pick up speed; it was heading straight toward them.

Lillian looked around. Where could they go? This was a wide, open area of the park; a vehicle would have no trouble chasing her, if that's what the driver wanted to do. Speed would be on the machine's side. What did she have on hers?

Surprise. And a bad attitude. She was darned if she was going to let some irresponsible, weird stranger in a public park disrupt her and Carl's morning walk.

Lillian reached down and unsnapped Carl's leash. "Get him, Carl!"

The dog didn't need any second invitation. He went back into full voice and stormed toward the car.

CHAPTER 2

LILLIAN HAD NO IDEA Carl could move that quickly. In seconds, he was dashing into the Bentley's path, then swerving to confront the driver's door. He stopped short of actually scraping his nails and paws along the door, but he seemed to be on springs, repeatedly jumping up to bark ferociously at the driver, with just a pane of glass separating their faces, before falling back down.

He was so intent on declaring his hostility that Lillian wondered whether he recognized the driver or the car. Maybe it was just that, somehow, he felt the Bentley had invaded his territory or threatened his pack.

Lillian was about thirty feet from the car when it suddenly stopped moving in their direction. The headlights were almost blinding her, but she thought she could see two figures in the front seat. The driver put it in reverse, got it back to the parking lot, and headed for the entrance to the street.

"Ma'am? Are you okay?"

Lillian heard a voice coming from behind her and turned to see an older man wearing pajamas with a robe, and carrying a flashlight.

"Yes, I'm fine," she said.

"It looked like that car was about to drive right at you," the man said.

Lillian nodded. Now that Carl had stopped barking and things had settled down, she realized she was shaking like a palm frond in a named storm. Even so, she had the presence of mind to snap Carl's leash back on his collar.

"Do you know whether he was trying to run you down?"

Maybe if she pretended she didn't have a voice, he would go away.

Lillian shook her head.

"We should find a bench and you should sit down. You don't look good."

Lillian shook her head again.

The man stuck out his hand. "My name is Arlo Serranno. My wife and I live in that house over there, right beside the park." He used the same hand to point out his home, which saved them both embarrassment if she delayed any longer in shaking his hand.

Lillian felt Carl pull toward the bush he'd been inspecting when the Bentley had arrived.

"I'm over here most days pretty early, walking my dog, Digger. Today she was a bit slow waking up, and I was just in the kitchen, making coffee. I looked out the window and saw that giant car driving up onto the grass and I couldn't figure out what was going on. I thought he was all alone in the park, then I saw you and your dog and, I don't know, something told me I should get over there and just add myself to the picture, you know? I had no idea what was going on, but if that driver of that car thought you were all by yourself there in the park, you know, I thought I should show him different.

"Being all by yourself is a bad idea, most of the time, if you ask me. Especially for older people, you know? Not that you don't look like you're barely old enough to vote, but you know, people our age, we shouldn't be all alone. Nobody should, really. Not at any age. You want to be with other people, be with family, do things together. And *do* things, am I right? Not just keep busy, but do important things, help people, make things.

"My brother is always going on and on about retirement, but I think it's a bad idea. Just hang around and watch TV, count your money to make sure it lasts long enough, sleep all the time. There's enough time for sleep and being alone after you're dead, you know what I mean?"

If Arlo had noticed that Lillian didn't want to chat with him, he would not let on.

Lillian let him ramble on while she kept an eye on Carl, who was acting absolutely frantic and crazy. He was running back and forth, as far as the leash would allow, from the bush by the palm tree to Lillian's side and away again.

Then, on a dime, he stopped, just inches away from the palm's trunk. Lillian stood very still. She'd worn capris, a short-sleeved blouse, and flip-flops for her walk on this balmy morning, but she suddenly shivered as if an icy wind had blown through.

Carl whined and as Lillian approached him, she could see what looked like a pile of something under the bush. What should she do? What was her responsibility in this situation? At the very least, maybe they should call 911, get some professional help.

But what if it was nothing more than a pile of leaves or garbage somebody had dumped? She'd look like an idiot.

Carl raised the ante, from whining to barking. He was almost hysterical, a mood she'd never seen him in. Lillian pulled her phone from her pocket and bent her head to look at the screen while she tapped in the numbers.

"Who are you phoning?" Arlo asked.

"I'm calling 911."

"Good idea."

Arlo didn't seem inclined to wait for the cavalry, though. He followed Carl to the edge of the bushes, then got down on his hands and knees.

"It looks like a pile of garden stuff," he said. "Maybe the landscaping crew was just putting it out of sight till they could come back to clean it up. They made it nice and tidy, putting that tarp on top."

Suddenly, Lillian felt the leash pulled almost out of her hands as Carl lunged toward the pile, grabbed the piece of canvas at the top of it in his teeth, and pulled.

A beautiful dog lay there, its head at an odd angle and its two back legs strapped together with what looked like a person's belt.

CHAPTER 3

FOR A LONG MOMENT, it was as if everything in the park was frozen, even in the warm Florida morning. Lillian clutched her phone tighter and spoke to the dispatcher on the emergency line. It was an instinct, and if anyone had asked her what to do in such a situation, she wouldn't have had a clue. But it felt right, and the dispatcher reassured her she'd done the right thing.

She sat down on the grass and clutched Carl in her arms. Somehow, he seemed to know it wasn't a time for expressing the puppy side of his personality. Arlo stood beside them, silent now. After about five minutes, he asked just one question: "Are the police coming?"

It was the firefighters who arrived first. They arrived without sirens, as did the police, and within minutes had spread out over the park, assessing the situation. One officer took photographs and another took notes while he asked Lillian and Arlo dozens of questions. The sun was coming up now; other dogs and dog owners had arrived at the park for their morning exercise. Most hung back when they saw the police cruisers and fire truck, but curiosity prompted a few to wander over to take a look at what was going on.

It was feeling to Lillian very much like a crowd, and she wondered how much longer she'd have to stick around. The officer seemed to have finished with his questions, but when she asked whether she could take Carl and go home, he gave a short negative shake of his head.

A dark green SUV drove into the parking lot, up onto the lawn and across the park to the trees where they stood. Doc Rosenthal, the Alamos Island veterinarian, got out and walked over. A young man whom Lillian recognized from her visits to the vet's office as Doc's assistant got out from the passenger side and joined them. He carried a small stretcher.

The police officers nodded at the vet, then Doc and his assistant moved toward the dog's body. Lillian had to turn away—she just couldn't watch this. And she couldn't answer any more of the police officer's questions. She was sure he'd touched on every point possible, except for the biggest one of all—what kind of person would kill a dog?

Later that day, Lillian couldn't remember the walk home. As the day went by, she felt as though she was in a fog. Everything just seemed too hard to do. She sat in her favorite chair, a blanket over her legs even though the temperature was 88 degrees and the air conditioner was on. Lunch was a handful of crackers, straight from the box.

She reached for her journal and started to write. It was her habit at any time of stress; it seemed to help so much to get the thoughts and feelings out of her before they had a chance to curdle.

Why does something so sad have to happen to a dog?

The entire day had exhausted Lillian, and she looked over toward her couch with its cozy light blanket covered in a pattern of starfish and seashells. She wanted a nap more than anything else right now.

But it was a better idea to have some kind of dinner, then stretch out the evening until a reasonable time to go to bed. She didn't even have the energy to take Carl out to stretch his legs, but he seemed to understand, and cooperatively headed out the back door into the yard, did his business and trotted back inside to lie down beside her chair once again.

**

One of the genuine pleasures in life, a newspaper. It was there on the step when Lillian opened her door the next morning. Yes, she understood the benefits of the internet,

———

the news outlet websites, and the way she could choose which news reports she wanted to see. But there was something about the tactile experience of holding that newsprint in her hands, every inch covered in information.

It was also a wonderful experience to sit down alone in her favorite burgundy velvet wing chair beside the bookshelf in her comfy living room, pull the newspaper up in front of her face to read, and know that she didn't have to hear another human voice for hours. Days, even.

The morning would be bright and warm, as it usually was in Florida. It was the tail end of the rainy season, however, and the skies could darken, bringing a lightning storm that could begin with almost no notice at all. But that usually happened in the late afternoon and even though it could be very dramatic (and very wet), the pop-up rarely lasted long. Lillian organized her day to get her walk in before noon and watch whatever weather show there might be from the comfort of her lanai.

The headlines were what you would expect from a small-town paper. The high school basketball team was on a winning streak; city council had listened to delegations from residents concerned about changes they thought would ruin their way of life; the annual food festival was coming up on the weekend and the farmers were rolling into town for the Farmers' Market. Restaurants were advertising lots of special meal deals and competing to see who could do the splashiest, most colorful ad to showcase their plates of shrimp stacks and crab cakes.

Lillian flipped to page A8. There it was, her weekly column. This time, she focused on saying hello to the seasonal visitors who were coming back. Most had headed home to their summer places in the north last April and were now, in late October, heading for the sunshine. It was a subject much on the minds of the locals. The streets would fill up with more cars and trucks; there would be line-ups at the restaurants. If you were in any sort of business that benefited from the annual influx of visitors to Florida, you celebrated, and if not, you complained about the crowds.

Most of the houses in Lillian's neighborhood were occupied by their owners and they rarely saw snowbirds or vacation rental visitors. Her house was the perfect match for her needs. It wasn't a structure that any architect would rush over to see, but it was okay for her, and occasionally, it gave her some joy. When she'd decided to leave Key West for some place quieter, she drove up and down the west coast of Florida, looking for the right combination of hominess and liveliness: a main street with real shops and easy access to the water. She didn't mind a few strip malls and chain stores along a nearby highway, as long as there were some alternatives that weren't sixty miles away.

Alamos Island had answered all her questions, quietly and decisively. Did it have a good bookstore? Was there a movie theater where she could see actors the way they were meant to be seen, on a screen thirty feet high? Could she shop for fruits and vegetables at an outdoor market?

The downtown wasn't nearly as glamorous as Fifth Avenue South in Naples, the next city along the coast, and the people weren't as well off, but that suited Lillian very well. In the year that she'd been here, she'd come to love the quiet, steady vibe and the slower pace.

Not that it was crowded with elderly people. Heavens, no. It was a myth that Florida was a place that only appealed to people who'd moved there to retire. One of Lillian's other requirements for a home neighborhood was that there were many generations represented, with families of every size and lifespan. Alamos Island had that, and plenty of playgrounds for the children, too. She knew if she wanted to see a four-year-old discovering the joy of swings, she only had to take a walk down the block toward the school. She didn't actually want to see or hear the four-year-olds, mind you. But she wanted to know that she could.

After about six months, she'd decided the house was too big for just one, and since she had no desire to share space with a two-legged companion, she bought a four-legged one. Carl had enchanted her from the moment she'd seen him in the animal rescue shelter, one of a litter of four brought in by a backyard beginner breeder who had no idea what they were doing and no patience for looking after the pups for eight weeks until they were ready for sale. He'd brought in the mother with the babies and they were all adopted almost immediately.

He was the perfect companion, one she could control, ignore, or lavish with attention, on her own timing. Lillian was seventy-one, after all, and she'd earned her independence. She wanted to do what she wanted when she wanted, and she didn't want to have to answer questions or justify her choices to anybody. She didn't want to take up new hobbies or keep up old ones; she actually enjoyed napping and sleeping quite a bit—almost the best, she'd say. And she didn't want to have to explain that to a roommate or a spouse.

"Come on, Carl, I'm ready to go," she told the Labrador, and he jumped up from his bed instantly. He romped over to the hook where his leash and her door keys hung, then chased his tail around a few times, in his excitement to get outside into the fresh air. He seemed to have completely forgotten the events of yesterday morning; that was one of the gifts dogs had been given, that ability to live completely in the present. Lillian was finding it much harder to put the sight of that murdered animal out of her memory.

They headed toward the beach, Lillian's favorite walk. Even though dogs weren't allowed out on the sand, she could see the cobalt blue water of the Gulf from the sidewalk and in between the passing cars, she could hear the distant roar of the surf. Soon, there would be more traffic as season got underway and more of the snowbirds arrived, but for now it had the pace that she imagined old Florida had once had, before the airports and the super-highways opened up the state.

A heavy pickup truck thundered past, its ridiculously large tires coming a bit too close to the curb for her taste. The license plate read "Wisconsin". In just a few weeks, every second one she'd see would be from Michigan, New York, New Jersey or one of the other northern states, their owners escaping the freezing temperatures and piles of snow. She didn't begrudge them their getaway to the Paradise Coast; she'd made the same choice herself, seven years ago, to Key West.

Okay, maybe she did begrudge them, a little. It's just that there were so many of them and they took up so much *space*. In just a few weeks, the grocery store would be so busy you could barely turn around and there would be lineups outside her favorite breakfast place all morning long. Lillian had come to Alamos Island for retirement, not vacation.

Lillian wanted a quieter place and a quieter lifestyle. Since the great disappointment that was Adam last year, in the midst of the commotion over the stolen Spanish heirlooms, she certainly wanted to stay as far away from men as possible. That was a decision she'd made several times in the past; the most painful had been Marv. Best to let sleeping dogs lie.

Women weren't much better. Whenever anybody called or emailed, suggesting a get-together she found some plausible way to duck the invitation. Faye had even invited her to join a book club and do a meeting every month. Lillian wasn't interested.

Unfortunately, this neighborhood had quite a few women like Faye, roaming the streets and hunting outliers to bring them in to the bridge-playing, garden club, or fund-raising fold. Lillian had taken to wearing large hats so that she could try to tuck in her chin and hide her face when one of these friendly ones saw her at a distance. It rarely worked.

She was getting tired of being forced to come up with excuses for her very normal wish to be alone. She'd tried to explain this to her grandson, Donovan, on the phone from his home in Miami one evening about a month ago.

"Have you ever seen that bumper sticker?" she said. "It reads 'The more time I spend with people, the more I like my dog.' That's what I'm about. I like my life just fine the way it is. I don't want more excitement or more friends. Carl is enough company for me."

"But Grandma," Donovan said. "You need to get out and see people. Everybody needs to see people."

"Depends on which people, kiddo," Lillian said. "The ones around here are nice but just not as nice as my books."

"There's more to life than books," Donovan said. "And retirement? What even is that? Just because you don't need to work to get money is no reason to do nothing."

Coming from anyone else, she might have been offended by that. But Donovan could do or say no wrong, in Lillian's book. "I disagree, it's exactly a good reason to do nothing but please yourself."

"But why doesn't it please you to be really active?" Donovan wasn't backing down.

"Doing what?"

"Take up a cause, ask for more work at the paper, start a business. Just anything that's not just 'busy' stuff. Don't join a club to play cards just to pass the time. Don't just go to parties. Take note of every dress-up or decorate the house occasion on the calendar. Set goals, compete. Decide you're going to meet five new people every day—"

Lillian started laughing. "I'm sorry, Donovan, but it sounds ghastly." She'd interrupted him to slow him down, but she didn't feel pressured. She knew that his motivation was kindness and that he wanted her to be happy. He just wasn't willing to accept her definition.

She reached the intersection in front of the tallest high-rise condo building on the beach and turned right toward the main street just a block away. The library was in the central part of town, right across the road from the art museum and City Hall. She was carrying books she needed to return; even though she couldn't take Carl in with her while she browsed for some new ones to read, she could get these back so that someone else could have a turn with them. Later today, or tomorrow, while he was napping in the late afternoon, she would walk over again and pick up a few new ones for the coming week.

She didn't really understand, or want to understand, why a quiet Labrador dog with very good manners wasn't allowed into the library. She thought it would improve the library to add the canine spirit to the atmosphere, although she realized that it was Carl's gentle, friendly spirit she had in mind. If there was a precedent set for her dog, would that mean that all library patrons would or should be allowed to bring in their dogs; and what about the cat owners?

They walked up to the drop box on the library wall and Lillian placed her four books in the drawer. When the books slid into the dark chute, she felt a little sad to see them go, as if they were living beings. Ah well, there would be new ones later today or tomorrow.

Lillian decided to take the long way home. With a column to file in three days and so far, no idea, she was hoping the walk would turn something up. She'd had nothing on her mind for over twenty-four hours but the dead dog they'd found in the park, but she was completely stumped at how that to turn that into any kind of column topic.

Since she'd started writing the column eight months ago, she'd rarely come up dry for an idea. She hadn't been on Alamos Island for very long, but she'd already discovered many sources of ideas. Bobby, her managing editor, didn't mind at all if she was commenting on reports or articles that had already been in the paper; in fact, he saw that as good cross-promotion and encouraged her to speak, or write her mind, when she saw something in the city or state politics stories that interested her. International news often provided an idea and if she was really scraping the corners for something, she could always search online for something quirky or weird.

She really didn't have a clear definition of what this column was all about, and that might be part of the problem she had with nailing down an idea. In previous times, when she was a teacher in Vancouver and she needed an idea or a theme for a class lesson on something, she'd found it easy to collect her thoughts and focus on a beginning, middle, and end. "Grade Four, the water cycle, the four seasons"—it was pretty clear what to say and do. "A column for, about, and by seniors" was a lot less specific.

The day was hot and humid, typical early fall weather. But Lillian didn't mind; she actually enjoyed being warm. It was one of the main reasons she'd moved to Florida. Her feet were hurting a little, just enough to remind her she'd probably walked about two miles by now. But Carl needed his exercise, so she would keep on going.

She was aware that she needed to be cautious about too much exercise for him, though. She'd read an article recently about runners who thought they would have a doggie companion for their half marathons as soon as the dog was past the puppy stage, only to find out that the dog's legs and hips just couldn't take it. They often found out after the poor animal had done some damage, through running much longer distance than their very young legs could handle, just because of the sheer eagerness and can-do spirit of the dog.

They walked along in the shade of the awnings over the sidewalk. This section of half a dozen blocks was one of the most charming of the commercial areas. It was mostly restaurants and small shops selling clothing or gifts and souvenirs or jewelry. Lillian liked the little Italian place on the corner, with half a dozen tables set out, patio-style, and covered in blue-checked tablecloths.

Carl's favorite was the pet supplies store.

A bell jingled as they walked through the door, then the store owner came out from the back to greet them.

———

"Hello, Carl!" he said, holding out the treat that was Carl's reason for preferring this store. "Hello, Carl's person!"

Lillian smiled, then selected the right bag of dog food under Carl's watchful eye.

Next stop was a coffee at the café.

Central Bark had occupied the prime piece of real estate on the Alamos Island main drag for almost thirty years. It was on the corner, right beside the pharmacy, a few doors down from one of the many medical clinics in town, and across the street from the dog park. Open daily for breakfast and lunch, from six a.m. to two p.m., and decorated in tropical shades of turquoise and coral, it made you crave a slice of key lime pie the minute you got there.

Lillian liked to sit outdoors on the patio, where Carl could get a welcome drink of water from one of the stainless-steel bowls they provided. He could be quite a sloppy drinker, especially on a hot, sunny day like today, when he liked to dive right in. Maybe both he and Lillian were still in some sort of state of shock after their discovery in the park; whatever the reason, she dropped into a chair as soon as they reached the café and Carl headed straight for one of the water bowls, set just by the side door, in the shade.

Lillian saw Tracey Simmons at a table a few feet away. She ducked her head and wished for a menu she could hide behind. A friendly conversation was the last thing she was in the mood for, right now, even with someone as easy to take as Tracey.

"Carl! Come!" Lillian groped for his leash and tried to make a swift and elegant exit.

"Hi Lillian, how are you?"

Too slow. Tracey had already glided across the patio and was standing behind one of the empty chairs at Lillian's table, smiling.

She was a 'woman of a certain age', as they say, which pretty much seemed to cover all females between forty and eighty. Someone no longer young, but not yet old.

Tracey kept her hair short and her fingernails long and polished. A Great Dane who was as lethargic as he was large usually accompanied her. Tackle, was that his name? At this moment, Lillian could see that he had raised his head to see where his owner had gone, when she left her seat by his side. He had enough energy to make sure he knew where she was, but not quite enough to actually follow her.

Lillian decided that Tracey's question should be treated literally. "Well, to tell you the truth, I'm the pits today. Actually."

Tracey frowned. "Why? What do you mean?"

Lillian waved at the server who had just passed by with two mugs of coffee and plates of muffins for the two older gentlemen at a table beside the street. "Could I get a cup of coffee when you have a minute? And a Danish?"

"Sure thing, hon. Y'all want cream and sugar with that?"

"Today I do," Lillian said.

Tracey pulled out a chair and sat down across from Lillian. She smiled at Carl, then reached into her fanny pack and brought out a doggie treat for him.

"Is it okay if I give him this? It's a bit big, it's Tackle's size, but I think Carl can manage it."

Tracey knew the name of all the regulars at the dog park. Even though Lillian hadn't chatted with her much and usually roamed off on her own in a different direction whenever she saw Tracey and Tackle approaching, Tracey had managed to initiate enough conversation once or twice to establish Carl and Lillian's names, where they lived, approximately, and their shared love for the Florida sunshine.

She held out the treat to Carl and he accepted it gratefully. Carl had fallen for Tracey long ago and Lillian enjoyed seeing it reinforced whenever they met. Even if she preferred not to spend a lot of time talking to other people, she didn't object to having her dog bond with them.

Tracey tilted her head to one side, looking at Carl. "He seems a bit off this morning. Does he seem that way to you?"

"We both are," Lillian said. Suddenly, she felt an urge to discuss the morning's events—maybe because it was Tracey and Tracey loved dogs.

"We found a dead dog in the park," Lillian said.

Tracey was shocked. "A dead dog! In our park?"

Lillian nodded. "The police were there. Nobody was willing to say much to me but they seemed to think it was suspicious."

"Suspicious? In what way?"

"Not a normal, natural death. Somebody killed him."

"But why?"

Tracey paused for a moment, while the server delivered Lillian's mug of coffee and breakfast muffin. After she walked away, Tracey pursued the question. "Who would want to kill a dog?"

Lillian sipped her coffee. "Exactly."

"Was he . . . was it . . ."

"Violent?"

Tracey nodded.

Lillian shook her head. "There was some blood on the sidewalk and the police took samples. But Doc Rosenthal thought the cause of death also could be poison."

"The vet was there?"

"He got there almost before the cops did."

"What kind of dog was it?"

"A Saluki, Doc said. I'm not familiar with that breed, but apparently, they're terrific family pets. And quick. I looked them up, and their top speed is forty-two miles an hour!"

Tracey didn't seem to take in what Lillian was saying. She still seemed to be in a daze from the news. "I just can't get over it. This is a quiet, safe place, you know? You know it, I know it. Bad things don't happen here."

Lillian made a face. "Sometimes, they do. Obviously."

Tracey gazed off into the distance. "It was this kind of thing, random crime, random violence, that made me leave Detroit. I wanted to live in a place where I could feel safe all the time, never give it a second thought." She shook her head. "And that's this place. This is just a weird, strange happening, once in a blue moon.

"I'll tell you one thing, though," she said as she turned her head to watch Tackle standing up. "It makes me glad that I live in the seniors' condo community over on the beach. Behind the gate."

Tracey tossed Carl one more treat, then zipped up her backpack and got ready to leave. "You really should take a look at the place with me one day, Lillian. I really think you'd like it. We have activities seven days a week, parties and special events all the time. Security. And dog people, a lot of dog people. There's a bunch of us walk together every day and weekends we're out at agility training or a dog show."

"Tackle does agility training?" Lillian raised an eyebrow.

Tracey laughed. "Tackle watches the border collies run around. And gives them his approval." She motioned to him to come and the two women both gave him their attention as he majestically moved across the patio, big enough to destroy the place yet somehow moving daintily among the tables and chairs. "I really wish you would think about it."

"Thank you, Tracey. I know you love your place and you'd like to recommend it and share it, but it's just not my cup of tea," Lillian said. "I wouldn't know what to do in a place with so many people."

CHAPTER 4

LILLIAN HALF-EXPECTED TO SEE a report about the killing in the dog park on the front page of the newspaper the next morning, but there was no mention of it. Well, she'd have something to say about that when she went in to the office for the weekly meeting today.

She didn't really know why she had to attend any of these meetings anyway. Her weekly column, on page A8, was almost entirely up to her: topic, slant, style—anything except length. Had to be eight hundred words to fill the hole, no matter what. Lillian had no problem with that; she'd started writing to meet length requirements and deadlines fifty years ago.

She knew she didn't have completely free rein to write whatever columns she wanted. While none of the other writers could tell her what to do, when Barbara Nugent, the newspaper's owner and publisher, had brought her on board last year, she made it clear who was boss. Lillian was hired because Barbara wanted a column on subjects of interest to people over sixty. Seniors were the biggest age group on Alamos Island and Barbara said she felt the paper wasn't serving them with enough material specifically geared to their lives.

Lillian had plenty to say about seniors' lives and interests. Since she started the column, she'd had no shortage of ideas, and lately people had been emailing her with suggestions.

Until this dog killing, Lillian didn't have much interest in getting involved with the assignments for the rest of the content of the newspaper. That was Bobby Murrow's headache, as managing editor. She had balked, all along, at having to attend these weekly meetings, even though Bobby had done his best to convince her of the importance of team-building.

His idea of team-building was multiple margaritas at a dark bar in a strip mall in the middle of town. She might have been up for it if he'd chosen a waterfront place with a good wine list.

Bobby had also given her a lecture once about the need to get to know her co-workers as individuals. She'd have had more curiosity about them if they'd been dogs. Or, at least, owned dogs.

The truth was that Lillian was waiting for someone else to make the first move. She'd been rejected enough times that she wasn't inclined to reach out and give someone the opportunity to take a bite out of her hand. She would wait—but, as it turned out in this office, anyway, nobody was inclined to extend in her direction, either.

She didn't consider invitations for margaritas in a dive bar a 'hey, we might be friends' move.

Lillian had made her opinion of these weekly meetings known to everyone, too, and so, when she walked in, surprise was on every face.

"Lillian." Bobby looked startled and not particularly pleased. "You're here." His parrot-covered tropical shirt was quite wrinkled and he exhibited more than the fashionable two days of stubble on his chin.

"I am," Lillian agreed. "Isn't there a meeting I'm supposed to attend?"

"There's one every Wednesday." Angela Lynch leaned against Bobby's desk, just a few feet away from his right elbow, as she had been on almost every occasion that Lillian had ever seen her.

Lillian smiled with what she hoped was a friendly, truce-calling vibe. "I haven't been able to make it to every meeting, but I'm here today," she said. "What's on the agenda?"

Carrie Sylla, the other reporter, looked up from the phone in her hand and gave Lillian a brief smile in return.

"We'll take it into our fancy boardroom." Bobby gathered up his laptop and phone, then headed toward the small, windowless room near the back wall.

Lillian sat down carefully on a black chair with a round seat and wheels that skittered away from her like live things. Bobby perched himself at the head of the table, within easy reach of a whiteboard, while Carrie and Angela took the seats on either side of him.

He passed around sheets of paper with the next week's rundown of assignments and some tentative layout ideas.

"Where's Ben?" Carrie asked.

"Out getting shots of the nests on the beach. He'll be back soon," Bobby said. "All right everybody, what's our front page this week?"

Community newspapers relied on city council and school board meetings for their lead stories a lot of the time. Lillian usually had to resist the urge to doze off during these discussions.

"I saw a police report that there was a killing in Jasmine Park," Carrie said.

That got everybody's attention, even the resistant Lillian.

"A killing!" Angela said. "Who was it?"

"Not so much a who as a what," Carrie said. "It was a dog."

"A dog! That's disgusting! Who would kill a dog!" Angela became outraged about many things, but her fire seemed stoked a little higher than usual. Lillian looked at her with new respect.

"Or kill a person," Bobby said mildly. "But what we have today is a dog murder. Not to be cold about it, but is that really front-page news? I mean, we can put something in about it but I'm not sure the front page is the place."

"I can cover it in my column," Lillian offered. "First-person account."

They all looked at her, waiting for more.

"I was at the park for an early morning walk and my dog, Carl, found him."

"Yes," Bobby said, eyes wide. "Write that." He turned to the whiteboard and put up the slug. *Dog Death.* "Angela, you do school board tonight and Carrie, I need coverage on the vacation rentals debate at council. Hey, Ben, glad you're here now. How was the beach?"

The tall young man with multiple tattoos on his forearms set his camera bag in the corner. "It's almost the end of nesting season," he said. "Not the most exciting photos you'll ever see, though."

"I know, right?" Bobby said. "But it's one of Barbara's interests, so we'll cover it."

Even though Barbara wasn't at the meeting, Bobby made sure her point of view was. The rest of the meeting revolved around a discussion of beach clean-ups and Halloween coverage. Lillian tried once more to get someone assigned to the dog killing, but the most she could squeeze out of Bobby was that he'd send Ben over to get a few shots of the park. If there was some free time.

By the end of the hour, Lillian was ready for some fresh air. She just wasn't a meetings kind of girl. She was looking forward to her chair on the back patio and a few hours with her book. But first, she had to stop off the vet's office to pick up some vitamins for Carl.

"Hi, Lois, how're things?" she asked Doc Rosenthal's receptionist.

"Busy, as usual," the woman said, as she stared at her computer.

"Better than the alternative," Doc said, as he came out from an examining room, carrying an enormous cat. "Mrs. Martinez, you have to stop feeding this cat so much."

He passed the cat back to its owner, then smiled at Lillian. "How are you, Mrs. Howe? Still shook up a bit from your discovery in the park, I'll bet."

Lillian nodded. "It wasn't the high point of my week. Thanks for asking. Is there any news about the cause of death?"

Doc waited while Mrs. Martinez left, then turned to Lillian. "He's been sent off for an autopsy. Necropsy, we call it, for animals. Looked to me like the beating wasn't the cause, and it might have been something else, but we'll see. Terrible shame, such a beautiful dog."

After leaving the vet's office with the vitamins, Lillian and Carl walked the two blocks to the pet supplies store. Carl was drooping; in fact, he'd been quite low energy. Did dogs get depressed? Ever since their discovery in the park at dawn, he hadn't been quite himself, and Lillian hoped a new toy would distract him. Carl loved toys and finding new ways to play with them. A ball or a piece of rope—he started out playing, used the toy for its intended purpose, then invented new things to do with it. A ball became something to hide and then discover. A rope was to be buried and then dug up.

It was a good thing she put flower beds lower on the pecking order than dogs. Not that Carl was tearing up her prize roses or anything. She just had a few hydrangeas and begonias in beds that he occasionally attacked. She liked to think of it as a canine method of aerating the soil, and it didn't upset her too much.

She had one plant, though, that she treasured. It was a bird-of-paradise, an amazing flower with one purple petal that looked like the upper jaw of a bird and a comb of orange petals that seemed to form the top of the bird's head. It had been growing in the garden of her little house on Royal Avenue when she moved in, and she had tended it with care every day. Carl watched her with interest while she watered it, fertilized it, and weeded the bed around it. He seemed to understand that it was special and not to be disturbed.

He was a very bright dog, in general. Lillian had had many dogs over her lifetime, and loved every one of them, but Carl was the best, so far. Of course, she always thought that about each of her dogs before they passed away.

"Can I ring that up for you, ma'am?" The young clerk behind the counter was smiling at her and she realized that she must have been standing there, looking at the squeaker balls and rubber ducks for quite some time.

"Yes, I'll take this yellow one," she said, reaching for a replacement for the toy Carl had mangled most recently.

Her phone rang. She rarely answered if she was in a store—or out doing anything interesting. But when she looked at the screen and saw Donovan's name, she answered.

Her grandson topped anything else she had going on that day.

"Donovan! What a nice surprise!"

"Hey, Grandma. How are things?"

Simple question, but it was a stopper. She needed to sit down somewhere quietly and collect her thoughts before she brought him up to speed on the events at the dog park.

"Everything's fine, Donovan, but I'm in a store right now, buying a toy for Carl. Could I call you back in fifteen or twenty minutes?"

"Absolutely, Grandma. I'll wait for your call."

Fifteen minutes later, she was on her favorite bench in the park. It was only about two hundred yards from the spot where she and Carl had found the dead dog and at first, she couldn't squelch the feeling of sadness and horror that had come over her that morning. Tears were rising and she had to make a strong effort to push them down; once again, she was overcome by the question that had assaulted her that morning: who would do something like that to a beautiful dog?

But this was her park and she would not let this drive her away. If she did, then the killer won twice.

Lillian took her phone from her purse and brought up Donovan's number.

"Hi Grandma!"

"Hi there! What are you up to today?"

"I'm just doing some repairs around the boat and I've got a particularly dirty job coming up. So, I thought I'd use you to procrastinate."

She laughed. "Well, I don't mind, go right ahead. What's new with you?"

"Not too much. Had a couple of nice clients earlier this week. One bunch wanted to go all the way to Bimini."

"How's your weather been?"

"Just glorious. Hurricane season is definitely over, I'd say, even though the calendar doesn't."

"It was a pretty quiet year."

"Yes, it was. Knock on wood."

Lillian found she was relaxing, just hearing his voice. This was a good idea. She breathed deeply and enjoyed the warmth of the sunshine on her cheeks. Gradually, the rancid aroma that had teased around the edges of the park seemed to be lifting and drifting off on the breeze.

"What's new with you, Grandma?"

"Well, I had quite an experience here at the doggie park earlier this week."

Donovan was instantly alert. "What happened? Is it Carl? Is he okay?"

"Yes, he's just fine. No, it wasn't anything about him. Well, he was there, but it didn't happen to him."

"Happen? What happened?"

Lillian took a deep breath. "We were over here for our morning walk and we found something. A dead dog."

"Oh wow, Grandma, I'm so sorry. That's horrible."

"Yes, it was," Lillian said. "We found him under a bush. Carl found him, actually. There was a tarp over him, but Carl pulled it off. And there he was."

Lillian figured that the long silences meant Donovan was struggling to decide what to say.

"What kind of dog was it?"

"I didn't stare at it for long. I didn't recognize the breed but heard later that it was a Saluki. A kind of hound."

"So, what did you do?"

"Called 911. The cops and firefighters got there right away."

"What happened to the dog? Could they tell? Was it obviously a very old dog?"

Lillian realized she hadn't given Donovan much detail. "Not old. It didn't look like a natural death. He'd been clubbed."

"*Clubbed?*"

"Hit with some kind of heavy object. There was a lot of blood."

"Oh, wow, Grandma."

Now he really was speechless.

"The police took care of things very quickly. They wrapped him up and took him away. Asked me and Arlo a few questions and then drove away. After ten minutes it was as if nothing had happened there."

"Arlo?"

"The neighbor who came out to see what was going on."

"How did Carl react?"

"I think he was pretty anxious about it all. His nose was on overdrive, I think. He was running around, sniffing everything, going back and forth from me to the bushes, even though he'd already showed everybody what was there. It was as if he was trying to do a job, you know?"

She could picture Donovan nodding his big shaggy head, then thoughtfully rubbing his beard in that way that he did.

"He was getting in the way so much that finally one police officer asked me to hold him on a tight leash until they were done," Lillian went on. "Then another one said there wasn't any reason for me to stay there any longer and that I should take Carl home."

"And this was … how long ago?"

"Two days."

"How've you been since then, Grandma? Do you want me and Hailey to come and stay with you for a while?"

"No, thank you, sweetie, but I'm fine," Lillian said. "You both have your work to do and you can't be running over here from Miami all the time."

"It's not all the time, Grandma, and you know I never feel you're too demanding," Donovan said. "I'd feel better about it if I felt like you had a lot of friends there, but I never hear you talk about anybody."

"I have just as many friends as I need," Lillian said. "And you know I like my time alone. Stop pestering me, young man!"

"Too much time," Donovan said. "Oh-oh, Hailey's giving me dirty looks across the room. She thinks I'm too direct with you too much."

"She's right," Lillian said.

"But you know Grandma, you could socialize a little more and you'd still be close to a full member of the hermit club."

"I'll think about it," Lillian said.

"The house you're renting is a long way off from other people." Donovan pressed his advantage. "Do you ever think about moving to one of those communities for people over fifty? Where they have card games and concerts and stuff?"

"You're beginning to sound like your mother," Lillian said. "And Tracey, one of my dog park friends. Don't go there, Donovan. Just sound like yourself."

"Which is how?"

She could hear the smile in his voice and returned it with her own. "Which is chill. Minding your own business."

CHAPTER 5

THE NEXT MORNING, Lillian pulled out her backpack and started to pack a portable lunch. Carl, as he always did, read her mind and her moves, jumping around the room like he'd won a lottery. Did he know they were headed to the beach? The one that allowed dogs to be there? The one that encouraged owners to let their dogs off the leash, to run and jump and meet other dogs, the way dogs were meant to do?

Lillian loved this little beach more than she did the house she was living in. Even though she spent far more time in her kitchen or on her back deck, and only managed to get to the beach once a week or so, it felt more like home. Maybe it was the joy she could see in Carl when he was there. Whatever it was, she wouldn't miss her visits to this beach for anything.

She usually drove the twenty miles to this stretch of sand on a Saturday or Sunday morning. Even though it was many years since she'd kept a Monday to Friday schedule, working for the weekend, Lillian still liked to create a sense of special time on those two days. She'd bring Carl to the doggie beach; she'd take herself to one of her favorite restaurants for lunch; then she started a new book.

She read a lot of books. She had a lot of free time in the evenings and, although she enjoyed a good movie as much as the next person, she wasn't one of those who could watch a screen for hours and hours. Books, then radio, then her laptop computer, then the TV—that was her hierarchy of entertainment.

Lillian stuffed her latest paperback into one of the backpack pockets. She had just a few dozen pages left to read in that one and then tonight, she'd start in on the next book in the stack on her shelf.

Carl's frisbee, a bag of treats, and his water dish went into the pack next. Water, sunscreen, towels, and a snack for herself and she was ready to go.

She still hadn't decided what to do about this week's column. Bobby had called twice to urge her to write her first-person account of finding the dead dog, but something was holding her back from doing that. It almost felt as though she were considering writing about a close family member—as if it were intrusive or too personal, somehow. She was angry about the dog killing, but she wasn't sure she wanted to share that with anyone.

He'd said he'd leave it up to her and she'd come up with three alternatives: an opinion piece about moving next year's Fourth of July fireworks off the beach and into a local park, to make life nicer for the nesting sea turtles; an analysis of the big picture on southwest Florida real estate prices, now that seven years had passed since the crash of '08; or a roundup of Halloween movies that seniors might like.

Yes, real estate. That was a subject that older people always loved to discuss. She had some history with it and she had one or two local contacts she could call, if she felt she needed a quote.

There was no rush to do that now. It could easily wait until she'd returned from her day at the beach with Carl.

When she pulled out of her driveway, then drove slowly past her house, along Shell Street, she appreciated the quiet and the lack of activity. Nobody was cutting grass or washing windows. She saw only one person, a man standing beside a bed of roses, drenching them with a stream of water from a hose. Carl was calm, too, settled down on his blanket on the back seat, barely even bothering to look out the window. He was saving himself for the special treat of a day at the beach that he seemed to know was coming.

The entrance to Catamaran Beach was easy to miss from the highway if you didn't know what you were looking for. Lillian pulled off onto a narrow, two-lane road that wound its way through some bush and then emerged in a parking lot right beside the Gulf of Mexico. A strip of sand half a mile wide led to the blue water and she could tell that Carl, his Labrador spirit in full flight, couldn't wait to get wet.

She parked the car and went around the back to let Carl out. Just as he'd been taught to do, he waited for her signal, then bounded out of the SUV and began following his nose around this amazing place.

Lillian's phone rang. Tracey's name was on the call display.

"Hi Tracey."

"Lillian." Tracey's voice sounded breathless.

"Where are you, Tracey? At the dog park? Is Tackle dragging you around?"

"No, I'm at home. Just listening to the radio news."

Lillian waited.

"There was an item about the dog killed at the park on Monday," Tracey said. "It was a dog named Turtle."

"Turtle," Lillian repeated.

"Yes, Turtle. A champion Saluki. Owned by Barbara Nugent."

"Barbara Nugent."

"Isn't that your boss?" Tracey asked. "At the newspaper?"

"Well, technically, I suppose she is," Lillian said. "She's the publisher. And the owner. But I've only ever met her once. When she hired me. She doesn't show up on a daily basis."

"They said on the news that the police are asking anyone who was at the park before sunrise Monday to contact them. But they already know about you, don't they?"

"Yes, they do."

"Hey! Hey you!" A woman in a polo shirt, shorts and a ball cap worn backwards was waving at Lillian. She had binoculars slung around her neck and carried a camera with a lens the size of a small planet. "Your dog!"

"Tracey, I've got to go. Some woman is yelling something about Carl," Lillian said. "Thanks for calling to tell me about this."

"I thought you'd be interested," Tracey said. "I'll let you go, but let's get together for lunch next week."

"Bye," Lillian said, shoving the phone into her shorts pocket. Where was Carl?

It took only a second to catch sight of him, frolicking in the shallow surf at the water's edge. He wasn't bothering anybody, and she couldn't see any reason this stranger would be shouting at her.

She was about to find out why.

"Your dog is disturbing the birds!"

Lillian looked around the beach, but the only birds she could see were a pair far offshore. Looked like they might be brown pelicans, but it was too far away to be sure.

She strolled over to the woman, making sure she maintained her sense of confidence and calmness. Lillian wanted to get along, out here on the dog beach, and she wanted Carl to get along.

She stopped within about ten feet, about to speak to the woman, when the stranger put her camera up to Lillian's face and took her picture.

This was a bit weird. "You're taking my photo?" Lillian asked. "Why?"

"I take photos of everything. It's my hobby."

"But I'm not your hobby," Lillian said, smiling to keep things on a friendly note. "And I didn't hear you ask my permission to take my photo."

"It's a public place," the woman replied. "I can photograph what I want."

"I don't think that's true," Lillian said. "And I'd rather you didn't take my picture. You're invading my privacy."

"You can't have privacy in a public place." The woman was arguing, but at least she'd had the grace to swing her camera out toward the horizon, focusing on the distant birds. "I'm trying to get some shots of the pelicans, anyway, and they were heading toward shore when your dog scared them off."

"You know, there are a lot of beaches up and down this coast that don't allow dogs. You'll find a lot of birds there," Lillian said, as mildly as she could.

Apparently, it wasn't mild enough. "Are you telling me where I can and can't go to a public beach?" The woman let go of her camera and it dropped, on its strap, down onto her chest. She wasn't looking at the birds or Carl anymore; she was staring straight at Lillian.

"I'm not telling you anything," she said.

Carl came running over to her, panting in joy, and lay down at her feet.

The woman glared at the Lab. "Shouldn't you have him on a leash? He's a big dog."

"He's not a big dog, and no matter what his size, he doesn't need a leash," Lillian said. "First of all, it's an off-leash park. Second, he's not bothering anybody. He's here, beside me, under control. You're the one who invaded my space."

"Invaded! Come off it," she said. "You people with your dogs, you think you own the place. Well, you don't. And neither do the dogs. Too damn many dogs in the world. People act like they're almost human, but they're not. Closer to insects than to humans. This one here"—she motioned toward Carl with her foot and for a moment, Lillian thought she intended to kick him. If she even nudged him with a toe, she'd let her have it. "This one here is just a waste of space. Like they all are. Including that pampered show dog they're making such a fuss over on the news."

She stood staring at Lillian, challenging her, but Lillian refused to rise to the bait. She said nothing and after about ten seconds, the woman stomped off down the beach.

Even though she'd been calm while the confrontation was happening, now that the woman was gone, Lillian discovered her hands were shaking. "Come on, Carl, let's go home," she said.

When Lillian got back to her house that night, her shock had dissipated and she was livid. Who did she think she was, that birdwatcher, telling her that dogs deserved no more attention or consideration than insects? That a murdered dog was not worthy of their concern? That Carl was an over-indulged waste of space?

She pulled out Carl's bag of dog food and shook it out into his bowl. "Can you believe it, Carl? Why would a person go to a dog beach if she didn't like dogs?"

Lillian paced around while Carl ate his dinner. She worked off some of her energy that way, but when he was finished, she could tell that she was still shaking inside. She had to do something to settle herself down and it didn't feel as though that something was exercise. And Carl was so tired out from his day at the beach he had just headed for his blanket in the corner and gone to sleep.

Lillian sat down in her desk chair and lifted the lid on her computer. Maybe writing something was the solution.

Almost before she knew it, words were moving from her mind to her fingertips and out onto her screen. It wasn't until the piece was completed that she knew she'd changed her mind about filing a column about Turtle's death.

It was the column she would have written the day he was killed, if she'd been spurred to it the way she was today. It was good, and she was happy with it, but now that it had blown out onto the page, she was having second thoughts about submitting it.

Would Bobby think she'd written about the dog killing because she'd heard he belonged to Barbara Nugent? Would that strike him as a good idea or a bad one?

Lillian had a feeling she might obsess over this question for hours without coming up with a clear answer. What did it matter, really, what Bobby thought? She'd written what was on her heart. She would email it to him and he could use it or not, as he chose. They could always put one more restaurant or tour boat ad in the paper if they didn't want her column.

But she knew he wouldn't do that. Readers get used to seeing the same items in the same spot in the layout, issue after issue, and if Bobby didn't like what she'd filed, he'd be on the phone to her, demanding something else.

"I'm putting the cart before the horse, as Mom used to say," Lillian said to Carl. "I'll just look it over, then send it."

Even though she knew she wasn't responsible for writing a headline, she added one anyway.

Champion Show Dog Found Dead in Local Park

by Lillian Howe

Earlier this week, on my regular morning walk in Jasmine Park, my dog and I made a terrible discovery.

It was just before dawn and the morning was glorious—that fresh, tropical sort of morning that signaled another gorgeous day in paradise. The weeks of high humidity (oh, alright, *months*) were over and season, with its happy vacationers and visitors, was just about to begin.

My dog Carl's nose is his floor-to-ceiling window on the world and he was completely absorbed in what it was showing him. My dog is normally a very relaxed chocolate Lab. You could even call him placid. But this morning, something had him racing around the park like a crazy thing.

For a few minutes I tried to keep up with him, then I gave up and just stood still, waiting for him either to calm down or make clear to me what he was up to.

He came to a stop beside a shrub near a palm tree and sat down. When I got close to him, I saw he had his eye on a pile of some sort, covered with a tarp.

I thought maybe it was a pile of mulch left there by the landscapers or maybe the remains of someone's picnic lunch, carried and dropped by crows or gulls.

Then Carl crawled over to the pile and started tugging at the tarp.

There was a dog underneath.

A beautiful dog, with blood gushing from its head and shoulders.

I've been upset about this for days. I wasn't going to write about it but an encounter today with someone on a beach showed me that not everyone loves dogs as

I do and not everyone would have the reaction, which I consider to be obvious, of expecting that the authorities will put as much effort into finding the killer as they would for a murdered person.

I understand that resources are limited and that the police have many other responsibilities that might interfere with their ability to find out who killed the dog.

But it seems to me that none of us who own pets can feel secure that our pets are safe if law enforcement doesn't move decisively and quickly on this.

This would be my position regardless of who owned the dog and whether it was a champion or a feral mutt. As humans, we can't begin to be good if we don't take care of those who depend on us.

Dogs give us many things, much love and much joy. But they have needs, too—needs that we must, and should, meet. Shelter, food, trust, respect, predictability, leadership . . . and action when they are wronged.

Just as we would do if it were a son or daughter, a grandchild, a parent— someone should investigate this dog's death and bring the killer to some sort of justice.

Not because a dog is some sort of furry human, or child-substitute, but because he is a living creature. That's reason enough.

I hope we'll soon hear that the Alamos Island police are looking into this further and have made some progress on revealing what happened that morning before dawn in the park. If they don't, we should protest and make as much noise as we can, to get action and show that we understand our responsibility to look after God's creatures.

-30-

Lillian saved the document, then typed one line into an email to Bobby.

Here you go. – L.

She pressed the 'Send' key.

CHAPTER 6

SHE WASN'T SURPRISED the next morning when Bobby was on the phone before the sun rose.

"Bobby," she said. "What on earth are you doing up at seven o'clock in the morning? Are you feeling guilty about something?"

"Ha! Hilarious, Miss Lillian," he said. "You know I've seen your column and I need to talk to you before I run it."

Or spike it, Lillian silently finished his sentence.

"Yes, of course. What's up?"

"Not over the phone. It's too complicated. What time could you come in to the office?"

"Today? Oh, I couldn't today, Bobby. I was just there yesterday."

"What difference does that make?" Bobby inhaled, and she knew he was sneaking one of the cigarettes he thought nobody knew about. "But it's not a staff meeting this time, Lillian, it's just you and me."

"What difference does that make?" Lillian snapped back. "It's not how big the meeting is that matters. It's that I had some plans for today and this is awfully short notice."

She could hear sounds in the background and she could picture Bobby out on the balcony outside his second-floor office. A high-rise residential complex was right next door.

"What plans?"

"That's snoopy, even for a newspaper editor," Lillian said. "It should be enough for you that I say I'm busy already today."

"And it should be enough for you that I've asked you to come in for a meeting. I'm afraid I'll have to insist—holy crap!"

"I beg your pardon?"

"Not you, Lillian, I wasn't talking to you. No—sorry—I have to go. Somebody just threw something from one of the upper-story apartments next door."

Lillian paced around her living room for a few minutes after Bobby hung up on her. It was a tiny living room in a small, seventy-year-old-bungalow and there were many days when she felt it was just too overcrowded, what with her furniture, her piano, and Carl's toys. Montana or Wyoming, maybe that would suit her better. But for Florida, it really was a good fit. Back in the day, this had been a house for a family of four; now, even some of the people living alone would think it too cramped. But most days, Lillian was just fine with the square footage, except on the days when she had something on her mind and needed to stretch her legs.

"Come on, Carl," she said, throwing a vintage leather bag over her shoulder. "We need to get out and walk for a while."

Lillian wasn't surprised that her walk led her right up to the door of the building where the *Tropical Times Gulf Coast* office lived, but Bobby seemed to have forgotten that he'd insisted. It wasn't that she felt she had to comply or please him, in any way, though; it was her curiosity, once again, leading her where her sensible brain might not venture.

"Miss Lillian," he said as she walked in, looking up but not getting up. "And a dog."

"Carl is one of the prior commitments I'm shifting to get to this meeting with you," Lillian said. "Carl, sit over there."

Bobby watched while the Lab got himself settled underneath a window and Lillian took over the chair across from his desk. She could see him tussle with himself, then give in.

"Alright, here we are," he said.

"Here we are, but before we get started, I want to ask you about whatever it was that was thrown from the apartment balcony," Lillian said. "What floor was it?"

"What? Oh . . . it wasn't the balcony. It was a window." Bobby looked amused. "So that's what brought you over here."

"Do the police know which window it came from?"

"How do you know the police came out?"

"Just a lucky guess."

Bobby opened his computer and read from the screen. "I made notes while they were talking. Twelfth floor, third window from the left, looks like one of the bedroom windows in the end unit. The ones facing the Gulf."

"What was it?"

"Don't know. Apparently, it came plunging down—a few people called the cop shop to report it. By the time they came over, somebody had gone out onto the lawn and picked up whatever it was."

"What did the person look like who picked it up?"

"Eight different eye witnesses and eight different descriptions."

"Typical." Lillian was losing interest. "Well, it wasn't much of a story in the end, was it? A very little bit of entertainment on a quiet Friday afternoon." She got up to leave.

"Hold on a minute, hold on." Bobby stood up, then went over to close the door to his office.

Lillian motioned to Carl to relax.

"I have to talk to you about the column you filed last night," he said. "Barbara's seen it and she has some concerns about it."

"Barbara Nugent might be the publisher and the owner of the paper but she's never taken advantage of that and interfered with editorial," Lillian said. "That I know of."

She'd meant it as a challenge to Bobby, but his reaction was mild. "That you know of."

Now that was just too much of a distraction and there was a lot of territory that might be covered if she reacted to it. Lillian decided to try to stick to today's point, and get out of Bobby's office as soon as she could.

"What are Barbara's concerns?"

Bobby sighed. "She thinks the column is too opinionated."

"Columns are supposed to be opinionated. Provocative, even."

"Yes, but Barbara feels that this particular one won't be well-received. That readers will think they're actually her words, just disguised by your byline."

Lillian raised her eyebrows and stared straight into his eyes. Her words, when they came out, were delivered in a low tone, as close to a snarl as she could manage. "I don't allow anybody to hijack my byline and I don't put forward anybody else's words as my own. Not even a publisher's."

"I know, I know, and Barbara knows, but she's concerned about perception," Bobby said. "And, with the connections, I can't say that I blame her."

"What connections?"

Bobby patted the front pocket of his shirt, as if he were looking for a pack of cigarettes. Nothing there. He picked up a pencil and fidgeted with it. "I thought you knew. Turtle was Barbara's dog."

"I did know, I do know. I don't know why that should have any effect on what we write or publish about it."

"I don't think so either, but Barbara is worried that it will look as though she's using the newspaper to push the authorities into investigating something she wants investigated."

Lillian didn't believe that Barbara Nugent worried much about anything. The few times she'd seen her, even at a distance, she'd been impressed by the woman's self-confidence and air of experience.

She sighed. "Alright, Bobby, what do you want to do? And why did you call me in here?"

"I want us to do what Barbara wants, which is to avoid using the paper as a platform for pushing the police to solve her dog's killing." Bobby stood up from his chair and went over to look out at the view. "But at the same time, I want us to investigate this dog murder."

Lillian was surprised. "You do?"

"I do."

"I thought you weren't particularly interested."

"I've given it some more thought. I do agree with you, that it's appalling that someone would do that. I also think it's the sort of thing a community newspaper should get behind. But I've got nobody to assign to it. We're short-staffed as it is."

Lillian heard the air-conditioning kick in and wondered how long Bobby was going to dance around his point.

"I want you to investigate it."

Apparently, not long.

Lillian thought it over for a few moments, then broke the silence. "I have a few questions."

"Shoot."

"Will Barbara know I'm investigating the story? Or anyone else?"

"No. Not unless you tell them. And I'd rather you didn't."

"What's your expectation for filing?"

"Nothing until you've got the solution. Then a long article, "on special assignment". Or a series."

"Will I do my usual column while I'm working on this?"

Bobby considered. "I'd like you to, if you can manage it. Keep everything looking the way it usually does, so there's no hint of what we're doing behind the scenes. What do you think?"

"I agree." Lillian glanced at Carl, maybe hoping for some kind of sign or help from the canine point of view. "Another question. Why me?"

"Like I said, we're short-staffed. If it all comes to nothing, or nothing interesting, not a good story, I can't afford to have one of my reporters tied up on it for weeks with nothing to show for it, in the end."

Not flattering but at least it was honest.

"One more reason, Lillian. I think you sincerely care about this dog, about all dogs, maybe, and I don't think an investigative reporter can do a good job if they don't care about the victim or victims or whatever crime it might be."

Lillian agreed with him. "But I'm not sure I have the writing skills or the reporting skills to pull this off."

"We'll stay in touch and I'll help you with anything you need. Even though we won't be public about anything, the paper will be behind you on this. Barbara has said she wants to know who did this to her last dog."

"Her last dog?"

Bobby laughed. "Oh, yeah, she has a new one already. A pup, a Collie pup. She had it in here the other day, gave us all a chance to make a fuss over it."

"Another purebred?"

"Of course. 'Show quality' was what she called him." Bobby's attention had wandered toward the laptop and the phone on the corner of his desk. "So, what do you say, Lillian? She may not want to use her newspaper and her status, but Barbara wants to see the creep who did this, whoever he is, exposed and made to pay. So do I."

"Can we run some form of my column this week, then?" Lillian asked. "Even if it's watered down?"

Bobby thought it over. "Okay. I can run that by Barbara and see what she says. If I get a yes on that, will you take on the reporting job?"

"I might. But look, Bobby, even though I agree somebody should find out what happened and inform the public about it, I'm not sure I can be the one to do that."

Bobby made serious eye contact. "And what if everybody said that?"

Lillian's early 60s, seventeen-year-old heart had to echo his point.

She and Carl walked home through the downtown district, but despite his hopeful glances, she didn't stop in at the pet supplies store or *Central Bark*. The sky had turned dark and even though it was three o'clock when they got home, Lillian had to turn on all the lights. The palm tree branches that had been gently swaying in the breeze just an hour ago were now almost horizontal to the ground. Usually, the sound Lillian heard most of, when she didn't have music playing, was the rumbling sound of waves reaching the shore, a distant low pulse. But now the wind had taken over. Usually, she could see a cobalt blue Gulf from her window and sometimes the water was turquoise, but today there was no view of anything. It was as if the clouds had sunk right down to the ground.

A boom of thunder startled her out of her thoughts. Moments later, she heard a knocking at her front door.

Lillian peered through the peephole to see who was there. Her neighbor, Robert, was standing on her porch. He was holding a pair of pruning shears in one hand and his Metallica tank shirt was drenched in sweat. If he were four decades younger, that might be age-appropriate, but with the bald head, the gray ponytail, and the middle-aged face, he had quite a bit of dissonance going on.

"Hello," she said as she opened the door.

"Hey, Mrs. Howe."

"Hello, Mr. Nicholson. Are you here to prune my hedge?"

He looked at the shears. "No, I'm just in the middle of doing mine. But then I saw the newspaper, and I came over to see if you'd seen it." He seemed to feel awkward about something, and that would be unusual, based on the little she knew about him, with his heavy metal T-shirts and his hair choices.

"What news?"

"About the reward for the dog they found."

"No, I hadn't seen it. I'll take a look at the paper." Lillian nodded in a goodbye kind of way, then moved to close her door.

Mr. Nicholson stepped forward. "It must have shaken you up a bit. Beautiful animal like that, just . . . killed. Who would do that?" He shook his shears in what might be interpreted as a protective way.

It occurred to her he was the one who was upset— or at least a little less comfortable than usual. What was the protocol in this situation? Was she responsible for comforting him?

"Nobody I'd want to spend any time around either," Lillian said, again moving to close her door.

"Anyway," he said, in a rush, "if you decide you know anything or saw anything that might help them catch that killer . . . if you need anybody to help you, go see the police or whatever, I just wanted to say, I'm here if you need me."

"Thank you, Mr. Nicholson," Lillian said. "I have to go now."

And she managed to get the door closed.

The full-page ad on the *Tropical Times Gulf Coast* was unlike anything she'd ever seen on the front of any newspaper she'd ever read. It would have been an eye-opener even if it hadn't included a photograph of a sad-eyed dog so adorable that you just wanted to give him a hug or invite him up onto your lap.

The text was even more startling. "Reward offered. For information leading to the arrest of the person or persons who killed a member of our family. Turtle was only four years old. He loved ice cream, his red ball, and chasing rabbits. He was a champion on the show floor and in our hearts."

The ad was signed by Barbara Nugent, Publisher and Owner.

Lillian took a deep breath and then put the newspaper down.

The phone rang, and she tapped the screen. "Donovan, I swear that sometimes I think you have telepathy."

"Why, what's going on?"

"Nothing bad. It's just that I'm just seeing this notification of a reward for finding Turtle's killer . . . Turtle, that's the dog I found in the park . . . and it's shocking. I'm feeling a bit shaken up, and then the phone rings, and there you are, and I feel better already." Lillian sat down on the couch and reached over to pet Carl, after he jumped up to sit beside her. "I don't know why Tracey keeps bugging me about living alone and telling me I should move to this seniors' place to have more friends and be around people. I've got Carl and I've got you, phoning whenever I need a little TLC."

"Yeah, you got me, Grandma, but that's not quite the same as having friends close by,"

"I have neighbors," Lillian said, but while her voice was telling him one thing, her brain was saying something else. Darn that Mr. Nicholson.

"What?" Donovan asked. "What about the neighbors?"

"It's nothing. They're good neighbors," she said firmly.

Donovan let it go. "What about this reward, then? Is there something you might know that's relevant?"

"I told the police everything . . . I know," Lillian said.

"What?"

"I'm just realizing that I didn't mention everything. There was a car, a big luxury car. But maybe it was just someone who'd come over to exercise their dog. Anyway, the other man probably mentioned it to the police."

"The other man?"

"Arlo Serranno, the neighbor who found the dog with me."

"How's he feeling about all this, a few days later?"

"I should ask him," Lillian said.

"You should, Grandma. Aren't you interested? Aren't you interested in finding out what happened to that poor dog?" She could sense that Donovan was getting worked up. "You used to be keen on finding things out. Don't you remember how you helped with the stolen pendants in Key West? And back in the day, when you worked at the radio station, you must have investigated a lot of things then?"

"Do you know, Donovan, that was fifty years ago," Lillian said with a laugh.

"So what? The idea is still the same."

"I haven't done any investigating, but I wrote an editorial about it," she said. "But I'm having second thoughts about whether I want them to run it."

"Get it into print, Grandma! Come on! Whoever did this shouldn't get away with it."

After Donovan hung up, Lillian thought about it for about ten minutes, then picked up her phone to call Bobby.

"Run it," she said as soon as he said hello. "For Turtle's sake. She cares enough about him to offer a big reward and let the public know how much she cared about him. So, I can give you a column. Fan the flames a bit."

"And will you hunt for the killer?"

"I'm still on the fence about that, Bobby."

Over the next few days, morning and evening, she tried to let her walks with Carl be her time for trying to come down on one side or the other. Her column appeared on

Wednesday, just over a week after Turtle was found, and as Bobby had expected, it created quite a stir.

Lillian hadn't thought it would draw so much attention, but Bobby said that was another example of why he was a newspaper editor and she was not. "If it bleeds, it leads", he reminded her. "Nobody ever went broke underestimating the public's appetite for violence. Even against a dog."

She didn't think she'd ever want to be a newspaper editor.

Everywhere she went over the next few days, she heard people discussing the dog murder and the column they'd read in the paper. Not many people knew she was the writer, at least not the strangers she encountered in various stores and parks, but Bobby told her he'd had a few calls from organizers of various events wanting her to come and speak about her views. Ha! Not a chance.

Friday night, she cooked herself a special pasta dinner and treated herself to a glass of wine. Carl got a chewy bone. She was looking forward to a new episode of her favorite TV show. But first, Carl had to get the chance to stretch his legs.

The neighborhood was dark and still, just a few stars showing in the spaces between the clouds. The moon was just a sliver of a silver crescent. They went for about five blocks; she usually skipped the park after dark and Carl didn't seem to mind.

Lillian felt content. She hadn't liked to admit it to herself, but before the phone call with Donovan, she hadn't felt right about her decision to sit in silence, given her feelings about Turtle's brutal killing. Now that she'd had her say, and perhaps sparked a few others to examine their thoughts and take some sort of action to side with the animals, she felt calmer in her heart.

Saturday night, at about the same time, she said another goodbye to Carl, then closed the front door and locked it. She'd finally given in and agreed to meet Tracey for her regular night at the pub. Tracey insisted that Lillian would enjoy all the people they'd be meeting there and that they would enjoy her. Nobody would try to draw her into a discussion of her newspaper columns or her experience finding Turtle, she promised. She'd prepared them for the fact that those were topics Lillian would rather not explore.

"They'll stick to fishing and Florida and cars," Tracey had promised. "That's the men. With the women, it'll be their grandchildren and the TV shows they watch. And everybody will want to know if you golf. But they won't hold it against you, that you don't."

As Lillian drove home from downtown, she was admitting to herself that Tracey had called it, pretty much perfectly. There were no questions about the reward, no unwelcome theories about the killing, and no pushing for more details about finding the dog.

Dwayne, Doris, Sam, and the others talked a lot about their seniors' residence, though, and that was unexpected. She knew Tracey was a vocal advocate for life at the Aragonese, but she hadn't realized the half dozen other people who'd joined them for drinks also lived there. They were quite polite, and didn't exclude her from extensive, extended discussions of their activities there, but every once in a while, it came up. They were quite a pleasant bunch, and it was nice to be around people who were happy with their choices. But Lillian was happy with hers, too, and she wouldn't have found it a relaxing evening if she'd had to spend most of it, defending.

Ahead, just above the western horizon, she could see some sort of reddish-orange haze in the sky. Fireworks? Odd, in early October, but maybe some Halloween fans were getting an early start. As she drove closer, the color intensified. What was it? Not fireworks, not with that grayish smoke curling up into the sky, too.

She could hear sirens in the distance.

One more turn and Lillian was on her street and she could see the answer to her question.

Firetrucks were parked on both sides of the street. People in bunker gear and fire helmets were running over the lawns, pulling hoses and carrying ladders.

It was a fire. It was a house on fire.

Places that usually were in shadow at this time of night were lit up with headlights and flashlights. Every house nearby had its lights on and crowds of people stood near the sidewalk.

The burning house had flames shooting from the windows and a line of firefighters holding hoses, shooting back.

It was her house.

CHAPTER 7

LILLIAN GUIDED HER CAR over to the curb, barely realizing what she was doing. She opened the door and got out, feeling a wave of dizziness sweep over her. For a moment, she thought she might pass out. Her stomach lurched, and nausea wasn't far behind. She put out a hand to try to steady herself on the car's front fender and waited for the shakiness to settle down.

A firefighter strode by, dragging a hose. Lillian tried to grab his arm. "This is my house!" she said. "What's going on?"

She had his attention. "Stay back, ma'am. Over there with the others."

She looked where he was pointing and saw a dozen of her neighbors, most of them in nightclothes, standing on Nicholson's lawn, staring at the flames.

"But I can't . . . I have to . . . ." She resisted his gentle attempt to push her toward the crowd. "My dog is inside!"

"Yes, we know, ma'am. Actually, he's outside now. We saw the notification on your door and we got him out, first thing. Smart idea, your neighborhood, having those notices up on every door where there's a pet inside. Just in case of a situation like this." The firefighter was talking to her but had his eyes fixed beyond her on the burning house. He looked at her sharply. "There's no one else inside, right?"

Lillian shook her head, then tried to look past him, toward the truck.

"Come on, I'll take you over to get him. Then, please go wait over there with the others. We'll have to talk to you, after we get this under control."

Lillian rushed over to the truck where she saw Carl, sitting in the front seat. The firefighter opened the door and Carl leaped down. He huddled as close to Lillian's knee as he could get.

"We got the call from one of your neighbors who heard him barking for quite a while. Said he went over to complain to you. Then when he smelled smoke and nobody answered the door, he called 911."

Lillian nodded at the firefighter; she couldn't quite manage a smile, or any words beyond "Thank you."

When she went over to stand with the neighbors, she saw many concerned faces, not one of which she recognized. No, wait, there was Bob Nicholson, who'd come to see her about the reward. Several people nodded and she realized she'd noticed them in their yards from time to time. The sight of the flames mesmerized everyone. The firefighters poured heavy streams of water from the firehoses on the structure and so far, the roof was holding up.

A paramedic approached with a blanket that he put over Lillian's shoulders. She realized she was shaking and when one neighbor stepped up with a plastic lawn chair and urged her to sit down, she didn't argue.

"Is there someone you can call, ma'am?" he said. "To come and be with you? Family? Friend?"

A woman in a plaid robe, her hair tied up in a scarf, spoke up. "Please come over to our place, Lillian. For a while. Till you get yourself sorted out."

Lillian forced herself to stop fixating on the colors and the dance of the flames. She and Carl wouldn't be going back in there. That was clear. What should she do next?

And who was this woman? What was her name?

Lillian closed her eyes and took a few deep breaths. She knew she didn't want to get herself 'sorted out' in the unfamiliar living room, kitchen, or spare bedroom of strangers. A hotel, that was it. Alamos Island had plenty of those.

"Thank you very much . . ."

"Kate. Kate Nicholson."

"Kate. But I have a plan and a place to go." She got hold of herself and tried to focus. *Make eye contact.* "But thank you."

Lillian suddenly felt that she had to get away. There would be plenty of time in the next few days, or even weeks, to assess the damage and to take in the enormity of what had just happened, but for now, she just had to get away from all these people.

She went over to the nearest firefighter. "Is there any possibility I'll be allowed to go back inside any time soon?"

"No, ma'am. I know it looks now as if we have it under control, but we still have quite a few things to do here. We have to make sure it's completely safe. And the arson team isn't even here yet. They'll be going over everything carefully before you're allowed anywhere near the place."

"Arson investigators?"

"Standard procedure." He looked at her. "Any chance you left something cooking on the stove when you went out?"

Lillian shook her head. She was a long way from that point—in fact, she was quite sure she wouldn't ever get there.

Lillian took a moment to be grateful that Carl was so well-behaved that he could be counted on to come along with her, quietly and without a leash. She could shop tomorrow for his food and water dishes, something to eat, a change of clothes, and anything else she might need.

"I'm quite tired out," she said. "So, if I'm not going back into my house, I think I'll go somewhere else for the night now, if there isn't anything you need me for."

"Just give me your full name and a contact phone number," the firefighter said.

An hour later, when Lillian had checked into a pet-friendly hotel and curled up under the covers, with some music playing softly on the clock-radio on the night table, she called Donovan.

"I'm on my way," he said, as soon as she told him what had happened.

"Oh, Donovan, you don't have to come all the way over here," she said.

"It's only a two-hour drive. I'll get a room in the same hotel as you. I'm on my way."

As the sun was rising the next morning, she was sitting with her grandson at a table in the hotel coffee shop. Even though she hadn't wanted to bother him, she was very grateful he was there.

"Have you talked to anybody in the fire department yet this morning?"

"They called about six. Said the fire was finally out and that I could drive by, if I wanted. Not safe to return to it. The investigators will take a while to determine a cause and the insurance people will be around later today, too." Lillian sipped her coffee. "It's a nightmare."

But even as she said it, she didn't really mean it. She'd been through nightmares before and this wasn't really it. This was annoying and upsetting, but she didn't feel terrified.

Donovan read her mood. "Okay, Grandma, it's not really a nightmare but it's not Christmas Day either, you have to admit that. Where are you going to go?"

"I'm here now," she said. "I'll figure it out while I stay here in this very comfortable hotel."

"Do you have any ideas about what might have caused it?"

Lillian shook her head. "I stay on top of the house maintenance. There was nothing that could have turned into a problem. But you never know."

"You said the firefighter said the arson investigator would be there."

She stared at Donovan. Something was up. "What is it?"

"Do you think there's any connection with the column you wrote, Grandma?" He seemed miserable, somehow. "It's been bugging me that I pushed you to get it into print and within a few days, this happens!"

Ah, that was it. "Donovan, you should never feel guilty for even five minutes about anything you say to me. I'm a grown woman and I make up my own mind about what I'm going to do or not do. You didn't write the column, you didn't push me to publish it, and you can't take on any responsibility or guilt for what happens. You're just not that important!" She gave him a little shove that turned into patting the back of his hand while she smiled at him. "Really. Don't give it another thought. I doubt very much that the fire at my house had anything to do with my column about a dead dog. Really. You've seen too many movies."

Donovan grinned back at her, but his eyes still seemed hurt. She would have to do something to make things right for him again. "Look, we'll have the results about the cause of the fire very soon and I'll get them to you as soon as possible."

"Lillian!"

Her name was being called across the coffee shop. She looked over to the doorway and saw Tracey standing there. This was unexpected. She waved her over and Tracey lost no time in getting there and holding out her arms for a hug. Lillian stood up and returned the hug. Tracey dropped into a chair.

"How are you? I heard about the fire and I wondered whether you were all right, where Carl was, where you were!"

Lillian smiled. "As you can see, I'm fine and I'm here. This is my grandson, Donovan."

Tracey signaled to the server for coffee. "I figured you might have gone to a hotel and so I thought I'd just take a walk through a few lobbies. I was going to try *Central Bark* next. I really didn't think I'd run into you at all, but it gave me something to do, something that felt mildly useful. I just feel so terrible. Your house burned!"

"Yeah, on a crummy day scale from one to ten, it's a ten," Lillian said. "But, as you can see, I'm doing fine here."

"I just can't get over it!" Tracey said. "I just saw you last night, just a few hours ago, and then your house burned!"

Lillian smiled. Her concern was very sweet. "I'm fine, Tracey. Nobody got hurt, and some stuff is gone. It's not that big a deal."

"But you're not thinking of living in a hotel for long, are you? Not when you have friends and family around."

"She's right, Grandma," Donovan said. "Maybe you'd like to come and stay with Hailey and me for a while?"

Lillian looked back and forth between them. The last thing she wanted to do was disrupt Donovan and Hailey's life. And she certainly didn't want to go be roomies with Tracey. What was wrong with a hotel stay?

"What's wrong with staying in a hotel?"

"It's very expensive, for one thing," Tracey said. "A week or two is one thing, but longer than that . . ? Is that something you want to spend that much money on?"

Lillian really didn't feel that Tracey knew her well enough for a discussion about her finances. "I'll be fine. And Donovan, thank you, but I don't want to be in Miami right now. I'll know more after I talk with the police and the insurance people."

Tracey didn't seem to feel rejected. "Okay, but remember, you can come over to stay with me anytime. I've been wanting to show you the community at the Aragonese for a while now, you know that."

"The Aragonese?" Donovan asked.

"Fifty-five plus," Lillian said. "Pickleball and clubs."

"Lots of clubs," Tracey echoed. "Card games, movie nights, dining out, choir, dancing . . . there's a lot going on."

"Sounds great," Donovan said. "Maybe you could at least take a tour, Grandma."

Lillian sipped at her coffee and gave it a few moments' thought. Maybe she owed him that, after all the guilty feelings and the middle-of-the-night drive from Miami to Alamos Island.

But first, she owed Carl a trip to Jasmine park. After smelling smoke, rousing the neighborhood, watching a fire, and sleeping on the floor of an unfamiliar hotel room, he deserved a few joyful moments of just running. Lillian said goodbye to Tracey and Donovan, then drove over to the dog park.

Carl galloped across the lawn with the delight that only a newly released dog can express. He made Lillian smile, as he always did. She'd had a wisp of an idea that she would wander over to take a look at the palm tree and shrub area where they'd found Turtle, but the park was busy with a couple dozen dog owners, exercising their pets and Lillian didn't want to be conspicuous.

A small group had gathered near the end of one of the footpaths, though, and eventually, Lillian's curiosity overcame everything else and drew her over to see what was going on.

"Very well, Mr. Nugent, let's walk your dog from here to the street," The man said. "His name, again?"

"Mr. Hyde." The owner had his head down, looking at his Pomeranian, but when he straightened, Lillian saw that it was Gerald Nugent, Barbara's husband. Was this one Barbara's dog, too? It looked like an unlikely dog for a man, even an older, out-of-shape man like Gerald Nugent, but then people didn't always look like their dogs.

I wonder who gave him that name?

The fluffy little dog was a model of good behavior, though, rotting along beside Gerald with just a perfect combination of obedience and independence.

"Bien, très bien. He is doing very well, Mr. Nugent." The trainer was wearing white pants and a T-shirt with a logo, initials IRF.

"I know, right? I think the dog is just fine. He's a three-time champion, for God's sake! But my wife thinks he has a problem with squirrels, Zhivago, and she thinks we need you to train him not to chase."

The trainer nodded. "Bien sûr, here we go." He took the leash from Gerald and walked off with Mr. Hyde, toward the swing set at the eastern edge of the park. Lillian watched while one bystander smiled at Gerald and dared to comment.

"He's a handful, that Mr. Hyde, is he?"

"He is a three-time champion!" Gerald hissed, then walked off in the trainer's direction.

"A three-time champion," Lillian murmured as she backed away from the crowd of onlookers. "My, my."

She walked toward the parking lot, then her heart almost stopped when she saw a gray Bentley slowly driving away.

On her way to the newspaper office, Lillian pondered what she knew about shows and show dogs. Not much, truth be told. She thought she had about the average person's level of information; she'd seen the Westminster Dog Show on TV a few times. She knew dogs only as pets, although she was aware that for many other people, they were working animals or show dogs, worth incredible amounts of money because of their potential as breeding dogs, once their show credentials were established.

Turtle was a champion, although she didn't have it quite clear whether that was for his looks. Was it possible that someone had wanted him dead so that he'd be off the show floor and out of competition?

In spite of herself, she was becoming interested in this. She'd told Bobby that she didn't have the time or the interest to try to find out about the dog's killing. Maybe she'd spoken too soon.

**

The next morning, her phone was ringing almost before she'd finished her coffee.

"Lillian, I want to set up a tour for you to see the Aragonese this afternoon." Tracey sounded like she would not take 'no' for an answer. *What had this woman done in her previous, pre-retirement life? Drill sergeant in the Army?*

"I'm sorry if it seems like I'm interfering, but I don't think you're quite realizing how upsetting losing your home in a fire can be."

Okay, maybe therapist or something. She obviously meant well.

"Alright, I'll take a look," Lillian said.

"Great! My friend, Arlo, he's a real estate agent, and he'll be over to pick you up at three o'clock," Tracey said. "I'll meet you out front when you get here."

CHAPTER 8

LILLIAN THOUGHT THE NAME 'Arlo' was unusual enough that it was unlikely there were more than one or two of them on Alamos Island. Sure enough, Arlo was the same man—the one who had come out to investigate, in his pajamas, the night Turtle the Saluki was found, dead.

"Hello there, Lillian! Long time, no see!" Now that she was meeting Arlo in the daytime, she picked up on his resemblance to a Chihuahua. Small, energetic, self-confident.

"Hi, Arlo," she said. "Thank you for offering to do this tour with Tracey and me. I gather that you have some properties listed in this complex."

"I do," he said. "Great places. A one-bedroom and a two-bedroom, both with a view of the Gulf. It's a fantastic building, great amenities. Great people," he said with a smile and a little bow toward Tracey."

Lillian was feeling a bit rushed. "I hope you understand that I'm not looking at buying anything yet," she said. "I'll probably rent, if I do anything or move anywhere right now. Everything's in a bit of a mess for me right now, as I'm sure Tracey told you . . ."

His broad smile instantly changed into an expression of concern. "Yes, she did. A house fire. I am so sorry. I know that you might not be a buyer, not right now, maybe not ever. But when Tracey called, I wanted to help her show you all that the Aragonese has to offer . . . and perhaps, answer any questions you may have about the complex or the neighborhood or the other suites that are available. You will see her place, of course, but it can be nice to see what others have done with their apartments, too."

Something about his manner made her feel like being direct. "Thank you, Arlo, that's very kind. But you know, I'm not sure I even like anything about the idea of a 'suite'. I think I'll want a house. I haven't even spoken to the insurance people or the fire department people yet. Maybe my place is repairable, maybe I'll be back in there by the end of the week."

Arlo and Tracey exchanged a glance.

"All right, maybe that's too optimistic," Lillian said. "But I'm not going to rush into anything."

"We are forewarned," Arlo said, with another big smile. "Come, let me show you the swimming pool and the movie theater."

Lillian had to admit to herself that it would not be too hard to enjoy life at the Aragonese. The grounds were a mix of open spaces, cozy corners embellished with benches and palm trees, and dedicated areas for the pets of tenants and owners. In the office, the posters featured photos of groups that included couples, single people, dogs, and cats; the word 'family' clearly took in the four-legged members, too.

"It's nice to see how welcoming they are to dogs, here," Lillian said. "You remember, Arlo, that I have a Labrador retriever."

"I do, beautiful dog," Arlo said. "I have a Chihuahua, myself. And yes, the Aragonese is one of the best multi-family complexes in town for welcoming dogs."

Inside, Arlo took Lillian to the two show units. The larger one, the two-bedroom, was about the same size as her house, and that surprised her. She had expected to feel cramped in the condos but the layout gave quite a feeling of spaciousness. There was no separate entrance, though, and there was no getting around that. She was used to having a front door and a back door. A condo building, with a lobby and an elevator, was just a different environment.

After meeting the two women who worked in the office, the man who handled the mail, packages, and visitors in the lobby, and three of the Tracey's friends, on their way to bingo, Lillian felt she'd thoroughly inspected the place.

"Thank you both so much for showing me around," she said. "You've given me a lot to think about."

Arlo shook hands and did his little bow. "We'll be in touch," he said as he headed out the door toward his car.

Tracey beamed at Lillian. "I can tell that you liked it," she said.

"I did. I'm going to go back to the hotel now for a little rest, before Carl's walk. But I will get back to you, once I get to the point of making some decisions," she said, peering around a corner as they passed a small room that housed the mailboxes.

Two people stood in front of the boxes, removing their letters. Wait a minute, was that the dog trainer from the park? The one with Gerald Nugent?

Lillian stopped in her tracks and Tracey almost bowled her over. "What is it, Lillian? Did you want to see the mailroom?"

Lillian hurried on past the doorway, toward the lobby entrance. "No, I just . . . I thought I saw someone I knew. But I was wrong."

Tracey looked back toward the mailroom. "No, I don't know either of them, either. But it's such a friendly place, Lillian. People meet each other so easily, you'll see." She laughed. "Or at least, I hope you will."

That night at the hotel, Lillian sat on the bed and stared at the blank screen on the TV. It was about as uninspiring a place as you could find, every element of it from TV stand to light switches to bathroom fixtures made to withstand heavy, daily use and to make the traveler feel that he was in a familiar environment. Despite her upbeat comments to Donovan and to Tracey, she wasn't really all that comfortable here and she'd rather be somewhere homier. It's just that she wanted it to be her home, not theirs.

She picked up the phone to call the number for the insurance company. After a few moments of being passed around, she was on the line with an agent, and after ten minutes of talking with her, she was overwhelmed.

She did get as far as understanding that a claim would have to be filed and that an adjuster would be going over to the house to look at the damages, but after that, it became so confusing that she decided to call Donovan.

"You'll want to get your own contractor, eventually, to look at repairing the place," Donovan said. "But the first thing you should do is arrange to secure the house. Make sure there are boards over any access points, that it's not smoldering any more, that there isn't any danger to the public anywhere. Get a claim filed, and don't forget to ask them for an advance for your living expenses while you have to be out of the house."

Her head was spinning, and he picked up on it. "Grandma, it's a lot to do. I was planning to drive over to see you again, anyway. Leave it all to me—and just give me the name and number of your agent. Maybe you could call her first and authorize me."

"Oh, Donovan, would you? That would be such a relief," Lillian said.

"Of course. We'll get it sorted out in no time," Donovan said. "Keep track of your expenses . . . and don't stop paying your premiums.

What are you planning to do right away, Grandma? Are you going to stay in the hotel?"

Lillian looked around the room. "No, I don't think so. Tracey showed me her condo building yesterday and it's quite nice. They'll take short-term tenants, so I think I'll go for that."

"Awesome," Donovan said. "Alright, sit tight for a day or two and then I'll be there, we'll find out what's what with your house and we'll get you moved into—what's name of the place again?"

"The Aragonese," Lillian said. "For the fifty-five plus. Why do I hate that idea?"

"Think of it as 'for the people with fifty-five bright ideas every day. Plus.' " Donovan said.

What a charmer.

She hung up, grabbed Carl's leash, then headed for the door. No need to call him; he was pumped and ready to go. Lillian drove to the dog park, wondering whether she'd see the French dog trainer, the yappy, squirrel-happy Pomeranian, or Gerald Nugent this time, but there was no sign of them. Not of Arlo, the neighbor/realtor, either.

What there was, to her delight, was a German Shepherd puppy. He was a lively, friendly type, his tan shoulders and legs, black saddle and ears just a gorgeous combination. Lillian had never been involved with dog shows or judging exceptional examples of a breed but she thought she could tell, when she looked at a dog, whether it was special. Of course, as with any species, just because it was a beautiful puppy didn't mean it would grow up to deliver on its promise, but for now, this one was gorgeous.

She smiled at the young woman, leading the pup around the park on a leash. "Nice dog!"

That was all that was needed. The young woman was thrilled to talk about her new puppy, and in five minutes, Lillian knew all about his age, his temperament, what the vet had had to say about him, his favorite toys, and his habits. His name was Duke.

Carl was very interested in meeting Duke and approved of him immediately. Lillian watched them play, and the young woman beam at them, and she could feel the pall that had been hovering over the park, for her, start to lift.

When she looked around, she could imagine poor Turtle bouncing around these fields, just as happily as Duke was doing. Full of life, trusting the world . . . and then, suddenly, dead. Killed, probably for no reason that had anything to do with any fault of his own—although she realized that she really didn't know what sort of dog he was. Maybe he was aggressive and had gone after someone walking in the park in the pre-dawn hour, scared the person, and received a deadly reciprocation as a result?

But if he were aggressive, would Barbara Nugent have kept him around?

And what was he doing over here in Jasmine Park that morning, anyway? This was a long way from Barbara's home territory, in a mansion over on Rappallo Square. Didn't they have anywhere to exercise dogs over there?

A gloomy thought roamed into Lillian's mind and shut down all the sunlight of the day. Maybe Turtle hadn't been in Jasmine Park for exercise. Maybe he was already dead when he was brought here.

She shivered. It made her sad, but even more than that (and she recognized this in herself from many experiences over the years), her curiosity was in gear. She didn't know anything about Turtle except his name and who his owner was, but she knew that finding out the answers would make her feel much better. Way back in the day, in her early married life, Marv had said her thirst for answers was just another form of enjoying gossip.

But it wasn't that. She had no interest in passing on the information she might pick up, as she searched for answers to her questions, and she took no pleasure in recounting other people's personal misfortunes or mistakes.

She just wanted to know.

And if she could, to get some justice for Turtle.

CHAPTER 9

LILLIAN TOSSED A HANDFUL of towels into her shopping cart, then fumbled to answer her ringing phone. My, how the world had changed; now everyone was on a tether all the time. She remembered when phones were on the wall, in the kitchen, one for the family to share, an extension in the parents' bedroom if they were particularly well-to-do or nervous about falling asleep.

She grinned to herself, remembering the last time she'd mentioned something like that to Donovan and he'd chided her, saying she sounded as if she were about three hundred years old. Well, she certainly remembered how she'd felt about hearing her grandparents reminisce when she was a teenager, about the first airplane they'd ever seen, about black-and-white TVs, and washing machines with a ringer. It was boring to her, and irritating, if it happened too often. She'd try to remember to keep a lid on it, with Donovan, or anybody else under sixty. Anybody over sixty, they'd probably enjoy it.

She looked at the call display.

Chelan Montgomery.

What a surprise—and a pleasant one.

"Hi, Chelan. So nice to hear your voice," Lillian said.

"You too, Lillian. How are you?"

"Just fine, dear. Enjoying Florida life, as always. How are things in Vancouver?"

"They were good when I left this morning. I'm in Atlanta right now. Stopover on my way to Fort Myers and then driving to Naples."

"A vacation?" Lillian asked.

"Not really. I have a friend in Naples—Iris—who asked me to come down for a few days. She's having a work crisis and she needs some support," Chelan said. "More of a personal crisis."

"How is your little one?" Lillian asked.

"I'm missing her so much! And it's only been a few hours! Drew couldn't handle her and his job, too, so Mom stepped in to help."

It made Lillian smile to hear that her young friend from Canada still went at the things in her life with as much enthusiasm as ever. "Are you going to be able to get down here to see me?"

"I'd love to, Lillian! That's why I'm calling. Nevada got to see you so much last year, in Key West, and I was jealous. I was hoping we'd be able to connect for lunch or something. It's not exactly the same neighborhood, but it's closer than Vancouver."

"I'll drive up to see you."

"Would you?"

"I have so much free time, it would be lovely. And I'm looking forward to seeing you." Chelan hesitated. "Are you okay, Lillian? You sound a bit . . . different."

Perceptive girl. "Lots going on here. I'll bring you up to date when I see you."

"I have some news for you, too."

What would that be about, Lillian wondered. It had been a few years since she'd been able to manage a visit with Chelan, although their paths had crossed online, and on the phone, last year when they were helping Nevada out with her situation in Savannah. It was wonderful to stay in touch with them both, and she'd never forget the way they'd been there for her, during that brief period when she'd been living in her car.

"Okay, Chelan, I'll see you in Naples. Text me the day and the restaurant where you want to meet for lunch."

When Lillian got to the Aragonese, Tracey was waiting for her outside, with a dolly to help load her belongings. The suite was furnished, which was a good thing—a necessary thing, actually. She didn't know if any pieces of her furniture would be usable, once they were past these first few days, post-fire.

Tracey held the door open for Lillian to push the dolly through. Carl trotted along behind. He seemed to be very interested in these new surroundings, just as he had been in the hotel. Just an adaptable, interested dog. Lillian felt very lucky that he was so well-behaved.

He deserved a good romp in the doggie park. Plus, Lillian was eager to get rolling on her plan to investigate Turtle's killing. She carried the boxes and bags of new things from the dolly into the suite, thanked Tracey for her help, then headed back out to the car with Carl.

When they got to the park, she scouted around for Gerald or Zhivago Picard, but there was no sign of them. She wanted to clarify Zhivago's presence at the condo building, too: maybe he was there the other day, visiting someone? But if so, would he have been near the mailboxes? Not likely, but it was possible that he was helping someone else who lived there by picking up their mail. That could wait until tomorrow; for today, she needed to take another, slower look at the edges of the park.

Now that she was here, she wasn't sure she remembered which shrub or palm tree it was that had sheltered Turtle. She walked slowly among the trees, scanning the ground. Lillian didn't really know what she was looking for, just that she'd know it when she spotted it. She took her time and covered every square inch around four of the trees.

"Miss Lillian!"

Truly, this world and this town got smaller every day. It was Arlo Serranno, the real estate man, this time holding a leash with a Chihuahua at the end of it.

"What a surprise to see you here, Mr. Serranno."

He shrugged. "Not really that remarkable. I live right over there. This is my local park. And this is my dog, Digger."

Lillian smiled. "Is that what she does?"

"It is what she does. It's in her nature. I try to explain that to my wife, again and again, when she is angry with him for ruining the flower beds. Ever since she was little, her first day with us, she was digging. So, that's her name." Digger seemed to be content just to sniff around the grass rather than tear it up right now. "And how is Carl today?"

"He's just fine. But ready for some water and maybe a rest at home, so we're on our way." Lillian headed toward her car.

Was it too paranoid of her to wonder if it was just coincidence that Mr. Arlo, living in his house just across the way, with the windows looking out over the lawn, showed up in this park almost every time she did?

CHAPTER 10

LILLIAN STOPPED IN AT THE LIBRARY on her way home and found a quiet spot to set up with her laptop. She could probably do this in her suite, but it still didn't feel like home.

Today, for her, it was going to start with the Saluki. The image of this 'second fastest dog on earth' showed an alert, almond-eyed, long-legged dog with an engaging face. It actually resembled the third fastest, the Afghan hound, with a longish nose, long neck and ears that gave it the appearance of a long-haired human. As soon as she saw the photograph, Lillian thought of Turtle, lying under the bush, bleeding, and she had to stop for a few seconds to let her sadness pass.

The Saluki was often a contender for Best in Show. Lillian watched some video of champion Salukis running the ring. A lot of personality and verve there.

Now that she had some background on the Saluki, she wondered whether there would be any information about Barbara Nugent's Saluki, in particular. Oh yes, there it was. A few searches and some nosing out of a few details took her about an hour. She now had a very solid file on Turtle, whose formal, registered name was Ch. Bosylia's King Khamudi Luxor. Best in breed at several shows. The pride and joy of Barbara Nugent, owner and publisher of the *Tropical Times Gulf Coast*. Lillian found several articles on the newspaper's website about the dog and its adventures in dog show world. In the photos, Barbara stood behind tables bearing large trophies and purple and gold ribbons; she was smiling like. . . . well, like someone very proud of their champion purebred dog.

Lillian's next hunt was for Zhivago Picard, the dog trainer. He was as well-covered as Turtle, probably even more so. His website showed a series of photos of joyful dogs at his feet or heels, plus a wide-angle shot of a training facility that looked as if it might stretch for a mile or two. Somewhere in the open spaces near Cape Coral, Lillian would guess. Instinct Revival Facility, it was called.

What on earth could that be about?

Well, apparently, many dog owners would like their dogs to get back in touch with their basic canine natures: herding, hunting, guarding, retrieving. They could come to the Instinct Revival Facility to re-learn whatever they'd forgotten or let go dormant for lack of use.

They could also learn some new tricks. If you'd always wanted your Shih Tzu to herd sheep or your Poodle to retrieve ducks, the Instinct Revival Facility would get you there.

Zhivago Picard's CV was impressive. Twenty years as a dog trainer, ten of them owning his own facility. A list of clients that included some well-known Naples, Tampa, and Miami families. References and testimonials that glowed like a shower of fireworks. If Carl had any problems, this was a trainer Lillian would consider calling.

The contact page of the website featured a large photograph of Mr. Picard and Lillian examined it carefully. It was definitely the man she had seen in the mailroom at the Aragonese: about five foot ten, forty-something, hair salt-and-pepper, full beard and mustache, muscular build. She didn't pick up anything from the photograph or the website about his personality, but when she'd seen him at the park, she got an impression of authority and competence. Not kindliness or depth, but perhaps he had those qualities, too. She hadn't seen him long at the park, and while they were there, Gerald Nugent had rather distracted her attention.

Next item on the research agenda was the local branch of the American Kennel Club. Lillian wanted to find out whether there were any upcoming shows, places where she might mingle, and pick up some insight into the dog world of south Florida.

Tracey had told her, too, that there was an active dog fanciers group at the Aragonese and that she would be more than welcome, along with Carl. Not that they met the formal definition of a dog fancier, breeding dogs or keeping more than four as pets . . . maybe dog lovers would be a better phrase.

As a rule, Lillian didn't have much, if any, time for joining clubs, but this might be a good reason to make an exception.

Tracey had been on the phone last night, urging her to come along to the garden club meeting this afternoon. She seemed to be quite worried that Lillian was, or would become, depressed about the fire at her house. Lillian wasn't the sort to give much time to depression, but she appreciated Tracey's concern.

The club was meeting at Gulf Coast Gardens, a spot that Lillian had been intending to see since her move to Alamos Island. She'd read an article last year that they had a few examples of the rare ghost orchid, and that if you were lucky, your visit to the Gardens might coincide with the opportunity to see the plant in bloom.

She'd told Tracey that she had plans for the day but that if she was done early enough, she'd try to get over to the Gardens in time to meet the club.

As she drove into the parking lot, the afternoon air was hot and humid. The weather was changing into the more moderate, high 70s days of the year, but a few humid ones still sneaked in, from time to time. Lillian put on a hat to shield the sun and walked over to the gate.

"Hi, I'm looking for the Aragonese garden club meeting?" Lillian said to the woman sitting behind the glass at the entrance.

"I think all the garden club members are meeting in the Orange Blossom Café," she said.

Lillian followed her directions, then peeked through a door to a side room filled with about forty people beside the main café. She saw Tracey sitting at a table.

"Hi," she whispered as she slid into an empty chair beside Tracey.

Her friend's eyes widened, followed by her smile. "Glad you could make it! They're just talking about volunteers for the Christmas lights display. They pretty much talk about volunteers all the time."

Lillian grinned back. "I'd rather tend flower beds than put up Christmas lights. How long will the meeting go?"

"We can leave right now if you want," Tracey whispered. "We'll just stop by the desk on the way out and put our names down for a weeding shift or something. Then, they'll let us escape."

As they strolled along the pathways, admiring the landscape architecture, Lillian felt glad that she had accepted Tracey's invitation. They discovered a mutual admiration for orchids and a preference for sunflowers. They exclaimed over a giant mural, painted in tropical colors of turquoise, coral, and yellow, and set up to provide shade for a lovely grove of wild ginger in the Herb Garden.

They both moved far off the path to give space to a large group of people coming through, led by a man carrying a sign that read Florida Floral Tours. He wore a dark purple jacket with the company name stitched on one lapel, and a pin with a Highland terrier on the other. His hat looked serious enough to take on the Namibian desert.

"And next, after the Herb Garden, we'll see the Caribbean Garden," he said. "Then, the Orchid Garden and the Singapore Garden."

"Are the ghost orchids blooming right now, Marlon?" One tourist wanted to know.

"Not today," the tour guide said. "But they have some beautiful books in the gift shop with incredible photos of them."

The group slowed down and Lillian stepped on the gas, to outdistance them, on the way to the Caribbean Garden. She didn't know why she was so impatient with the appearance of too many people in a public place, but she was.

She noticed Tracey didn't seem to mind moving away from the tour.

But later, when they stopped in to the gift shop to pick up some seeds for a herb garden Tracey was trying on her patio, they bumped into the crowd again.

"Well, we can't seem to escape them," Lillian said.

"Let's stop for just a minute," Tracey said. "My friend Joyce said she saw some really cute Great Dane garden posts here."

The tour guide, Marlon, was rummaging through some framed posters nearby. "They're right over there, beside the window," he said.

"Oh! Thank you," Tracey said. She looked at him for a few seconds. "Could I ask you?" She read his name badge. "Marlon, is it? Could I ask if your company . . . Florida Floral Tours . . . do you also take people to see the Everglades?"

Marlon put back the bird-of-paradise photo he'd been examining. "We do. Regularly. Are you interested in taking a tour?"

"I've lived here for years and I've never been," Tracey said. "But I have no idea what I want to see and where to find it."

"Florida Floral Tours could certainly offer you several possibilities," he said.

Lillian smiled at him. "I see that you're a dog lover. Owner, too?"

Marlon smiled back. "Nothing but terriers, though. Mrs. Tanaka wouldn't have it any other way."

———

"Mrs. Tanaka is your wife?"

"My mother, actually. She has two Scotties and I have a West Highland White. We show them regularly." He seemed ready to settle in for a long chat. "Are you dog show people, too?"

"We're dog people," Tracey said. "But I haven't gotten around to attending any dog shows since I've been here."

"Oh, you really should! We have a lot of really active clubs, if you have the interest and the time. What kind of terrier do you have?"

Tracey grinned. "Great Dane."

"Lab retriever."

Was it Lillian's imagination or did he wince?

Marlon smiled. "I guess there are big dog people and there are small dog people," he said. "I've always thought the smaller ones are smarter, and I like that. And you don't have to ever feel intimidated or at risk when you're around a small dog."

"I never feel intimidated by Tackle," Tracey said. "Lillian, are you intimidated by Carl?"

Lillian shook her head.

"Maybe not, but they're your own, your pet dogs, right? It's a different story if you're meeting a strange dog. If it takes against you and it's only fifteen pounds, it might be annoying, but it's not going to get you injured. Even if you get bitten, it's no big deal.

"But if it's a big one, a strong one, you're at quite a disadvantage, if he doesn't like you. Although if a small one doesn't like you, he can set off quite a racket."

Lillian looked at Tracey. How had they gotten into this conversation with this stranger?

"Anyway, I'm sorry I went off on such a tangent," Marlon said. "I think you'd enjoy the dog shows very much. And the Everglades. Please give us a call or go online and look us up."

Tracey found a pair of garden posts with the desired Great Dane decoration that she wanted and they went over to the cashier to pay. "Come on a day trip with me," she said, while they waited in a long line. "For a tour of the Everglades."

Lillian stared at the row of Gulf Coast Gardens key chains and fridge magnets lined up in front of her. Across the store, she watched Marlon Tanaka fuss around his group.

Her purpose these days was clear to her, and this visit to the garden club meeting was just a brief diversion from it.

But perhaps coincidence had put someone in her path who might lead on to some answers, or open some doors? She just had a feeling about Marlon Tanaka and she wanted to spend a little more time with him.

"Alright," she said. "A tour of the Everglades."

When she left the Gardens, she drove back to the Aragonese for a Carl stop before going on to the newspaper office. *For a woman who is retired, I certainly don't get to stay home much!* she joked to herself.

It was good that she was starting to think she might be able to consider the condo as home. Good, and surprising, after so short a time and after so much resistance to the idea. Looking at the front entrance, with its beautiful stone work and the lobby with its Italian marble, she took a moment to appreciate the place.

Carl seemed to like it, too. He was waiting at the door to greet her and she could feel his happiness as he sat for her to snap on his leash. He took a few laps of the doggie area behind the building, then dashed around while she knocked out a tennis ball for him to retrieve.

After getting his heart rate up into a good zone and tiring him out for his afternoon nap, Lillian tucked Carl back into the condo and pulled out her phone. She was ready to let Bobby know she wanted to look into the killing of Turtle.

"I'm glad to hear it," Bobby said. "When can you start?"

———

"I already have," Lillian said. "I've done some preliminary research and I'm starting to interview people. I'll need to speak with Barbara very soon. Interesting, that the Saluki is one of the fastest dogs on earth but Barbara decided to name him 'Turtle'."

"I think that was Gerald," Bobby said. "But, good start. Why don't you come over this afternoon? She's in the office and I'll ask her to meet with you."

Lillian had mixed feelings about talking to Barbara. Her impression of the newspaper publisher/society queen was that she was used to getting her way, instantly—like a general, barking a command. She said she didn't want Lillian to write an essay or an editorial about her dog's killing and she didn't want Bobby to run it, but they went ahead anyway. She might be a little ticked off about that.

But if she agreed to talk with Lillian, it would be a signal that she believed that someone, other than the police who were actively investigating it, should be looking into her dog's death.

"Lillian! Good," Bobby said, as he ushered her into the waiting area outside Barbara's office. "Barbara will be back soon."

"Thanks, Bobby." Lillian lowered herself into a deep, padded armchair, one of four placed in perfect symmetry around the waiting room. "Anything new to tell me about this?"

"Barbara is still quite upset," he said. "Try to tread softly when you interview her. She's got herself that new puppy. Said the best way to get over losing a dog is to get another one," Bobby said. "They did an autopsy on Turtle. She's quite upset about that, too. A lot of detail in the report, as you can imagine."

Lillian made a face. "Cause of death?"

"Poisoning. Complicated by trauma due to blows from a blunt instrument," Bobby said.

"How are the police handling it?"

"It falls under the umbrella of 'animal cruelty'," Bobby said. "It's a crime and they're investigating."

"Am I investigating for the paper or for you, Bobby?"

"I'm not really thinking about getting material from it," Bobby said. "I just think whoever killed this dog should be called to account for it. If the police find him—"

"Or her."

"Or her," he agreed. "If they crack the case first, that's great. But I think it can't hurt to have you nose around a little." Bobby stood up. "I think you care."

"I do," Lillian agreed. "Let's see what Barbara says."

"Let's see what Barbara says about what?"

The newspaper publisher owned the room, as well as the paper. Dressed in a beige linen suit and turquoise heels, Barbara Nugent was magazine-cover ready. Unlike many women over forty, she didn't put her makeup on with a butter knife and she didn't look like she spent one full day a week with strands of her hair in foil under lights in a hair salon. She just looked effortlessly young.

As she passed by on her way to the inner office, Lillian caught a subtle whiff of a spicy perfume.

Lillian nodded to Bobby, then got up to follow. She sat down in the chair across the desk. Barbara ignored her for the first few minutes, tossing a bag on a side chair, glancing over the files on her desk, and checking the messages on her phone.

Finally, she sat down, stared into Lillian's eyes, and asked: "Why are you here?"

"Your friends on the paper have asked me to use my abundant, senior-citizen free time to try to help find out who killed Turtle," Lillian said, as gently and inoffensively as she could. She had no idea why it mattered whether Barbara approved of her involvement, but somehow, it did.

Barbara made up her mind. "All right. What do you want to know?"

Lillian took out her notebook.

———————

Barbara smirked. "Old school, I see."

Lillian smiled back. "Always. Now. What was Turtle doing that morning?"

"He woke up about five, as he usually does. My housekeeper let him out into the yard, then gave him some water. One of the team, Riccardo I think it was, was there to do the early morning walks."

"Walks, plural?"

"For Turtle and for Hyde, my husband's dog," Barbara said.

"And did Riccardo take Turtle for a walk?"

"Yes, he says he did. Brought him back and put him into the doggie pen on the beach side of the house. He and Hyde hung out together."

Lillian made her notes. "Then what?"

"Then what what? I don't know what you mean." Barbara wasn't going to make this easy.

"What went on during the rest of the morning? When did you get up? What did you do? Where did you go? What is Mr. Nugent's morning routine? When did you notice Turtle was gone? Who might have taken him?"

Barbara stared at her, then spoke slowly and loudly. "I get up at six, go downstairs to the gym and work out for an hour. Mr. Nugent goes to his office downtown about 6:30. I usually dress, visit the dogs for a few minutes, then leave for work. But this time, when I went out to the pen, Turtle was gone. I thought Riccardo had kept him out for an extra-long walk. He does that sometimes. Gerald had already left. He had to stop at the pharmacy and do a few other errands.

"So, I just got in my car and went to work. Then, the police phoned."

"Let me say, too, Barbara, that I'm so sorry this happened to your dog. I have a Lab retriever of my own and I know they are part of your family."

"Thank you, Lillian." Barbara looked at her a bit more closely. "Is that why you wrote such a strident column?"

"Oh . . . would we call that strident?" Lillian smiled as warmly as she could, trying to create some sort of rapport. "I just wrote from my heart."

And suddenly, it was as if Barbara put down her fists. "Yes, you did. That came through loud and clear. I was a bit rattled by it at first, as you know, from Bobby, but I just didn't want people thinking I was using the newspaper as my personal platform."

"I understand," Lillian said.

"And I didn't want a repeat of what happened the last time."

CHAPTER 11

PATIENCE. LILLIAN believed that was often the best thing—just listen to people.

But Barbara outwaited her. After about ninety seconds, Lillian asked, "What happened another time?"

"We lost another little dog about twenty years ago. He'd been missing for five days and I was just hysterical. We put an appeal in the paper and within hours, somebody found him. He'd just wandered off and was living off the land, near a local park.

"But I took a lot of flak, especially from the guy who picked him up and brought him back. I guess he thought there should have been some sort of finder's fee, or something." She made a try at a sort of laugh. "I didn't want to go through that again. I thought it would be better this time if I offered a reward, and clarified that I would not take advantage of anybody, or of my position. I was going to put the reward notice in the daily paper and on the radio stations only, then your column was a sort of demand-bid and I thought it was best to put it in our paper, too. Gerald thought I was being silly, but I really want to find out who did this as quickly as possible."

Barbara got up and walked over to look out the window. "I've been just devastated ever since Turtle was killed," Barbara said. "Do you have any theories about who might have done it?"

Lillian just shook her head. Even if she had, she wouldn't be sharing them with Barbara—or with anybody—at this point.

Barbara kept her there, chatting, for almost an hour. At the beginning, it had seemed to Lillian that she'd be fortunate if the interview lasted a full ten minutes. Something had happened to warm Barbara up, suddenly; she'd shared confidences, offered help, and put her head together with Lillian as if they were girlfriends.

Maybe it was just a matter of taking a little time to connect. Some people were just like that. There was a natural reserve, rooted in shyness and lack of self-confidence, and they had to give it some space and time. But once those moments had passed, they could connect as well as anyone. Maybe that was Barbara's story.

"Gerald says it's just part of life, if you have some profile and some money," Barbara said. "It's unfortunate some weirdo pulled Turtle into it, he says. He's backing me up, on pushing harder to find the person who did this, but he says it's not the end of the world. Maybe we'll never know, and maybe that's for the best. We'll see."

Finally, Lillian closed her notebook firmly and made a move to stand up.

"Well, I've taken enough of your time," she said.

"You let me know if there's anything I can tell you about or people I can introduce you to," Barbara said as she walked Lillian to the door.

As she left the building, Lillian was shaking her head. It was like feeling the wind change from easterly to westerly in the space of two minutes. Barbara had started out being some sort of ice queen and had ended the interview, offering to mentor Lillian. A woman thirty years her junior, too. Lillian couldn't help finding that amusing.

On the way back home, her phone rang.

"Hello, Ms. Howe, this is Miranda from your insurance company. How are you today?"

"I'm fine, Miranda. How about you?" Lillian loved these hands-free phone calls that she could have, now that Donovan had wired up her car somehow to answer the phone for her.

"Fine, thanks for asking. I'm just calling to let you know that the police have finished with their investigation and we're done with our inspections. Next, we have to get on with repair."

"Whoa, slow down a bit. Before we talk about repair, what can you tell me about the fire?"

"It's completely out. I suppose that's the good news."

"What was the cause?"

"I'm told it was inconclusive, but there was enough evidence for them to open an arson investigation on it."

"Arson."

"Yes, ma'am. There have been some other fires on the island that were deliberately set. Small ones—nothing taking over an entire house, like yours. But I guess the police feel that's important to take in, as circumstantial evidence, and they want to keep a file open on your place."

"What will that mean for my repairs?"

'We have contractors and sub-trades all ready to go, Ms. Howe, if you want us to handle everything."

"Well, my grandson has advised me to get my own contractors, and he's going to help me with all that."

"That's just fine Ms. Howe. Let's keep in touch, alright?"

When Lillian arrived back at the condo complex, she was exhausted. All she wanted was to stretch out on the couch, give Carl a cuddle, and sip a cup of tea. She saw Tracey sitting in a group in the lobby and she silently moaned; she would have liked to pretend she hadn't seen them and avoid them all. This was the downside of living in a place like this and being friendly with her neighbors.

"Lillian! Hi! Come and meet the Aragonese dog lovers," Tracey said.

Lillian required herself to smile. "Hi, everybody," she said. Although there were only four people there, it felt to her like a crowd of two hundred.

An older woman with elegantly done, silver-white hair that matched the shade on the Samoyed sitting at her feet smiled at Lillian. "Nice to meet you," she said. "I've seen you go by with your Lab. He looks like a wonderful boy."

"He is," Lillian agreed. "But this one is pretty special, too." She reached out to let the Sami sniff her and make friends.

"We've just been talking about a little field trip we want to make at the end of the week," Tracey said. "Kyra has been taking Ice Cream to some training sessions at the Instinct Revival Facility and she wants us all to see the place."

"Instinct Revival Facility?" Lillian asked. She knew about it, of course, from her media research at the library the other day, but there was a big difference between reading about something and having the chance to ask questions of someone who'd been there. Not as big as going there herself, but still significant.

"Zhivago Picard, the owner, is the most amazing trainer I've come across in years of having dogs," Kyra said. "I told him I wanted to bring three friends over to meet him and he said that would be fine. Four friends," she said with a smile and a nod to Lillian.

"What did you think of the facility?" Lillian asked.

Kyra reached down to stroke her dog's head. "Very impressive. Ice Cream has had a problem with refusing to get off the furniture and Zhivago has developed a plan to cure her in a month."

"Nothing like a positive review," Lillian said. "I'd be very interested in going to see it. Thank you for inviting me."

Tracey was beaming. "I'll text you the details," she said, as Lillian moved away, toward the elevator.

Lillian decided to take Carl out for a vigorous game of fetch in the dog run. He needed it, but she needed it, too. Her mind was racing and when she lay down on the couch to rest, she found she couldn't turn it off.

It helped a little, but she was still so restless. A cup of tea at *Central Bark* might be the cure.

Carl needed no coaxing to jump into the back of the car for a ride and she rolled all four windows down all the way so that he could enjoy the wind in his face. Once she had her table and her tea, he curled up at her feet and went to sleep.

She took her notebook out, opening it to a fresh page, then labeling it "What I Know So Far".

Someone torched my house

That was a good start. A cut-to-the-chase start. If nothing else, she'd like to find out who set fire to her house while her dog was inside.

Someone killed a beautiful, purebred dog

She listed in point form: Owned by Barbara and Gerald Nugent. Champion show dog. Last seen by the family's dog-walker assistant. Discovered in Jasmine Park by me and Arlo Serranno, who lives beside the park.

Lillian stopped writing and looked across the café. She'd just realized that she hadn't asked Arlo whether he'd seen Turtle come into the park, either alone or on the end of a leash.

She had quite a few questions for him. What time did he leave his house and come over to speak to her? Had he seen anything from his window prior to that?

If he did see Turtle, he would have been the last person to see the dog alive. How did the dog look? Did Turtle walk into the park under his own steam or was he carried?

Lillian started a fresh page, listing her next steps. Go see Mr. Serranno.

What else did she know?

Barbara Nugent raised the dog from a puppy four years ago. Her husband had named hers and she'd named her husband's dog, Mr. Hyde.

Mr. Hyde is being trained by the owner of the Instinct Revival Facility, Zhivago Picard.

Alamos Island is home to hundreds, maybe tens of thousands of dog lovers and dog haters.

Lillian sipped at her tea and stared at her notebook. It really wasn't much. She had a lot to do.

Her phone buzzed and she looked at the message screen. From Tracey.

We're on for tomorrow at 10 at the IRF. Do u want to drive out together?

Truth was, Lillian always would rather meet people somewhere than go in the same car. But.

Tracey had made it possible for her to go along on this excursion, and she had a feeling it would be easier to ask her questions and avoid looking suspiciously snoopy if she were with a group of ladies having an outing.

Sure. Let's meet in the lobby at 9:30

She put the phone aside and tried to get back to her thoughts. It was like trying to watch one particular firefly; she just couldn't stay focused.

Her phone rang, and she blessed this next interruption. She just wasn't getting anywhere, anyway.

"Lillian? Is that you?"

"Nevada!" Lillian laughed. "How nice to hear from you. Particularly at this moment."

"Why is that?"

"Oh, I'm trying to get something written, and it's just not flowing."

"Yeah, Chelan told me you're writing a regular column for the community newspaper. Good for you!" Nevada had always been generous with her supportive comments. In all the time that Lillian had known her, since 2008 in Canada, Nevada had never failed to let out a little cheer whenever she heard of any new project of Lillian's.

"Thank you. I'm enjoying it. But it's quite easy, compared to what I'm trying to do now."

"And what's that?"

It occurred to Lillian that Nevada might be able to help her quite a bit with this. She had worked as a journalist and a news director for nearly thirty years. This was a brain she should pick.

"I've been asked to ask around about a really horrible case of animal cruelty," Lillian said. "A dog belonging to the owner of the paper I work on was killed last week. Head bashed in."

"Oh, my God," Nevada said.

"Exactly."

"Is it your boss who asked you to 'ask around'? I love the way you put that, by the way."

"No, it was the managing editor on the paper. She's answered a few questions for me but we're not really sympatico, you know what I mean? She's a country club lady type, although she does seem to work very hard at publishing this newspaper. But I'm sure she does it mainly for fun. She's married to a billionaire, sportsman type."

"Wow, slow down a bit. I'm trying to keep up with all this." Nevada sounded as if she were making notes of her own, at the other end of the call. "Okay, got it. What else?"

"Well, I was the one who found its . . . his body."

"Oh, I'm sorry. That must have been horrible."

"It was. I was walking Carl and I just stumbled on it."

"How is Carl?"

"He's doing great. Loves Alamos Island."

"And Donovan? How is he?"

"Still working the boats. Almost married. Still talks about his treasure-hunting adventure last year."

"Say hi for me."

"Where are you now?"

"Owen and I are in New York. He's running a hospital and I'm working with books."

"Books!"

"Yeah, it was time for another change. Listen, I'm still processing your news about this dog."

"I haven't told you all of it yet. I wrote a column about it and then a few days later, there was a fire at my house."

"There was a fire…"

"Actually, it was torched. Police confirmed."

Nevada exhaled. "Wow. Is there anything I can do?"

"You know, there is, since you ask. I need some help with how to go about trying to find out what happened. I'm not going to step on any police toes but if there's anything I can do to help find the scum who would do such a thing to a dog, I'd like to. Not to mention how much I want to know what happened to my house."

"I can help with that," Nevada said.

"I have quite a few ideas but I'd love to run them by you, get some insight into how you'd go at it, if you were reporting a story like this."

"I'm on board," Nevada said. "What have you done so far?"

"Talked to Barbara Nugent, the dog's owner."

"And how cut up about it was she?"

Lillian hesitated. "Sort of. I mean, I don't know. I don't know how upset about anything Barbara Nugent gets, to be frank. She's quite a cucumber."

"When you talk to anybody, watch for their reactions to your questions just as much as you take note of the actual answers," Nevada said.

"Great tip, thank you. Who else should I talk to?"

"As many people as you can. Anybody the dog came into contact with on a daily basis, weekly, monthly. Neighbors. Groomer? Doggie day care? Barbara's husband. And I'm sure you've thought of the fact that it might have nothing to do with the dog itself . . . what's his name? Her name?"

"Turtle is his call name."

"Turtle?"

"Barbara's husband named him. He's a Saluki, the second fastest dog in the world. Can go forty-two miles an hour."

"Hah. I get it."

"And the husband has a fluffy Pomeranian that Barbara named Mr. Hyde. Although I've seen that one in action. He doesn't have an ironic name."

"Interesting people. Okay, see if you can talk to the husband, too. I'd also try for the vet's name, and maybe the breeder. But, as I was saying, I'd look beyond the dog itself, too. Does Barbara have enemies? Anybody angry at the paper?"

"Well, I hadn't thought of that," Lillian said. "I've been much too narrow."

"Yes, go broad. Put out a wide net. And call me anytime you want, if you come up dry again or if you want to ask my reactions to something you've heard. Or found."

"Thank you! That's great."

"So, I've got to get going, Lillian. I just called to say 'hi' and 'what's new'."

"Next time, we'll talk all about you the whole time."

Nevada laughed. "It's a deal, Lillian. Nice to hear your voice."

Same to you, Nevada. More than nice.

At nine-thirty the next morning, Lillian was ready and waiting for Tracey in the lobby. She didn't know whether Turtle had even been one of Zhivago Picard's clients, but she meant to find out.

After a half hour drive on Interstate 75 and two or three turns onto quiet rural roads lined by avocado trees, they pulled in at an acreage somewhere north and a bit east. A large sign set up in the front yard of a faux-Spanish, mid-sized house announced *Instinct Revival Facility* and a half dozen dogs of various breeds romped around in a pen a few hundred feet from the house. Outbuildings that probably housed kennels surrounded the main house; two vehicles were parked in the circular driveway: a low-slung sports car and an off-road Jeep.

Lillian got out of the car and stretched.

"I'm still undecided about whether we should have asked if we could bring Tackle and Carl," Tracey said. "This property would be such a playground for them."

"Best that we're here without them," Lillian said. "Without a specific invitation to bring them along, I mean."

"You're right," Tracey said. "Oh, there's Kyra and the others. Hey everybody. You all know Lillian—I'm not sure I introduced everybody the other day—this is Wanda and this is Heather."

The five of them turned at the sound of a call from the direction of the kennel.

"Bonjour, mesdames!"

Zhivago Picard, up close, was a lot friendlier than he'd seemed at the park, with Gerald Nugent. Maybe he was having a better day. Or maybe he got along better with groups of older women who loved dogs than he did with a solitary man who was tussling in a public place with a disobedient dog. Whatever it was, the scowling, furious face Lillian had seen the other day was replaced today by a smile lighting up dark blue eyes, almost navy blue, she'd say. He was unusually tall, very muscular, and tanned.

"Kyra, thank you so much for bringing your friends along to see my training facility," Zhivago said.

"You did such a marvelous job with Ice Cream, I've been telling everyone I know who has a dog that you are somebody they should meet," Kyra said.

"And everyone you know *should* have a dog," Zhivago said. "Everyone should have a dog!"

"We agree!" Kyra laughed.

Lillian was feeling a little dizzy with how jolly they both were.

"Let me show you around," Zhivago said. "As you know, I do one-on-one training for clients, but we also run special training sessions for groups of people who want their dogs to be around other dogs and learn something new. Or maybe it is old."

Lillian dove for her opportunity. "Yes, what does it mean, the name of your place? Instinct Revival Facility?"

"I have found that many of today's dogs don't have the opportunity to express their natural tendencies, the good ones, because of the way they live. In apartments. As the only pet of a family or a single individual. Here, we give them the chance to do the activities they were made to do, by instinct. Sometimes, they've lost something and we help revive it."

"Like a sheep herding dog whose owner doesn't know any sheep?" Wanda asked.

"Precisely," Zhivago said. "And sometimes, we can help a dog that's not known to have the instinct to herd or to hunt or to retrieve learn how to do it."

"Does that make the dog happier?" Heather asked.

"And their owners!" Zhivago laughed. "You would not believe how many people take delight in seeing their little terriers run around with sheep. Or their dogs they thought were nothing but decorative go out and bring back some lost object."

Just then, a woman's voice carried across the open air.

"Hey, Zhivago, is it okay if I give the dogs a treat?"

The speaker was a young woman, only twenty-two, Lillian would guess. As she walked out of the kennel and toward them, she recognized her.

It was Iris Kendall, the supermodel.

What was she doing in a dog kennel in the backcountry on Alamos Island, Florida?

CHAPTER 12

ZHIVAGO WAS ACROSS THE YARD toward her in two steps. "No, I'd really rather you didn't feed them. Around here, we use the treats just to motivate them. It's a good idea to do that at home, too."

"I'm learning so much," the young woman said with a friendly smile at the others. "I don't think I'll ever want to leave my dogs at an ordinary kennel again."

"What kind are your dogs?" Kyra said. "I'm Kyra, by the way."

"I'm Iris," the young woman said, making eye contact with each of them. "I have two Jack Russell terriers."

"Mine's a Samoyed," Kyra said.

One by one, they introduced themselves. "Tracey, Great Dane."

"Wanda. Poodle."

"Heather. Beagle."

"Lillian. Chocolate Lab."

"Let me guess," Kyra said. "One of your terriers is named Wishbone, after the TV dog?"

Iris laughed, her green eyes sparkling and her mouth curving in a way that made you want to laugh along with her. Lillian couldn't help staring at her; she'd seen very few people so naturally beautiful.

"No, I resisted that temptation. One is Flash and the other is Speedy. Those are just their home names, of course. Jack Russell terriers are one of the five fastest dogs in the world, and these little guys just blaze around."

"If they have one name at home, can we assume they have other names and that you show them?"

Zhivago stepped in. "Oh, yes, she shows them. They come from the Macsperling kennels in Massachusetts."

"Do you handle them yourself?"

"Oh no," Iris said. "I travel eighty percent of the time, so I have staff looking after them and a professional handler to show them." Her smile faded, and she looked a bit upset. "The last show we did, they didn't behave for the handler at all and were quite rude to some of the other dogs."

"Both of them?" Lillian asked.

Iris nodded. "But Zhivago has been working with them for a few weeks and we have a new handler. He says they're ready." She turned her smile on the trainer.

"We registered for a small show day after tomorrow," Zhivago added. "It's at the Country Club. Just to get Flash and Speedy comfortable with the new regime. Invitation only, small numbers. And I think you have to be a member at the Club," he said, probably picking up on the eagerness on some of the faces that Lillian saw, too.

"I'm a member," Kyra offered. "It could be fun. What do you think, ladies?"

"I'd love to go," Wanda said. "Patrick is golfing again."

"I'm in," said Heather.

"I think I can arrange passes, if you'd like to come along," Iris said.

"Sounds like a plan," Kyra said. "But in the meantime, we don't want to interrupt your time with Zhivago. We just came over because I wanted to check out the place before committing to bring Ice Cream here."

Iris smiled again. "I'm just on my way out, anyway. The boys are staying for a few days, until after the show. But it's been very nice to meet you all."

"I'll walk you out," Zhivago said. "Look around all you like, ladies. Please don't go into any of the kennels."

"Well, she was friendly," Lillian said, after Zhivago and the model had walked off toward her car. Kyra trailed along just a few feet behind them.

"For a supermodel, I'd say," Tracey agreed.

"So, you recognized her, too?"

The other three women nodded.

They watched as Kyra approached Iris, spoke for a few moments, handed her a card, then walked back to their group.

"Zhivago is going to be tied up for a while longer, so he suggested we come over again next week," Kyra said. "Iris is going to contact me about tickets to the dog show. She was lovely, wasn't she?"

"She was," Tracey agreed. "It's getting super-hot here, Kyra. The sun's almost right overhead. I think it's time for lunch."

The others agreed and they headed back to town. Lillian begged off lunch, but they only let her escape after she agreed to attend the town hall meeting of the condo association that evening.

"It'll be fun," Tracey said. "The meeting part is not very long and they have great snacks afterward. And it's a good place to meet all your new neighbors," she told Lillian.

Lillian wasn't in that much of a hurry to meet all her new neighbors; she would rather spend the rest of the day and the evening with Carl, going over her notes and plans for investigating Turtle's death. She also had a column to file for next week, in a day or two.

But she felt it would be rude to say no, especially after this group had been so kind and welcoming to her. She wished them all a good time at lunch and promised to see them at the meeting after dinner.

Carl was thrilled to see her when she returned, and they had a nice cuddle, followed by a short game of fetch. Lillian looked around her suite, then gritted her teeth and went down to spend some time by the side of the pool. May as well make this a triple, as far as being around people went.

Morning, noon, and night. Donovan was continually coaxing her to get out more and when she protested that she did that, with Carl twice a day, he wouldn't accept it.

"That's not what I mean, Grandma, and you know it," he said. "I mean out, with other people."

"You are very bossy, for a twenty-eight-year-old," she'd told him, with a smile.

She was looking forward to telling him about her foray to the Instinct Revival Facility and her interview with Barbara Nugent.

She knew he also was referring to socializing and just being out, among people. So, she gathered up a towel, sunglasses, a paperback book, her journal, and a bottle of water, stuffed them into a cloth bag, and headed down to sit by the pool.

By four p.m., the sun was smothering the day in a blanket of heat and haze. Lillian sat by the pool, feeling the rays invade her skin and watching it turn pink. She wore a 50 SPF sunscreen and a wide-brimmed straw hat. She had no worries that a sunburn lurked in her future, as it did for many (if not most) of the tourists. She wouldn't underestimate the power of the sun. Half an hour would be plenty.

A little girl floated in the pool with water wings and sang, "Bop. Bop." She paddled back and forth around her grandmother, but she was the only thing moving. About twenty others were in the pool, but no one swam anywhere. They just stood there, waist-deep in the water, some of them with drinks in hands, cooling off from the heat.

Lillian tried to make some progress on the book she was reading. *The Girl on the Train.* It was headway of only about ten pages before her phone blew up with texts from Tracey.

We still on for this evening?
Yes, what time?
7. in the bigger club room. I'll save you a seat

Lillian remembered the room she'd seen on the tour earlier and she doubted any seat-saving would be necessary. It was a big room. But as she stood just inside the door, scanning for Tracey, she realized it was a good idea. Almost every seat was already taken. Maybe these folks didn't have enough to do in their own homes and wanted to get out, to anything, anytime. Maybe they didn't have pets to feed and walk.

"Thanks, Tracey," she whispered as she took her chair.

They hadn't been kidding when they said it was a short meeting. A brisk quarter hour of receiving minutes, reviewing a month's spending, looking at a noise complaint, and setting next month's meeting date, and they were done. As soon as the president declared them adjourned, people jumped up to move and fold chairs, creating lots of room for people to mingle. Four tables at the side of the room were suddenly laden with charcuterie boards, trays of sweets, and an impressive collection of wine and cocktail glasses.

"Wow," Lillian said to Tracey. "It looks like they're settling in for a week of socializing."

"At least three or four hours," Tracey said. "Lillian, you know Sam. Joyce. Dwayne and Doris." Two women had joined them and two men followed almost immediately. "Dwayne and Doris are a couple."

"A couple of what?" Dwayne said.

Everyone laughed but Doris.

"Welcome to the Aragonese, Lillian," the tall, silver-haired man said.

"Thank you," Lillian paused, trying to recall the names that had just gone by so quickly. She wanted to make sure she got this one right. "Sam."

"Where are you from, Lillian?" The short woman with the heavy glasses spoke to her, but was looking over her head toward the drinks table.

"I've lived here on Alamos Island for almost a year," Lillian said. "Decided I needed a change and just moved in here, to the Aragonese, last week. How about all of you? Where are you from, Joyce?"

Joyce had a lively, almost mischievous quality about her. "New York," she said.

"Well, I didn't know that!" Dwayne said. "So are we. How about you, Tracey?"

"I'm from Tennessee, originally," Tracey said. "But Lillian only had time to tell half her story. She's originally from Vancouver, Canada, and she lived in Key West for a couple of years. She's the person who writes the seniors' column in the newspaper."

Sam looked at Lillian more closely. "I thought you looked familiar when we met you at the restaurant a while back."

Lillian smiled politely but inwardly she was grappling with her reaction to Tracey. Was she wrong to feel that personal information had been given out that she'd prefer to keep to herself? Yes, probably, since her name *was* in the paper every week. And her photo, although it was a tiny one, and about ten years out-of-date.

"Do you miss New York, Joyce?" Lillian asked, trying to turn the spotlight in another direction.

"Not really," Joyce said.

Suddenly, it seemed as though the temperature had gone down in the room.

"Lillian is here because of a fire at her house," Tracey said. "The police say it might be arson, maybe somebody with an axe to grind because of one of her columns."

Sam, Dwayne, and Doris looked at her with concern. Joyce's mind was elsewhere.

"I'm sure it was an excellent idea to move here," Sam said.

"Yeah, it has to be plenty safe with all these dogs living here," Dwayne said.

Tracey seemed to wait for Lillian to say something, then plunged in. "Lillian has a dog of her own, a beautiful chocolate Lab. She was away from her house the night of the fire but her dog was there.”

“This must all be very upsetting for you, Lillian,” Sam said with a tone of quiet, steady control. Maybe he’d been an airline pilot or something like that. “If there’s anything I can do, please let me know.”

“Thank you, Sam,” she said. “The police are on it.”

“I’m sure the person who hurt that poor animal will be caught soon enough,” Doris said. “But if there’s anything Dwayne and I can do, just call.”

“Thank you,” Lillian said. *There’s nothing I can think of.*

“I’m sure Lillian has everything under control,” Joyce said suddenly.

“I do.” *What was this about?*

“Please excuse me, everybody, I’m going to turn in early tonight,” Joyce said, and in a few seconds, she was gone.

Lillian was surprised and a bit disappointed. Of all the people she’d met at the Aragonese so far, for some reason, Joyce seemed like someone she wouldn’t mind getting to know better.

“This news about this other dog is pretty disturbing, too,” Dwayne said.

“What news?” Lillian said.

Tracey was right behind her. “What other dog?”

“It’s been all over the TV news today. Kidnapped. Owned by a guy who’s a big deal in property development. Gerald something.”

“Gerald Nugent?” Lillian asked.

“That’s it,” Dwayne confirmed.

Lillian’s mind was racing. Barbara’s dog, now Gerald’s dog. Were the events connected? What kind of person would target a dog?

CHAPTER 13

LILLIAN WAS HAVING TROUBLE staying focused on the conversation, and she knew it was time to say goodnight. As she made her way through the lobby, she heard her name called.

"Lillian, wait up," Sam said. "I just wanted to say that if there's anything I can do to help, either with your house situation or your reporting on the dog killing, let me know."

"That's very kind of you, Sam." Lillian was no stranger to this kind of vibe. Sam was making intense eye contact.

"I could probably help more than the average guy," he said. "I'm a retired police officer."

Well, that might come in handy.

"Maybe we could grab lunch together tomorrow and you could run a few things by me."

Nope. Price was a little too high.

"Thank you, Sam, but I already have plans for lunch tomorrow," Lillian said. "And I think it's important that I be careful about confidentiality, as I'm going about this."

"Yes, of course." He looked a little disappointed and she felt some guilt, as she always did, about saying 'no' to someone.

But not so much guilt that she would change her mind. She had decided a while ago that she was done with socializing—how did she find herself in this rabbit's warren of a home, with so many people around, and now, one of them asking for one-on-one time with her?

How long ago was that now, in Key West, when she'd made such an incredible mistake in judgment? She thought Adam Brecklin seemed all right and he turned out to be a major crook. She would not make the same mistake twice and she would not agree to any kind of meeting with Sam Gavigan.

When she got back to her suite and checked her messages, there was one from Chelan, saying that she'd arrived in Naples and could they meet for lunch tomorrow. She would drive over to Alamos Island to meet Lillian. Lillian texted back a quick *Yes!* and a suggestion of a beachfront restaurant she thought Chelan would enjoy.

The morning dawned bright and what passed for crisp in Florida—seventy-five degrees and low humidity. Lillian had an appointment to see Bobby at the newspaper office, and as soon as she got Carl squared away with his morning run, she drove downtown.

"Hi Lillian, what's up?" Ben looked up from a large computer monitor where he was going through thumbnail photos.

"Hey, Lillian, nice to see you." Carrie sung out from across the room.

Seemed like everyone was in quite an upbeat mood. Lillian hated to be the one to squelch them by being the bearer of bad news, but she guessed they'd probably heard about the dog kidnapping already.

"Hey, Lillian, right on time," Bobby said, as he opened his office door and motioned her to come in. "I've got a lead for you to follow on the dog killing story."

"Is that how you think of it?" Lillian asked as she settled herself into the chair in front of his desk. Bobby closed the door, then pulled up his chair across from her.

"Yeah, well, I'm assuming you'll want to write something on it if you're able to dig anything up," Bobby said. "And I'm assuming you're wanting to dig something up because you were the one to find the dog."

"And because I love dogs and I don't want to see anybody get away with this," Lillian said. "What's the lead?"

"Got a call from someone in Everglades City, saying there's a dog breeder out there who's been heard in the local hang-outs telling a story about trying to get Barbara to come out and endorse his operation. I asked her about it and she said she didn't remember the guy's name or the request, but she gets hundreds every week, for money, for reviews, things like that. Her assistant handles almost all of it. It wasn't clear whether the guy was looking for her interest as a newspaper owner who could give him some profile or as a big noise in the purebred dog world. I thought maybe that's one thing you could ask around about."

Lillian nodded. "I'll do that. Have you heard anything about this dog kidnapping, Bobby?"

"Had a phone call from the police department with a few additional details they said we could use. I think they're pretty eager over there to see somebody caught on this . . . particularly, the K-9 unit."

"I heard it was Gerald Nugent's dog."

"Yeah, Mr. Hyde is his name. Snatched from Nugent's front yard. They figure somebody lured it, with food probably."

"Doesn't that seem like some sort of weird coincidence?"

Bobby nodded.

"Is there any thought that it might turn up later, like Turtle did?" Lillian asked.

"Turn up dead, you mean? I guess it's possible. We won't know until they either get a ransom note or find the dog somewhere," Bobby said.

Lillian shook her head, looking past him through his window, out toward the beach. "What a tragedy for that family. Two precious dogs taken within a few days of one another."

Bobby pointed at her. "That. Can you make that the opening for your column this week? Barbara is past the point of caring whether readers think she's using the paper for her personal issues. You just go ahead and write from your heart and we'll print it."

"Sure," Lillian said. "I've got a lunch date in an hour, but if I can use an empty desk, I'll just sit down and see if I can get it filed before I leave."

The words came easily.

Second Island Dog Becomes Victim of Animal Cruelty
by Lillian Howe

This week, we learned that another Alamos Island dog, a Pomeranian named Mr. Hyde, belonging to local businessman Gerald Nugent, disappeared from his front yard.

Canine kidnapping is suspected and police are waiting for a demand for money to turn up.

Even if Mr. Hyde is returned, safe and sound, the crime has already been committed. The dog is a victim of animal cruelty, even if nobody touches a hair on his head.

The connection between a dog and his human family is profound and breaking it is a form of animal cruelty.

For many years—too many years—we've looked on dogs as possessions and as tools to put to work. Dogs love to work, and I'm not arguing against that. But they need much more than a job to do.

They need our companionship, our affection, and our protection.

If there is a dog in your home, take a moment to hold him or her close. Promise him, in your heart, that he can trust you and that you will protect him.

And join me in vowing that we'll find the person or persons responsible for hurting these animals and we will make them pay.

-30-

Lillian pushed herself back from the desk, satisfied. The piece was solid and she felt purged by having put it out on the page. Now . . . or soon, when this issue went to print . . . it would have a life of its own, out in the world.

She had ten minutes to get over to the Sunrise Restaurant to meet Chelan for lunch.

CHAPTER 14

THE LINEUP TO THE RESTAURANT DOOR was about half a dozen long—not the crowd you could expect to see during the holidays and into the winter season, but enough to make for a twenty-minute wait or so. Lillian gave her name at the desk, then took up a place at the end of the line.

Five minutes later, Chelan came rushing up, arms wide for a hug.

"Lillian, it's great to see you! You look wonderful!"

It had been seven years since Lillian and Chelan had first met. At that time, Chelan was an eager twenty-four-year-old, newly installed in her first career job and determined to stay there. To climb up the ladder at the television station. Meanwhile, Lillian was a destitute sixty-four-year-old, living in her car and hanging on by her fingernails.

The only constant in life is change.

"Chelan, you look fantastic, too! It's so nice that you drove down here to see me. Oh—okay, yes," Lillian said to the server who'd beckoned them into the restaurant. They followed him to a table by the bay, and five minutes later were relaxing in chairs in the sunshine, looking out over the water.

"How is the little one?"

"She's just fine," Chelan said. "And thank you again for the lovely gifts you sent for Christmas and her birthday."

"I love to do it," Lillian said. "It's pure fun for me, to go into the toy stores and the children's clothing stores, to see how things have changed in forty-five years."

"And are you still enjoying living in Florida?"

"I am. Alamos Island suits me more than Key West . . . although I did have some wonderful times there, too."

"What about Canada?" Chelan asked, her expression suddenly serious. "Do you remember wonderful times in Vancouver? Do you miss it at all?"

Lillian smiled, but her eyes searched Chelan's. "Of course. Sometimes. Why do you ask?"

Chelan sighed, then laughed almost apologetically. "There's really no way to go at this delicately so I'll just barge right in. I've come across some information about you, and it's kind of—well, it's sort of—sort of . . ."

"Sort of what, Chelan? Come on, give me some adjectives."

Chelan was about to answer when the server arrived at their table. They picked up their menus.

"I'll do the Caesar salad," Chelan said.

"The same," Lillian said.

As the server walked away, Chelan took a deep breath and continued. "Embarrassing. Painful. Unbelievable. Maybe very private."

"My, my. That's quite a list," Lillian smiled. "Relax, Chelan. Just tell me about it, whatever it is."

Not in a thousand years could Chelan have come across the one thing that Lillian would rather keep concealed. The salads arrived and Lillian dug into hers.

"Alright, I'll just dive right in," Chelan said. "I was working on a freelance piece about the future of marriage for an online magazine and I came across some court documents on the Web. It was quite an obscure filing, from way back in the 80s, and it only showed up because my search was such a specific, unusual question." Chelan took a drink of water, then cleared her throat. "Your name showed up in the material. It's not a terribly unusual name so I thought perhaps it was another Lillian Howe. So, I searched you in a few different places online and followed a few different trails."

Chelan stared into Lillian's eyes. "It was the same Lillian Howe and I think it's you."

"And what were the court documents about?"

"It was a divorce. Lillian Howe was suing her husband, Marvin Edward, for divorce."

"And what was the specific, unusual question?"

Chelan's smile was sympathetic. "Are there any Canadian cases of divorce on grounds of bigamy?"

"And so, you discovered that I divorced Marv when I found out he had another wife," Lillian said. "Another whole family, actually."

"It must have been devastating, to find that out."

"It was."

Chelan waited, giving Lillian time to tell more, but Lillian just didn't have the words, just yet.

"How long did you know about it?"

Lillian sighed. "About six months, before I took any action on it."

"Did he tell you about it?"

Lillian shook her head. "An old friend told me and I didn't believe it, at first. She didn't have any proof. Just said she knew it to be true. Asked me to think about Marv's absences—business trips, working late at the office two or three nights a week, weekends at the office. Whether Marv ever invited me to join him on any trip, or at the office, just to hang out there with a book, while he worked. Asked me to listen to my heart, to really probe how I felt about the health of the marriage. Questioned me about how often Marv told me he loved me—which was never.

"I told her we had to be careful, here. Some men just don't say the words 'I love you'. I read that there are other ways to say it—or show it. She questioned me about how often Marv showed me that he loved me, and the answer was also 'never'.

"But I still wouldn't believe her. Then, she sent me photographs, taken over a number of years. Marv with his other wife and with their child."

Lillian gave herself a shake and brought the wall back up around herself. "I should tell you the rest of the story. I confronted him, he disappeared. I filed for divorce but I don't know if they ever found him, to serve the papers. I went into a depression, couldn't do my teaching job anymore. The money got tighter and tighter. Then, I thought I could get myself out of the hole if I could just do well with some investments. I put everything into an overseas company that promised double-digit returns within a year, and I lost it all. My house, my tiny savings account. I hadn't stayed long enough in teaching to get the pension.

"So, I ended up in the car, where you met me."

"My God, Lillian." Chelan had barely breathed during Lillian's story.

"Yeah. Just a nightmare," Lillian said. "But . . . it's all over now. It was a long time ago and I've long since recovered."

"You must have been very strong," Chelan said. "But, why didn't your children help you, financially?"

"Oh, they wanted to. But there were some things said and some accusations made. I wasn't inclined to take any handouts from them."

"What did they have to say about their father?"

Lillian pushed her salad around on the plate. She hadn't eaten a bite. "You know, I never told them. I don't know, I'd been so thoroughly convinced of the importance of loyalty that I just couldn't ever wade into that conversation with them. And, I didn't want them to feel as hurt as I did. When he took off, they blamed me, said I'd driven him away. We have a kind of uneasy, occasionally cordial relationship now but it took decades to get there."

Chelan pushed her own plate aside and leaned across the table. "You know, I think the time might have come to clear the air, Lillian. I think they should know what was really going on. The truth is always better than the alternative."

"Not when there's no benefit to anybody involved," Lillian said. "I don't have any burning need for them to know that he hurt me. I don't need to blame him or to have my 'day in court'. It's all so long ago and it just doesn't matter now."

"But it's part of their lives, too, Lillian. He didn't just disappear on you, he disappeared on them, too."

"Well, he didn't, actually. I found out years later that he got back in touch. Phone calls and letters and gifts, sometimes. Told them I'd refused to allow him back in the picture. That's how he put it 'back in the picture'!" Lillian could feel herself getting upset about the memories. That was why she stayed away from the subject. The bridge to bitterness was very short. "The picture he was in had another woman in it. And a child. Even if he'd approached and asked me, which he never did, what was I supposed to do? Forget that there was this other family, and that these other people were at risk of being hurt, too? I just had to let it go."

"Well, Lillian, I—"

But Lillian was done with the conversation. She stood up. "Chelan, I know you mean well, but I don't want to talk about this anymore."

When she walked out into the fresh air and sunshine outside the restaurant, Lillian felt like she'd been released from prison. A few moments later, Chelan came hurrying out, looking up and down the street until she saw Lillian sitting on a bench a few hundred feet away.

Lillian waved her over. "Chelan, I have to do an errand in Everglades City this afternoon. Do you want to come along? My editor gave me a lead on this dog story I'm following, but the person I want to interview seems to be based out there."

"Oh, Lillian, thanks, I'd love to," Chelan said. "I'm so sorry. I thought I'd really offended you. Of course, I won't push you any more to open up these secrets—"

"So, we can talk about the dog killing and we can talk about ways of covering a story. Those are our topics." Lillian stood up, and gave Chelan a smile. "Those are my terms. Are you coming along?"

CHAPTER 15

LILLIAN PULLED OFF TAMIAMI TRAIL at the sign for Everglades City. They could have taken the interstate, which turned into something called Alligator Alley and then barreled straight on through the Everglades, but Lillian had been told the Trail was a more scenic drive.

She didn't have the basis for comparison, but this was definitely scenic. Long reeds and cypress trees lined both sides of the two-lane road. Tracey had told her, when she called to mention that she was going to the Everglades this afternoon on a story and she was sorry that Tracey couldn't go along (but maybe, next time), that Marjory Stoneman Douglas had named this the River of Grass in the 1940s, and the name had stuck. Tracey said it was the third largest national park in the U.S. and that it was right next door to the Big Cypress Nature Preserve, which was sort of like the National Park, except that you could have businesses in it and the trees and animals were a bit different. Alligators and Burmese python snakes in the Everglades, rattlesnakes and cougars in Big Cypress. Got it.

Everglades City Hall was a square, white building with impressive pillars set out in front in a pleasant symmetry. On the way back from the National Park office, Lillian would like to stop in and see what lived there. But her plan was to stop at the Park first, get some brochures, talk to a ranger, and try to pick up some information about the place. She'd already looked online and had the names and addresses of the two Pomeranian dog breeders who lived in the area. If she had time, she'd scope out a few of the other breeds.

She felt good about having Chelan along with her on this little expedition. If there were any conflict, she planned to fall back on the 'little old lady in distress' routine, but if that didn't work, she was sure that Chelan had a few reporting and people management skills in her kit bag.

The conversation with the Park Ranger, while pleasant enough, hadn't really brought out anything she didn't already know. Discreet, that was the word for the reaction. Didn't know the breeder that Lillian mentioned, hadn't heard about a dog killing and a dog kidnapping on Alamos Island, couldn't suggest where Lillian might inquire next.

They walked back to Lillian's Karmann Ghia, both a little demoralized. Then, Lillian saw Marlon. Marlon Tanaka, the Florida Floral Tours guide. He was standing behind an SUV, opening the tailgate and shoving a golf bag inside. It looked as though he had dog crates in the back.

Lillian made her mind up quickly. "Mr. Tanaka!" She called out.

"No, Lillian, don't—" Chelan tried to shush her friend, but it was too late.

He looked up and across the parking lot at them. In seconds, he closed the crate door, shut the tailgate, and ran around to the driver's door to get behind the wheel. Literally, he ran. You don't often see that.

He had driven out of the parking lot before Lillian had even the beginning of an idea of what to do next.

"Well, I never," Lillian said.

"I can't even," Chelan agreed.

"You shushed me when I called to him," Lillian said.

"I had a feeling he would bolt," Chelan said. "I don't know why. But I have no idea who he is or how he's important to anything you're working on."

Lillian smiled at her. "You think of it as something I'm 'working on'?"

"Of course, I do. It seems like you've got quite a story going here, Lillian. But who was that guy and where does he fit in?"

"He's a tour guide that my friend and I met at Gulf Coast Gardens earlier this week. He's a dog lover, he said, and owns one or two Highland terriers. I don't quite remember all the details of the conversation."

"I guess he was here to enjoy the wide-open spaces with his dogs," Chelan said. "But I didn't see any Scottish terriers in that crate. I think it was something smaller. Reddish or blondish fur." Chelan shaded her eyes with her hand and looked off down the road, away from the Park office. "Maybe a Pomeranian."

They got into Lillian's car and tried to find Marlon's SUV out on the main road through town, but the moment for giving chase had long passed. The street wove through town toward the water's edge—the entrance to the Ten Thousand Islands that had once given shelter, adventure, and many mosquito bites to people running from any number of challenges on the mainland. Maybe they still did.

The Smallwood Store, at the end of the road, was a bookstore/souvenir shop/museum. It looked like it was more than a hundred years old. It was open, but the clerk behind the counter had never heard of the dog breeder Lillian was seeking and hadn't seen anybody driving an SUV pull in that afternoon. Or that morning.

Lillian was definitely drooping, but Chelan pointed out that she'd actually made quite a bit of progress that day. She'd seen Marlon Tanaka and knew he felt guilty about something—otherwise, why did he run? Innocent people just hang around and answer questions.

Lillian cheered up a bit, but she was exhausted and ready to go home. They had one more stop to make, though. They had come all this way and they had to find the dog kennel and talk with the breeder. Lillian put the coordinates and the address into the GPS and twenty minutes later, they were pulling into the Big Cypress yard of a dual business: dog breeder, with Pomeranians and Collies for sale, and Airboat tour operator, with alligator sightings guaranteed.

Lillian had never ridden on an airboat or hovercraft or marine tank or whatever the Everglades tour company vehicles were called. She knew the machines were in the vicinity; she could hear the loud roar they made. One of these days, she might like to have the experience, but for today, all she cared about doing was asking a few questions of the dog breeder.

It was not to be. The clerk behind the Airboat Tour counter said they shared space with the dog breeder, and the dog people had gone away on a trip. All of their old animals had been farmed out to friends and relatives for two weeks and there were no new ones. Lillian searched among the vehicles parked in the lot, their passengers all off on an airboat ride.

No sign of Marlon Tanaka.

CHAPTER 16

ON THE MORNING OF THE DOG SHOW, Lillian gave a little extra time and care to Carl. She always felt guilty when she left him on his own for five or six hours. But this was even a bit more intense because she was leaving him to go hang out with a bunch of other dogs.

She took him to the dog park and sent him chasing tennis balls for nearly an hour. When they got home, he immediately headed for his crate, curled up inside, and went to sleep.

Tracey was waiting for her in the lobby. "Kyra and the others will be here in just a few minutes," she said.

Lillian wasn't inclined to wait. "Why don't we just get going? I'm sure we'll see them over there, and I don't want to be away from Carl too long. Let's take my car."

"Well, if you're sure . . ." Tracey didn't seem like she was, but Lillian swept her along, toward the parking lot and then out to the highway, toward the Sandpiper Country Club.

The parking lot there was jammed with Bentleys, Jaguars, and BMWs. Lillian looked around, thinking she might spot the one that had been in the dog park that awful morning, but it was like trying to pick out a specific bird in a flock on a wire.

Why hadn't she thought to pull out her smartphone with its camera and take a photo of the license plate, the way Donovan and Hailey snapped pictures of everything mildly interesting to them in a day?

Ah well, spilled milk. Lillian turned her attention to the people passing by, since the cars had nothing for her related to her search. Most were dressed as if coming from Sunday church or a special night out for dinner. She saw floral print dresses and tropical shirts everywhere, with jewelry and special watches galore. They must be spectators rather than owners and contestants, because none were accompanied by dogs. She was disappointed by that, but she expected there would be plenty of dogs to see inside.

Lillian had been to a handful of dog shows over the years, usually just for an afternoon's entertainment once in a while. Carl was far from being a show dog, even though he had papers and she thought he was an exceptionally handsome specimen of his breed. Lillian had other priorities.

Scanning the crowd of people threading their way through the parked cars toward an open area near the driving range, Lillian spotted Gerald walking in beside a younger man in a white linen suit.

"There's Gerald Nugent," she said to Tracey.

"The one whose dog was kidnapped?"

"And the one married to my boss, Barbara, whose dog was killed."

Tracey shook her head. "So horrible. You know, this has really shaken up everybody at the condo. Watching their own dogs really closely."

Lillian nodded. "Me, too. Oh, and look, there's Iris Kendall."

They watched the supermodel make her way toward the dog show tents. Even in a parking lot in one of tens of thousands of clubs near small cities in any state, she shone.

"Is Barbara here?" Tracey asked.

"I would think she might give it a pass since it hasn't been long since Turtle was killed," Lillian said. "I also would think he would probably be one of the stars of this show. And now he's gone."

Then, Lillian's attention was hooked and landed like a fish. A woman in khaki pants and a T-shirt trailed along behind a short man in huge sunglasses and a seersucker jacket. It was the dog-hater she'd run into at the waterfront—the one who'd taken such exception to Carl, minding his own business on an off-leash doggie beach.

What on earth was a dog-hater doing at a dog show?

They flashed their invitation cards and made their way into the tent, where bleachers had been set up around a show arena. Eight handlers were trotting around the center ring with dogs on leashes showing their best stuff. The judge stood in the middle, staring intently at each tiny dog as it went by.

Tracey stopped to watch. "Which one would you choose?" she asked.

Lillian knew absolutely nothing about these dogs, but it was fun to play. "Okay, I'll say the Pug."

"I pick the Pomeranian," Tracey said.

The handlers put their dogs into a sit while the judge walked up to each and considered him carefully.

"One, two, three, four," the judge said, pointing to each.

Number one was the Pomeranian, a vivacious orange and cream-colored somebody with a lively smile and great presence, as he scampered around the ring beside his handler for the victory lap. *One of those dogs who has no idea he weighs only seven pounds.*

"Windmill's Best Bedside Manner, owned by Dr. and Mrs. Ellison Mills, shown by Noreen Marengo." The show announcer's voice was proud, almost as if he owned the dog himself.

Lillian watched as the owners joined the judge, handler, and dog in the center of the ring. The owners stepped forward to receive the ribbon for 'Best in Group'. it was the dog-hater from the beach! Lillian was still baffled as to why this woman would be front-and-center at a dog show.

"They did the 'Best in Breed' judging much earlier this morning," Tracey said . "Kyra told me she is thinking of entering Ice Cream next year."

"Do you know this Pomeranian?"

"Yes, his call name is Feisty. Owned by that guy, Ellison Mills."

"Do you know his wife?"

"Yes, they write her up in the social pages sometimes. Bit of an oddball, right? Look at the way she's dressed," Tracey smiled. "Selena Birkenshaw is her name."

"Maybe 'feisty' is a good nickname for her, too," Lillian said. "Did Gerald Nugent's Pomeranian have any chance of beating this one?"

"We've reached the limit of my knowledge," Tracey said. "But Kyra might know."

They found her roaming the rows of tables and crates where dogs and handlers waited for their event. Each dog had a little fiefdom of his own, with room for his grooming supplies, human attendants, and a place to lie down and relax. Lillian watched a woman blow-drying the long locks of an Afghan hound; both dog and handler looked as though they were enjoying the moment.

"Hi there," Kyra said, glancing and smiling at them quickly but not taking her eyes off the dogs for more than a moment. She had a notebook and pen in hand and kept moving as they talked, stopping occasionally to make a note or a check mark on her pad.

"We just saw the Toy Group," Tracey said.

"Ellison Mills's Pom won that one," Kyra commented. "Are you enjoying yourselves?"

"Absolutely. It was so nice of Iris Kendall to get us the invites." Tracey seemed to look around the tent for something. "Do they have any Great Danes here?"

"Over by the south wall," Kyra said. "Working Group."

"Oh, I like that idea," Tracey said. "That he be a working group dog. Even though the only work he does is keep me company and entertain me."

"That might be work," Lillian joked.

Tracey laughed.

"Maybe he needs to go to Zhivago's training camp. Get back to his roots," Kyra said.

"Sounds a bit strange," Lillian said.

"I guess it would be, if you're trying to get a Maltese to herd sheep or something," Tracey said. "But if you have a Chihuahua who does nothing but lie on the couch all day or a Newfoundland that doesn't want to go near the water, it might work. Try to get them back to their roots."

"That would be interesting, to see one of those sessions, see Zhivago in action," Lillian said.

"Oh, look at this gorgeous Samoyed," Kyra said, making a note on her pad.

"Are you scoping out the competition?" Lillian asked.

"Sort of," Kyra laughed. "Technically, they don't compete with each other. The judges are looking for conformation to a breed standard. But I like to look and try to see which of the others might catch the judge's eye and come closer than Ice Cream. She's pretty special, but she has a few minor flaws."

"Do you know anything about Salukis?" Lillian was keeping up with Kyra and Tracey, while she tried to scan the crowds strolling past the dog tables and pens.

"Are you thinking of Turtle Nugent, the one who was killed?" Kyra asked. "He was a champion. Barbara showed him regularly.

"You know Barbara Nugent?"

"Oh, yes," Kyra said. "I just spoke with her half an hour ago, over by the refreshments area."

"She's here?" It was an obvious question that Lillian probably should have left unasked, but she was surprised.

Kyra smiled at her. "She's one of the show organizers. Yes, she's here. So is her husband, Gerald. He had his Pom, Mr. Hyde, entered, but . . . I don't know if you heard, but the dog's disappeared."

"What do people think happened?"

"There's gossip, of course," Kyra said. "The dog's not terribly well-trained. People think they probably left him unsupervised, and he just wandered off."

"How are Barbara and Gerald taking it?"

"Upset, of course. Marlon!" Kyra almost bumped into a man carrying two small dogs. "Hi, how are you? Nice to see you here. These are my friends, Tracey and Lillian."

Lillian found herself face to face with the man she and Chelan had been pursuing through the roads of the Everglades. Marlon Tanaka had two Scottie dogs on plaid leashes. He seemed to be in a rush.

"Kyra, hello! Nice to see you, can't stop, sorry, we have to find our benching area," Marlon said, hurrying off toward the north end of the tent.

When Lillian had last seen him, he was stowing golf clubs in the back of a Jeep and then speeding through the Everglades. Before that, he'd been leading a group of tourists through Gulf Coast Botanical Gardens. Now, he was getting ready to go onto a dog show floor. Versatile guy.

"What was I saying? Oh, yes, Gerald and Barbara. They're very upset that Mr. Hyde has disappeared—Gerald is, anyway. Barbara's not a big fan of the Pomeranians."

"We just saw that group judged," Lillian said. "I take it that the dog who won was already the best in his breed. That's why he was in the ring with all those others?"

"Yes, Feisty is an outstanding example of the Pomeranian," Kyra said. "Mr. Hyde would have given him some competition, though. If he'd been here."

"Is there any news about him?" Lillian asked.

Kyra shook her head. "So far, they've only been willing to say he's 'missing', but you have to admit, it's quite a coincidence, two dogs in less than a week."

"And what a tragedy for that one family," Lillian said.

"Are you enjoying the show?" The voice was deep and authoritative, and if Lillian had taken a guess before she turned around, she would have guessed Zhivago Picard. The trainer had three dogs with him on leash: a Dalmatian, a Chow, and a Poodle.

"Hello, Zhivago, yes, we certainly are," Kyra said. "Are these your entries for today?"

"Yes, non-sporting group. I am just going to deliver them to their handlers," Zhivago said.

He smiled at them all as he passed by.

"Why don't we go grab a seat for the judging?" Lillian suggested.

As they threaded their way among the tables, Lillian spotted Arlo with his Chihuahua, Marlon with his two Scotties, and Ellison Mills, proudly carrying his Pomeranian Feisty to his home-away-from-home. His wife, Selena, sat in a folding chair beside the table, which was draped in white cloth and featured a small bulletin board set up on one side, festooned with photographs of Feisty's several wins as Best in Show.

Lillian observed the trio carefully, her curiosity in fourth gear. Ellison seemed very pleased with his dog's victory and with all the congratulations he was receiving; Selena seemed intent on burying herself in the book she was reading.

As Lillian stared at them, something caught her eye, struck her as not quite right. She nudged Tracey and spoke to Kyra. "Let's go over and say congratulations. You know them, don't you, Kyra?"

"Yes, I do. I'd be happy to introduce you."

Selena looked up from her book as they approached; Lillian was sure she was recognized. Ellison greeted them as just three more of Feisty's fan club.

"Beautiful dog," Lillian commented.

"Thank you," Ellison said.

"Lillian, Tracey, this is Dr. Mills and his wife, Ms. Birkenshaw," Kyra said. "This is their first visit to one of our dog shows."

"Welcome," Ellison said, as if he owned the place. Perhaps he did, Lillian thought.

"You must be just thrilled, Ellison," Kyra said. "We won't keep you long. I know you want to get ready. What time is Best?"

"Four o'clock. And yes, Feisty needs a little downtime."

"We've heard that you've had Feisty doing a little extra training with Mr. Picard over at Instinct Revival," Lillian said. "Tracey is thinking of taking her Great Dane over there. What do you think, do you recommend him?"

Tracey gave Lillian just a nano-second of a look, then stepped into character. "Yes, my Great Dane, Tackle, is showing some aggression toward anyone who comes anywhere near me. I think it's protectiveness, do you think that's what it would be? Is that the sort of thing Zhivago Picard deals with?"

"Yes, it absolutely is," Ellison said with enthusiasm. He locked into the question. "Canine aggression comes from two sources: one, it's a conditioned response to . . . "

Lillian waited until he was firmly distracted and preoccupied with his explanation, then lunged forward decisively toward the odd angle she'd seen in the drapery of the white cloth over Feisty's table. She pulled it back and they all saw a small wire cage underneath. A fluffy tail and a bright foxish face could be seen, poking through a couple of the gaps.

She took a chance. "Mr. Hyde? Come here!"

And the little animal jumped to its feet.

CHAPTER 17

LILLIAN HAD CREATED pandemonium.

"Mr. Hyde? What are you talking about?" Ellison dove for the table covering and pulled it back as far as it would go. He and all the other bystanders could now see what Lillian saw.

The news rippled like a falling row of dominoes through the tent, and in no time at all, Gerald Nugent and Zhivago Picard were at the edge of Feisty's table.

"My dog!" Gerald was on his hands and knees, trying to drag the cage out from underneath the table. When he got it out into the middle of the aisle, he opened the door and the little Pomeranian sprang into his arms.

He turned on Ellison. "What was he doing there?"

Lillian hung on for the answer to the question, just like the dozen other people who'd gathered. The crowd was growing by the minute.

"I have no idea," Ellison said.

Gerald glared at him. "Did you take my dog?"

"I did not. Why would I want your dog? I have a show champion of my own."

"What's going on?" Barbara Nugent had arrived. Lillian hadn't seen her since their conversation that day at the newspaper office. She was at her well-groomed best for this occasion, ready for the show to go on, despite her own recent loss and perhaps a lack of zest for an event like this right now.

Still, she must have been upset by the disappearance of her husband's dog as well. Odd, but she didn't look happy about his reappearance.

Barbara brought quite an impression of authority with her. Lillian watched as almost everyone in the circle tried to answer her question. People standing anywhere in the vicinity came drifting over to find out what was going on. Iris Kendall and Marlon Tanaka appeared, both with their excitable dogs left somewhere else. Marlon nodded at Barbara while Iris gave Lillian a wide smile. Gerald and Ellison both spoke at the same time and neither one would back down or shut up.

"Mr. Hyde is here! Under Mills's bench!" was the essence of what Gerald was shouting.

"Nugent is accusing me of something—I'm not sure what—but I won't have it!" Ellison seemed to look around for something to pick up. It was probably a good thing that the environment had nothing to offer but a blow dryer and a doggie hair brush.

Lillian caught some motion from the corner of her eye, and looked up just in time to see Selena, *Mrs.* Mills and Feisty's other family member, stand up quietly. She looked across the top of Feisty's dog cage at Barbara, then slipped away into the crowd.

Ellison turned on Lillian. "How did you know to look for him there? Who goes around looking under tables at a dog show?"

Lillian hung onto her confidence and met his aggressive eye contact as calmly as she could. "Something just didn't look quite right, under there, so I pulled back the cloth. Anybody would have. How could you not know what was lying underneath your dog's table? And why didn't Feisty react to the other dog being. there?"

Zhivago Picard had Mr. Hyde in his hands and was examining him, ears to tail. "Because Feisty is well-trained," he said.

"Did you train him?" Lillian asked.

"I did, and I'm in the process of bringing Mr. Nugent's dog to the same level of ability," Zhivago said.

"I know. I saw you in the park the other day," Lillian said.

Zhivago faced her straight on. "And you are?"

"I'm Lillian Howe from the *Tropical Times Gulf Coast*."

Lillian was surprised that she had decided to present herself in such a professional way. It just slipped out, without any forethought. Maybe it would make them all back down, a little.

A lot, it turned out. Zhivago and Gerald exchanged looks, then got busy retrieving Mr. Hyde's cage and getting ready to go. Dr. Ellison Mills picked up his dog and lifted his head to look out over the crowd. "Would you like a statement?" he asked Lillian.

Lillian knew this was an opportunity. "I'd like to do an interview with you," she said. "Could I come by your office tomorrow?"

Ellison nodded, and Lillian decided to nail it down. "Ten a.m.?" she said, then made a show of waiting for, and receiving his agreement. "See you then."

She strode away, leaving Tracey to follow, probably in confusion but certainly showing solidarity.

"What was all that about?" Tracey asked, as soon as they were clear of the Toy Group crowd.

"I need to talk to him about all this," Lillian said. "And to his wife. I thought I might be able to figure out what happened to Turtle without talking with anybody much, but I'm realizing you just can't."

Tracey looked her up and down. "Maybe the group at the Aragonese could help you, after all?"

Lillian shook her head. "I wouldn't go *that* far."

When they got out to the parking lot, it took a few minutes to locate Lillian's car. Donovan coached her about this all the time, but it just wasn't top-of-mind for her and she always forgot to make a note of where she parked.

Tracey hadn't noticed either, so they roamed up and down the rows, trying to spot it.

As they searched for Lillian's Karmann Ghia, a growl from behind made Lillian turn her head slowly to the right. One part of her wanted to know what was there and one part didn't.

Over her shoulder, she could see two Rottweilers, their backs and legs about as tense as they could possibly be, standing in the parking lot lane about eight feet away from them.

"Lillian," Tracey said. "Bad timing, I know, but there's your car."

Lillian followed her very subtle, pointer-finger signal, and saw her little car on the other side of the Rottweilers.

She knew she'd never get up the courage to make a move, if she stood still and thought about it for too long. She also knew, somehow, that they shouldn't go straight at those dogs. What on earth were they doing, off-leash? Off-harness? Out of the vehicle they should be in, like a heavy-duty pickup truck? Away, in a yard with an eight-foot, electrified fence?

"Come on," she said to Tracey, and turned to walk with purpose toward her car. She hated turning her back on the Rotties, but she had a feeling they shouldn't be making eye contact with them and shouldn't invade the space that the dogs seemed to think was theirs. Who knew why they were growling; maybe they had reason to believe this was their territory. Maybe they were protecting something or somebody.

Lillian didn't really want to find out. *Just ignore them,* she muttered to herself. Don't talk to them. Don't run. Just walk. Don't show fear.

Even better would be if she could stop feeling it. She was frozen, physically and mentally.

She felt a hand under her elbow and then an arm link through hers. "We're okay," Tracey said, under her breath. "Two of them and two of us. They have each other and so do we. Just keep walking—that way, away from them."

They made their way, slowly and deliberately.

"That's good, Lillian. We're almost there," Tracey said. "We'll just turn right here. Keep going. Don't stop. Don't think about it. We'll get there."

The Karmann Ghia's right bumper was just a few feet away. Lillian groped in her handbag for her keys and got ready to dash the last few steps. She sprang the door locks, then she and Tracey grabbed for the handles, yanked open the doors, and jumped inside.

It took three or four minutes for her to regain her normal breathing and her voice.

"Thank you," she said to Tracey.

Tracey smiled. "You're welcome. I wasn't sure we'd make it, but here we are."

"Thanks to you." Lillian watched as the Rottweilers strolled around the parking lot, obviously very much at home. Did the Club employ guard dogs on a regular basis? Or were these just a pair that some spectator had brought along and not left securely tied?

She could think of half a dozen explanations, but Tracey's thoughts were going in another direction.

"Who do you know who has Rottweilers, Lillian? And who wants to use them to scare you? Putting the least awful interpretation on it."

"I don't know, Tracey."

Tracey said nothing, but Lillian got a sense of the way her mind was going. "I don't think anybody was using Rottweilers to attack me."

"Call the cops, Lillian."

**

That night, she and Tracey had a glass of brandy together in Tracey's apartment, just to de-compress from the terror. Lillian felt it adding to the bonding of the entire experience, too.

She hadn't been in Tracey's suite before this. Tracey had invited her about a dozen times, but usually she liked to just stay in her own place. If she spent time with people, she met with them in public places like restaurants and dog parks.

But this was nice. Tracey's taste was like her own and she felt herself relaxing into the overstuffed armchair, while enjoying the sight of all the books in the bookcases. Her own suite had come already furnished, everything in basic neutral, and the police still hadn't released most of her own things since the house fire.

That night, she dreamed of skinny, powerful animals chasing her through a department store. Might have been dogs, might have been cats, actually. Regardless, it was a wakeful, unpleasant night.

In the morning, she drove over to the newspaper office and asked Bobby if he had a spare desk where she could set up for a few hours. Her first call was to Deputy Sheriff Burtt at the Sheriff's office.

"Hello, Deputy," she said. "What can you tell me about the latest about Turtle Nugent's death?"

"Hello, Mrs. Howe." He sounded as if he were kicking back for a long conversation. "I do have some news. But this can go no further than you and me. Off the record, you got me?"

"Yes, sir," Lillian said. 'And thanks for making it clear at the beginning of the call, and not asking me for favors after we've done all our talking."

He laughed. "All right, here's what I've got. Necropsy results are in on the Saluki dog that was killed."

"At the dog park."

"Not at the dog park."

He had Lillian's attention now. "Where was Turtle killed?"

"We don't know for sure where, but he was poisoned. Poisoned and then transported to the dog park, where he was battered around the head with some sort of blunt instrument. The back legs were hobbled after he was already dead."

Lillian was finding this a lot to take in, so she tried to focus on details, one by one. "Back legs tied with a black scarf or belt of some kind. What kind of poison?" Lillian asked.

"The vet who did the post-mortem isn't quite finished with his report yet but he says it looks like human prescription medication, probably a blood pressure med like a beta blocker or an ACE inhibitor."

"Something hoovered up? By accident?" "Maybe. Or maybe something administered to him on purpose."

"Doctors have that," Lillian said slowly.

"Hundreds of people have that," Burtt said. "Thousands. Millions." He took a long pause. "We've got some blood spatter evidence. From the beating he took to the head."

"I called you, partly because I remembered something that I neglected to tell you about that morning, " Lillian said.

"Well, thank you, Miss Lillian," Burtt said. "What was it?"

"I saw a car. A gray Bentley, leaving the park in what might have been a big hurry. Mr. Serranno saw it, too."

"Oh yeah, Mr. Serranno," Burtt said. "We spoke with him day before yesterday. In connection with a foot print we found at the scene."

"A footprint?" Lillian said. "How could that mean anything? He was a witness. I was a witness. My footprints were probably at the scene."

"There's more to it than that," Burtt said.

"Tell me."

"I can't just yet. But we might need to ask you a few more questions about that morning."

"Of course."

"One more thing . . ."

Lillian waited.

"About your house fire."

"Oh yes, I've been wanting to ask you about that," Lillian said. "When are you planning to release my personal property?"

He didn't answer her. "We found the lens cap from a pair of binoculars in the ashes," Burtt said. "Are you missing one?"

"No," Lillian answered, her mind racing. "Did you find anything else?"

"That's the only thing," Burtt said. "But Sparky's not done their investigation yet, so there might be more information yet."

"That's a lot of information as it is," Lillian said. "Why didn't you tell me any of this before?"

"You didn't ask," Burtt said. "You haven't called. You haven't returned my calls. But you have written two newspaper columns, without benefit of the official police comment, without calling us for a statement."

Lillian was silent. It hadn't occurred to her to call him.

"Do me a favor," Burtt said. "Call me next time you have a question or you're going to print something."

Something from deep in Lillian's radio reporter's past grumbled for attention. "I'm not going to check my copy with you before I print it."

"I'm not asking that," he said. "I'm just saying I could help you. Take advantage of that."

Lillian thought that over.

An hour later, Lillian had Nevada on the phone.

"What do you think?" she asked the veteran news director. "You did thirty-five years in journalism—should I take him at his word?"

"Depends on him as an individual," Nevada said. "There's no blanket comment I can make about all police people, everywhere."

"Or any group of people," Lillian said. "I get it. Okay. Just based on the vibe I get from him, I'd say yeah, I can trust him."

"Then, do that," Nevada said. "Anything else going on, other than the dog show stuff you told me about?"

"I've made a list," Lillian said, pulling out her notepad.

"Aha! Let me have it."

"Okay. Number one is Mr. Zhivago Picard, the dog trainer."

"You believe someone who loves dogs enough to make it his life's work, training them, would hurt one? Kill it?"

"Maybe he hates his job," Lillian said. "Or, maybe something happened with Barbara Nugent, specifically, that made him kill Turtle."

"But we don't really know," Nevada said. "So, we don't have a motive for Mr. Picard, but we do have means, if he could get his hands on this type of medication—can we find out if he has high blood pressure? And, if he was at the Nugent house, either working with Turtle or Mr. Hyde, he had opportunity."

"Number two, Ellison Mills. It looks like he kidnapped Mr. Hyde, maybe he had it in for Turtle, too. The competition between him and Gerald Nugent is pretty fierce. Maybe he's getting at his rival through his dogs?"

"But Turtle wasn't Gerald's dog, he was Barbara's," Nevada said. "Is there some connection between Barbara and Ellison Mills? You have to look into that. And he drives a Bentley, maybe he was at the park that morning you found Turtle?"

"There's an unusually large number of Bentleys around here," Lillian said. "Okay, number three, Dr. Mills's wife."

"Yeah, what's her name again? Selena. So, she hates dogs, would rather be around birds. Maybe she has a beef with Barbara Nugent?"

"Maybe she was driving her husband's Bentley that morning?" Lillian said, adding a note.

"And helped herself to his prescription pad."

"Number four." Lillian looked down at her list. "Gerald Nugent."

"Somebody would kill his own family dog?"

"Yeah, unlikely. But it was really Barbara's, rather than his."

"How's their marriage?"

"Normal, I guess. But who ever really knows about someone else's relationship."

"True," Nevada said.

"Number five. Arlo Serranno. Present at the park the morning Turtle was discovered. Lives right next door."

"So, opportunity. Motive?"

"Don't know," Lillian said. "Maybe something to do with his own dogs? Maybe he's involved with the dog show bunch that orbits around Barbara?"

"More connections you need to look for. Anybody else?"

"One. Marlon Tanaka, the tour guide I told you about, the one I met at Gulf Coast Gardens and then saw again when Chelan and I went out to the Everglades. He has dogs, too, and was at the dog show. I don't know if he knows Nugent or Mills, but he knows Zhivago Picard. And he just seemed shady to me. Plus, the way he took off when he saw us in the parking lot at the National Park.

"Why would he do that?"

"Let's not forget people we may not know about yet, too," Nevada said. "Who else might have a motive? Some other crazy dog competition person who has a Saluki that Turtle beat in some contest or other? Somebody who reads the newspaper and has a grudge against Barbara Nugent for something?"

"We've also got a lot of other people who aren't actually on my list, but I'm just curious about," Lillian said.

"What's a supermodel doing on Alamos Island? Miami, I could get, but here?"

"Why was your new friend, Kyra, from the condo, so eager to get you all over to visit Picard's dog training town?"

Lillian stopped to think that one over. "I just figured she likes him—or his methods—a lot and was trying to help him by sending more business his way."

"Maybe."

"And not just people, but things going on," Lillian said. "I've been wondering about seeing Zhivago Picard at the Aragonese. Was that a coincidence? What was he doing there?"

"Now, sometimes a duck is just a duck," Nevada said.

Lillian shook her head. "I'm not convinced."

"Has anybody come forward with anything in response to the reward that Barbara offered?" Nevada asked.

"I don't know. Good question."

"They're all good questions, Lillian! Call me again soon to let me know what you're finding out," Nevada said. "And stay in close touch with that Sheriff Burtt. He can probably help a lot."

When Lillian came out of the office, she found Carrie, Angela, Ben, and Bobby standing in a circle around a large pizza box. She'd completely forgotten that it was close to lunchtime and she realized she was hungry.

"Lillian!" Bobby was just about to close in on a large slice of Hawaiian pizza. "Join us."

Usually, she liked to avoid scenes like this, but she hadn't eaten in many hours. Angela passed her a paper plate with a slice of pizza and as she ate and listened to them talk, she realized how very many of her meals she ate alone. Mostly, she enjoyed living alone, and she always had Carl to chat to, but sitting down to a meal was the one time she was conscious of how very much things had changed since the days when she had four young ones around her table, enjoying the food she'd shopped for and prepared. Conscious and sad.

She listened to the four others talk. Bobby described a fishing day he'd had on the weekend. Ben had gone out to buy a new guitar; she learned that music was one of his hobbies. Angela spent her Saturday loading up with new books for the coming late fall and winter evenings when the sun set earlier and earlier. Carrie's family had a new puppy and it was growing much faster than the vet had expected.

She realized she really didn't know any of them much at all. She'd missed a lot.

"Lillian? What are you up to this afternoon?" Angela sounded as if she were sincerely interested.

"I'm going to take a drive out to Everglades City," she said. "The dog breeder I left my card for, the last time I was there, sent me a voice mail. saying he'd see me." Lillian checked her bag for notebook and phone. "He said he's known Dr. Mills for a long time. Maybe he can point me toward a past that creates the future."

**

Lillian gave a few moments' thought, then decided to swing by her apartment to pick up Carl. He hadn't had much exercise today and she might appreciate his company on the road. When she went in to pick him up, his chocolate-brown tail swung like a perpetual-motion machine and his joy at going with her made her glad she'd made the stop.

"Come on, Carl!" she said. "Let's go find out what they know in the Everglades."

The day was warm and sunny—When was it ever not? Lillian drove past the fields of marsh grass and narrow channels, on her way deep into the land of the River of Grass, the alligators, the Burmese pythons, the marsh birds, and all the other creatures that made this wild area their home. She'd only been here a few times since moving from the northwestern corner of the continent and when she thought about it, she often thought of the miles of unexplored territory and the Ten Thousand Islands as a dark, mysterious treasure trove holding the answers to her questions.

Now, she was narrowing her focus: maybe it was the dog breeder's kennels that housed the solutions, either to the mystery about Turtle or to her own dilemma about her past?

Ever since Chelan had appeared and suggested that it really was time that she faced her unresolved sorrows, she'd been contemplating her options: should she try to get some sort of closure, once and for all, or should she let sleeping dogs lie?

The thing was, it was not only her decision to make. Well, yes, it was only her decision but the outcome of the decision would affect quite a few other people. Her grandson, Donovan, for one. He was one of the lights of her life these days.

But he wasn't the only one whose life would be touched by this. Her daughter and her two sons. It had been almost thirty years since they were all under one roof, living their lives, going to school, learning about life from her. But even though they were all grown up, had been for a long time, and were raising their own families, she still felt a loyalty to them and an obligation not to hurt them or make life difficult for them.

The truth about their family was not something that would go down easily with them.

She had not yet decided if she was the one who should (or could) uncover the secrets for them. Perhaps the truth would come out anyway, some other way, if it were meant to? She had shielded them from it for all these years.

In the past, she had thought they were just too young to know; then, as they got older, she had come to believe there was no benefit to anybody, in having the truth come out. Marv was dead. She had absorbed the blow, recovered, moved away to start a new life, and landed on her feet. She'd had her reasons at the time to conceal the details, and they were excellent reasons.

———————

What good would it do anybody to bring the truth to light now?

But Chelan had argued, passionately and persuasively, that she believed truth is always better. That even though it would be harsh, at first, for her family to hear the truth, in the end, they would thank her for it. Lillian had argued, just as passionately, that she didn't see it that way.

And anyway, how had this become any of Chelan's business?

Those were rhetorical, unnecessary questions. Lillian knew it was Iris Kendall who had shone the light in the dark corners. Iris, the successful model. Iris, the friend who made the connection between Chelan and Lillian.

Iris, Marv's youngest granddaughter.

Lillian had always thought she was the only one who knew Marv's story. Marv was dead, his other wife was dead, and their only daughter was dead. The existence of Marv's other family was a secret Lillian had carried for thirty years, partly out of loyalty to her once-husband, but mostly out of a desire not to have to deal with the chaos and commotion it would cause her grown children.

He told her he had never revealed her existence to his other, and she believed him. She knew, vaguely, that there was a granddaughter, but it had never occurred to her that the young woman might have any impact or relevance to her life.

Until now. Until Iris Kendall contacted her and asked to meet her at this address in the Everglades.

**

The house was set several hundred yards back from the side-road off the highway. Signs promoting airboat tours lined the ditches on either side of the driveway. Lillian drove slowly up to the front yard and parked.

Iris sat on the front steps, right beside the sign that announced "Windmills Kennels."

"That's the name of the breeder in Feisty's name," Lillian said after she got out of the car and said hello. "Dr. Mills's dog."

"It is," Iris said. "And Mr. Hyde. They're litter-mates. It's actually a kennel that Dr. Mills owns."

"The breeder is his employee?"

Iris nodded.

"What's your connection?" Lillian asked.

"My uncle is the breeder," Iris said. "He has something to tell you about Dr. Mills and Mr. Nugent."

"Before we do that," Lillian said, "could we talk about your grandfather?"

Iris looked at her. "I know it must be painful for you, but to me, it's just not that important. We barely saw him when I was growing up. When I was about twelve, he came around for a while and we got to know each other a bit. We both enjoyed books. But then he passed away. And that was that."

"Did your mother know . . . that . . . that he . . . that he was from Canada?" Lillian still couldn't bring herself to say the words out loud.

"That he had another family?" Iris said. "If she did, she never mentioned it to me. We all have our secrets, don't we?"

Lillian nodded. "Yes, and I believe they are personal. They belong to the person they belong to, and it's up to her or him, whether they are discussed or not."

"I thought you'd probably think that," Iris said. "It fits in with the way you've lived your life." She reached around behind herself and brought out a photo album, which she held out to Lillian. For a moment, Lillian was afraid it was some sort of family photo album and she desperately did not want to look. She had reached the point where she could calmly accept that her husband had lived a double life but she didn't want to see pictures of it.

But Iris relieved her mind. "It's about the dogs," she said. "My uncle Leonard is very proud to have bred and raised two champion Pomeranians. It just kills him that Gerald and Ellison can't get along. He is hoping that you will take their stories to the newspaper and give some recognition."

So, that was what they wanted? Iris wanted to help her uncle get publicity and validation for his kennel, using a newspaper column from Lillian, and in return?

"And then what?" Lillian asked.

"And then, nothing changes. Nobody hears thirty-five-year-old stories about how a man could be in two places at one time. And why."

For Lillian, this was an easy choice. She didn't like being pressured into writing something, but she liked the idea of forcing her family to face details about their past publicly, even less.

CHAPTER 18

AS LILLIAN DROVE THROUGH Big Cypress, looking out into the wilderness and wondering about the animals that lived there, under the bushes and in the shallows, she felt relieved. She still was no closer to finding out who poisoned Turtle and who moved his body to Jasmine Park to dump it there after battering it. But now she knew the specifics of the connection between Ellison and Gerald and she had Iris's uncle's promise that if it was needed, she could have him testify about Ellison's threat to ruin Gerald.

This was all what was important in her life right now. The family connection to Iris was a tiny detail that just didn't matter.

What mattered right now was stopping Dr. Ellison Mills in his arrogant tracks. He was next on her 'must interview' list. She turned her car toward the medical center.

Lillian hadn't visited this area of Alamos Island during her twelve months here. She'd been fortunate not to need a hospital and she avoided doctors as a matter of opinion. Donovan was continually bugging her about regular checkups and she knew that he was right. After all, she took care with her dog, didn't she? Making sure he was examined if he showed any signs of pain or distress and keeping his shots up to date.

But for herself, she believed that if she paid attention to every little ache or pain, it would grow into a serious one.

The street where Dr. Ellison Mills had his office was one of the most affluent she'd seen since she'd moved here.

High-rise condo buildings lined both sides of the boulevard, with the beachside ones looking out over a majestic view of the Gulf of Mexico and the street side ones looking east toward the Everglades. She imagined that if you were on a high enough floor, you might be able to see all the way to Miami.

She had called a few days ago and made an appointment. Easy enough to do; Dr. Mills was probably like a lot of the south Florida physicians and surgeons—more than ready to meet with someone who wanted to spend his or her funds on improving their physical appearance.

"Lillian Howe, to see Dr. Mills," she said to the receptionist, then took a seat in the spacious waiting room. The posters covering the walls showed the highlights of the plant life of Florida: palm trees, orchids, and other exotic flowers.

One exception to the theme was a framed photograph of a dog: a Pomeranian, on a show table with a trophy beside him. Lillian had had only a glimpse of Feisty on Saturday but she would bet money that was him.

When her name was called, she rose and followed the receptionist, who showed her into a room lined with bookshelves on three walls and numerous diplomas on another. After a wait of about fifteen minutes, Dr. Mills came in and took a seat behind his desk.

"Mrs. Howe," he said. "What are we here to talk about today?"

She could see him looking at her with curiosity. He recognized her.

Lillian decided to get right to the point. "I'm not here to be a patient, Dr. Mills," she said. "I'm here to talk about dogs."

"My dog?"

"Not exactly," she said. "Barbara Nugent's dog. And Gerald Nugent's Pomeranian."

He smiled as if a weight had been lifted from his shoulders. "You are the woman from the dog show the other day. The one who found Gerald's dog under my table."

No guts, no glory, she decided. "Did you put him there?"

Dr. Mills smiled and leaned back in his chair. "No, Mrs. Howe. Why would I? Why would I have any reason to kidnap my dog's rival when my dog is clearly superior and could win, on his own merits, anyway? There is no achievement in winning something by cheating. I realized that a long time ago. Besides," he started glancing toward the smartphone lying to the left of his elbow, which was lighting up with messages, "we're talking about dogs. It would hardly be worth the effort."

"Do you know Barbara Nugent?"

"Of course. Everybody in this town knows Barbara Nugent."

"Would you have any reason to want her dog killed?"

Dr. Mills stared at her. "I don't have any reason to want any dog killed. Or harmed in any way."

"Did you know that a bottle of medication, prescribed by you, turned up at the dog park a few days after Turtle—Mrs. Nugent's dog—was discovered?"

Ellison Mills seemed to be shaken up by this. "Prescribed by me? For whom?"

"I'd rather not say, Dr. Mills," Lillian said. "But you have to agree, that doesn't look good."

He scoffed at that. "I prescribe pills all day long. It's not hard to imagine that someone – the person who actually did something in that park – might have dropped a pill bottle there."

He got up and started to pace around the office. "Or dropped it on purpose. To frame me, or somebody else. I'm telling you, Mrs. Howe, this is very upsetting. I love dogs, I've had dogs all my life. I have no reason to hurt any dog and I've never done that. My life is an open book, you can check anywhere."

———

"Another odd thing about you, Dr. Mills," Lillian said. "Why does your wife hate dogs so much? And why does she go to so many places where she'll encounter them?"

"To the first question – she was attacked as a child and she has a fear of dogs, She keeps it under control and is able to accompany me, and Feisty, to some of our events, the really significant ones. As to why she goes to other places where she'd have to see dogs, you'll have to ask her that."

"One final question, Dr. Mills," Lillian said. She was getting into this role and finding that asking questions as if she really were an investigator was becoming easier with each interview.

"Where were you Sunday night, the fifteenth?"

Dr. Mills stopped his pacing right by the door. "At home."

Lillian stood up and took his hint. Just before she left, she asked, "Do you have anyone who can verify that?"

**

Lillian drove Carl over to the dog park for a run. He'd been very well-behaved all day and she felt she needed to reward him. But when they got to the dog park, it appeared to be closed.

All right then, next stop, the beach.

The sunset was a glorious gold and red, with the orb glowing a deep yellow and arms of color stretching for miles.

Her phone rang. It was Deputy Sheriff Burtt.

"We've finished analyzing the footprint we found at the park, Mrs. Howe," he said. "It came from a very expensive brand of sports shoe. *Speed of Light* shoes. Are you familiar with them?"

"No, I'm not, Deputy Burtt. But fashionable sports shoes aren't really my thing."

She thought she could hear him grinning. "No, probably not. Anyway, they're the ones the younger people all want, nowadays. You can pay upwards of five hundred bucks for them."

"Do you know where people buy them locally?"

"Oh, yes. But, of course nowadays, nobody has to buy anything local. Could come from anywhere." He sounded a bit frustrated. "But we're checking into it."

"In the meantime, could you text me a photo?" Lillian asked.

"Oh, yeah. Yeah, good idea." She could hear his attention redirected for a moment. "There you go. Let me know if you see anything similar anywhere."

Lillian sprang Carl from his crate in the back and he joyfully jumped down to the beach parking lot. The only other vehicle there was a gray Bentley Flying Spur, parked by the trail to the sand. The rear passenger seat door was open and someone was bent over, retrieving something from inside. When the person withdrew, gadget bag in hand, Lillian saw that it was Selena Birkenshaw, better known as Mrs. Ellison Mills.

They stopped and stared at each other.

"Well, of all the gin joints in all the world," Lillian said.

Selena looked at her, blankly, then unzipped the bag and pulled out her binoculars.

"I mean, it's a coincidence, running into you here," Lillian said.

Selena shrugged. "Maybe it was inevitable that we'd cross paths somewhere," she said. "It's a small town."

"Not really," Lillian said. "Go on, Carl, go see." She sent her dog away from Selena, who if not visibly cowering, was certainly uncomfortable. "If you don't mind me asking, why do you come to dog beaches and parks, and dog shows, if you hate them so much?"

"I love my husband more than I hate dogs," Selena said, watching Carl take off into the bushes. "I don't really hate dogs. I like them, but . . . they terrify me. I guess I was attacked or something when I was a kid. I don't really remember. But they scare the crap out of me—particularly, if the owners don't seem to have them under control. And that's a lot of them."

Selena shut her car door. "I come to this beach because I'm trying to desensitize myself to dogs. For Ellison's sake. I'm trying to get used to them more, and I really don't have any problem with our dogs. It's just the unfamiliar, unpredictable ones. I come to a place like this, or the dog park in town, and I can feel my anxiety getting out of control. I'm on meds for it but at a certain point, nothing has helped. My therapist suggested a gradual desensitizing might work, so here I am."

Lillian was sympathetic. "Carl is very easy to be around."

"He looks like he might be." Selena smiled. "But I'll just take your word for it. Don't call him over."

"So, I take it from what you're saying, that you wouldn't ever hurt a dog," Lillian said.

"Lord, no. Absolutely not," Selena said. "I think it's appalling, what happened to Turtle. Even though I don't want to be around them, I like dogs. I imagine Barbara is devastated."

"It was tragic, yes, but she's trying to bounce back," Lillian said. "She has a new puppy, I'm told. A Collie."

"Ellison shows Collies, too. Collies and Pomeranians. Likes the long hair, I guess." She smiled. "You wouldn't believe our housekeeping bills every month."

"Labradors shed, too," Lillian said. "It's a small price to pay, I think."

Selena nodded. "I agree. I'm not obsessed with them, the way Ellison is, but I like dogs."

"Your husband is obsessed with dogs?"

"Ever since he was a kid. He keeps a notebook and writes down every detail of the dogs he has, the dogs everybody else has, his predictions on who is going to win what at every show. He's very competitive.

"Any thoughts on who might have been responsible?"

Selena stared off toward the beach and Lillian began to feel that the question was just too clumsy. She almost rushed in with another one, but then, decided just to wait.

They heard Carl barking and then saw him come dashing into the parking lot, in hot pursuit of a pelican that had strayed too far from the waterline just a few hundred yards away.

Selena gripped her bag, her mouth crunching into a grim line.

"There's an example of why dogs are a pain sometimes, even if they aren't the kind to attack anybody," she said. "Birds don't invade or ruin the mood the way dogs do."

"Oh, I think that's debatable," Lillian said, with a smile. "Carl! Come here! Leave it!"

Carl came romping over to Lillian, then lay down at her feet, panting. Selena winced, but at least she didn't jump in her car and speed away.

"You seem okay now," Lillian commented.

"Good drugs," Selena said, and they both grinned. "And yoga. I go to sunrise classes every weekday morning."

Lillian watched Selena reach into her bag, searching. She brought out a pair of binoculars and pulled the strap over her shoulder.

"Come on, Carl, let's let this lady have the beach now," Lillian said.

Selena watched as Lillian opened the back door for Carl to jump in and take his place in his crate. "You know, I do have one idea," she said. Lillian waited. "If I were looking into it. I'd wonder where the hotshot dog trainer was the morning that Turtle turned up in Jasmine Park."

**

The Instinct Revival Facility was even more impressive on Lillian's second visit. Two wrought-iron gates flanked the driveway from the road, each displaying the image of a large, proud dog. She followed the twists and turns, past palm trees, a small lagoon on the right-hand side and an open meadow surrounded by a chain-link fence on the left.

The kennels and an office building dominated the next area, with a house and a stable to be seen far off in the distance. The house appeared to be more of a mansion than a farmhouse, with colonial pillars standing in front of three stories.

She hadn't noticed any of this the other day when she'd come to visit with Kyra and the other women from her condo, but it had been a lot to take in all at once. She'd often found that second and third visits to a place generated a lot more observation for her.

A pack of barking dogs greeted her arrival. It had been very quiet when she'd visited the first time, but then, their visit was expected, that time. This time, it seemed, the guards were welcome to express themselves.

Four Rottweilers surrounded her car. Lillian parked and sat, patiently, quite sure that a person would be arriving shortly, to investigate the dogs' announcement.

Sure enough.

Lillian rolled down her window.

The person beside her car was a woman in her twenties, carrying a small, fluffy dog. "Do you have an appointment?" The question was abrupt but the smile was friendly.

Lillian waited while the dogs stopped barking and then, one by one, trotted off to check out something going on elsewhere in the yard, their 'sound the alarm' job finished.

"No, but I thought Mr. Picard might see me. I'm Lillian Howe from the *Gulf Coast Tropical Times*."

The woman smiled again. "I'll text him," she said, fishing a phone from her jeans pocket and sending a quick message.

In minutes, Zhivago came strolling from one of the kennels, three Rottweilers at his heels. "Hello, Lillian!" he said, as he looked over her shoulder into her car toward Carl's crate in the back. "Nice to see you again. Would you like to let your dog out to stretch his legs? Is he going to be okay with the rest of these guys? Or is he here for a behavior problem?"

"No, Carl has no behavior problems," Lillian said. "I'm sure he'd love to get out and run around this amazing property you have here."

"Would you like the grand tour?" Zhivago asked. "I have a free hour."

"Thank you, but no. This is just a quick stop," Lillian said. She hopped from the car, let Carl out, and then bent down to say hello to the dogs. "Are these all of yours or are they clients?"

"They're clients," Zhivago said. "All right then, what can I do for you?"

"As you might know, I've been writing a few things for the *Tropical Times* about the Saluki that was found dead in Jasmine Park."

"I heard that you found him," Zhivago said.

"I did. And it disturbed me so much that it's become my main interest, just now," Lillian said, wondering how to raise the question she had. On the way over, before standing face to face with him, it seemed it would be an easy thing to just ask. But now . . .

"So, what can I do for you?" he repeated.

"Mr. Picard—"

"Zhivago. Please."

"Zhivago, is there anything you can tell me about what might have happened to Turtle?" Lillian asked.

"Just that I have nothing to tell you," he said. "Why would you think that I might?

"Well," Lillian paused. She didn't want to say that Selena Mills had suggested she drive over here. "You trained Turtle. And Gerald Nugent's dog, Mr. Hyde."

"And Ellison Mills's dog, Feisty. And Arlo Serranno's Chihuahua. And several hundred other dogs in the area," Zhivago said. "I'll take care of your chocolate Lab, if you'd like me to. He's probably already got the retriever part down pat, but how is he on actual hunting? Does he have the prey drive? The killer instinct? Is that well enough nurtured?"

He was becoming quite worked up, all on his own. She hadn't asked any supplementary questions but he seemed to be insulted just by the first one.

There was a long pause, while Zhivago seemed to wait for her to justify or explain herself. Then, he opened the back door of her car and signaled to Carl to get inside. He closed the door on her dog, then opened the driver's side door for her.

"Thanks for coming by, Lillian. I have nothing I can tell you about the killing of Barbara Nugent's Saluki. I have to get back to work."

**

And so do I, Lillian thought, as she settled herself in front of her computer to write. Ever since the dog show, ideas had been swirling around in her head and she felt a need to get them organized and 'down on paper' (although nowadays, paper had nothing to do with it).

She hoped she was inspired enough to make this a really good column; maybe Bobby would put it forward for syndication to all the other community newspapers, if it was.

Sometimes, she had trouble with the first few words but this time, even though the headline would probably be rewritten, it was her starting point. She could visualize it on the page.

Dog Killer still at Large
by Lillian Howe

> Somewhere this morning, someone is going about his or her daily life. Having breakfast, going for a walk, putting out the trash, planning the day, reading this newspaper. That person is filth.

150

This is a person who poisoned a magnificent creature, then bludgeoned its skull to make sure that the deed was done. That life was extinguished.

I can't even begin to understand what would prompt someone to carry out such a crime.

I have tried

Lillian couldn't continue. With every few words, she found herself distracted by thoughts about her conversation with Zhivago Picard. Could he have been responsible for Turtle's death? There was no evidence he'd been anywhere near Jasmine Park that morning, but he just seemed . . . guilty, somehow. He was acting guilty, that was it. Was that enough?

If a person seemed embarrassed or uncomfortable, was that proof that they had something to hide? Did Lillian trust her own skills at reading people enough to be sure that was what she had seen on his face, and not something else?

She forced her gaze back to her computer screen and her column.

I don't know what methods the police are using to investigate. I have no doubt that they have resources beyond those that I have—knowledge, tools, techniques, experience, money.

So, I'm going to use this small platform that I have to urge them to put everything they have behind this effort.

I've heard a few people this week say 'Oh, it's just a dog. Why so much fuss?'

But it's much more than just a dog. The way that a community responds to an assault on one of its own is a reflection of its values, its character, and even its soul.

Our companion animals, our dogs, our cats, our horses, whatever it may be, are members of our community and are treasured members of our families. If you don't protect your family, it's the beginning of the end of community.

I've also heard people say 'I love dogs and I love my dog, but this one wasn't my dog'.

But, if we don't act on behalf of any and every dog that is in peril, we won't be able to look after our own.

And that's dog, or child, or spouse, or any loved one.

American novelist Pearl Buck wrote that the test of a civilization is the way that it cares for its helpless members. Indian leader Mahatma Ghandi wrote that the greatness of a nation can be judged by the way it treats its animals.

So, what are we, here on Alamos Island?

I say we are a great community and a civilized one. We care for our animals and for our helpless members.

And this dog killer must be brought to justice.

-30-

CHAPTER 19

LILLIAN SAT AT HER KITCHEN TABLE, sipping tea and looking over her copy of the *Tropical Times*. Bobby had given her column a higher profile this week, taking it off its usual page 8 spot and moving it up to page 3. He'd had it illustrated with one of Ben's photographs from the dog show last week, a wide-angle shot of the full benching area, dozens of dogs on tables being combed and prepped for their appearance in the ring.

She looked down to see Carl watching her, in his polite way, waiting for a treat from the bag she had on the table beside her. He made her smile, he always did. She reached down toward him, a snack in her fingers, and he gently took it from her.

The note with the list of possible suspects that she made in her conversation with Nevada was also on the table. Her attention was caught by the line "last one to see victim alive". That would be Riccardo Lopez, one of the Nugents' assistants.

It had not been difficult to track him down and to get permission from Barbara to speak with him. She wasn't sure that was the way the police would do it, but just operating from the golden rule, Lillian thought it would be best to check with Barbara first.

It was a good call, actually, because Barbara knew that Riccardo spent his Saturday afternoons at a golf course and was able to give her a name and directions.

Lillian found Riccardo on the third fairway. She had arrived at Shady Palms prepared to go much farther, though, and had convinced the young guy in the pro shop to let her use a cart. She couldn't walk far, she told him, and she really needed to get the medication to the husband who had forgotten to take it before he went out to play a round.

It was often very useful to be over seventy.

"Riccardo? My name is Lillian Howe and I'm looking into the death of Barbara Nugent's dog," she said.

Riccardo Lopez was a dandy. From his two-tone shoes to matching cream-colored shorts, dark-brown golf shirt, and red bandanna, the man signaled his attention to his appearance. Even his golf bag matched his shoes.

Riccardo replaced his driver in his bag and signaled to the rest of his foursome to carry on without him. "What do you want to know, Mrs. Howe?"

"I'm told you were the last one to be with Turtle, before he was found in Jasmine Park."

"That is true. I took him for his morning walk, as usual. Then I put him into the run outside and left to do some errands for Gerald."

"And the next time anybody saw him was when my dog discovered him at the park," Lillian said.

"Your dog, and you, and Mr. Arlo," Riccardo said.

"Mr. Arlo? Do you know Mr. Arlo?"

Riccardo seemed flustered for a minute. "Not real well, but yeah. He golfs here, too. And he's done some work for Gerald, over the years. Managing rental properties for him."

"Do they do things with their dogs together?"

"No, I've never heard anything about that."

"But you heard that Arlo was there the morning Turtle was found."

"Yeah. The police mentioned that, I think, when they interviewed me about looking after Turtle," Riccardo said. "I didn't know they'd do that, when a dog got killed, but I guess it's animal cruelty."

"The terminal kind," Lillian said.

She heard a buzzing sound coming from the direction of his golf bag. Riccardo reached into a pocket, pulled out a phone, and looked at the screen. "Hey, pardon me, but I gotta take this."

He muttered a few sentences into the phone, then ended the call. "I have to cut this short, but I hope you got what you need. Gerald has a couple of items he needs me to attend to."

"On a Saturday?" Lillian asked. "In the middle of a game of golf?"

Riccardo shrugged. "He's the boss. He says 'jump', I say 'how high'."

Lillian was a bit startled by this image and apparently, it showed on her face.

"Hey, it was just a joke, Mrs. Howe," Riccardo said. "Was there anything else you wanted to ask?"

Yes, Lillian thought. *Did you notice whether Turtle seemed unusually agitated? Or unusually quiet? Is there any possibility somebody gave him anything that might have poisoned him? Was anything missing from his bed or his crate? Did he have any enemies? Does Gerald have enemies?*

Do you?

**

Lillian's next stop had to be Arlo Serranno, but she wasn't sure how to approach this. She'd been thinking about it since the day that Deputy Sheriff Burtt had called her with the information about the footprint found in the dog park and the expensive athletic shoes. She'd been trying to recall what kind of shoes Arlo was wearing that day. She hadn't really noticed. She usually got as far as noticing whether women wore heels and whether men's shoes were polished. It wasn't much detail, she knew; she really did need to work on her observation skills.

She considered whether she would go up to Arlo's house and surprise him there, but then decided his office would be a better choice. She hadn't seen it yet, for one thing, and she thought it would be a good idea to see him in his working habitat. She'd met the friendly, early-morning-dog-walking Arlo and the networking, get-to-know the affluent crowd Arlo, but she had no sense of what he might be like in his office.

Jasmine Park was on the way to Arlo's office and Lillian slowed down as she drove by. She was rewarded with a glimpse of Dr. Ellison Mills's Bentley rolling slowly into the lot, parking and letting Feisty out on a long leash. A small woman Lillian didn't recognize climbed out of the driver's seat and followed the Pomeranian around the grassy area of the park for a few minutes.

Lillian pulled over to the curb and parked. She watched as Feisty and his walker explored the park for about ten minutes, then returned to the car and left the park.

Sand Dollar Property Management Ltd. had offices by the beach in a high-rise tower that was very new. It was in the same neighborhood as the newspaper office, actually. Lillian found a place to park right on the street and tucked her Karmann Ghia in against the curb. She'd left Carl at home, to snooze in his shady spot in the kitchen. The temperature had climbed in the last few days and it felt more like August than October. It was the kind of weather when dogs and humans appreciated shade or air-conditioning.

Tracey had invited her to go dog walking but Lillian was in avoidance mode, as far as the condo residents were concerned. There were just too many players in this drama and she didn't know whom to trust any more.

Lillian had considered calling to make an appointment but decided against it. She knew she was risking that he wouldn't be there. Still, she thought there was a benefit in surprising Arlo.

"Lillian!" he exclaimed as he came out to the lobby to greet her. He certainly was a jolly man.

"Hello, Arlo, how are you?"

"Just fine. How about you? And how is that handsome dog of yours?"

He showed her into his office, guided her to a seat on an expensive leather couch, then closed the door. "Tell me, what can I do for you? Are you looking for a different place to live?" His eyes gleamed. "Or perhaps you have plans to create a vacation rental in your house, once it's cleaned up and renovated? Should take about a month, in my experience. You could make quite a tidy income, your house being in the location it is. And of course, once it's a vacation rental, you can deduct every expense with it. Get cleaners in every week . . . you could even have a daily housekeeper. Hire a chef for your vacationers, get him to do an extra portion for you, expense all your yard care and landscaping, even your Christmas decorations!" Arlo sat down behind his desk, leaned back, and beamed at her. "You just let me know, and I can set it all up for you."

The entire time he was talking, Lillian didn't lose sight of her mission for this visit. After he motioned her to take a seat on the couch, and before he sat down behind his desk, she stared at his shoes as hard as she could. She wished she could risk taking out her phone and snapping a quick photo, but she doubted she could come up with a plausible explanation for doing that.

They were white shoes, sort of an odd choice with a business suit. But it was quite a casual suit, a Florida suit, and there was no tie, so maybe it worked. White shoes, athletic style, dark red laces. As soon as she could, she would call Deputy Burtt and describe them.

"Oh, no, thanks, Arlo, but I'm not interested in setting up my home as a vacation rental," Lillian said. "I just came by to see you to ask if you'd heard anything more about Turtle's killing. Because we found him together, I feel like we're in this together. It's an experience we shared. I haven't heard a thing since I moved out of the neighborhood, and I was hoping you had some news."

"Oh, I agree, somebody has to be brought to justice on this," Arlo said. "But no, I haven't heard anything. People were talking about it at the dog show, of course, but nobody had any facts. Then, of course, we all got distracted when you found Gerald's dog. And with that column you wrote! You stirred up the dog community quite a bit, I can tell you. Any reaction to that, at your end?"

Lillian smiled. "Oh, the usual stuff you get to a news column. Some in favor, some against. Lots of dog lovers. And people connected with the dog business, if I can call it that. Doggie day cares, breeders, trainers. Speaking of trainers, I was wondering about Zhivago Picard. And you. Ever since I saw him at my condo building … "

"Yes, I got him a unit there. As an investment." Arlo's smile didn't falter. "The man is fantastic with dogs but not quite as good with money."

"So, he doesn't actually live there."

"No, he owns the condo and rents it out," Arlo said. "Wants to sell it, though, and channel the funds into his business. He has the condo on the market right now, as a matter of fact. Don't suppose you'd be interested in buying?"

Lillian shook her head. "No, I'm just waiting for my house repair to be finished. Well, listen, Arlo, I won't take up any more of your time."

Or my own, she thought, as she rushed out of the building, into her car, and onto her phone. In minutes, she had Deputy Burtt on the line, described the shoes, and minutes later, watched as a sheriff's car pulled up at Sand Dollar Property Management.

She waited until the car left and her phone rang with a call from the deputy.

"Well, here's the story," Burtt said. "And it didn't make Mr. Serranno happy that he had to tell it to me. It seems that he manages quite a few vacation rental properties. Furnished accommodation. Some of the owners are in the habit of leaving personal items around, sometimes in locked cupboards and sometimes not. For their own use, when they want to use the condo. Those shoes are a match to the footprints we found at the park, and it was Mr. Serranno wearing them. But he didn't have them on that morning. He just stole them last week. He objected to my use of the word 'stole', by the way. He says he always puts the items back, just borrows them for a little while."

Deputy Burtt snorted, then continued. "Anyway, when we visited him just now, he says, yes, he does have the shoes on today but didn't have them on the morning the dog was found. Don't suppose you noticed his shoes that morning?"

"I'm sorry, Deputy, but no, I didn't."

"Anyways. No problem. We still have lots to go on."

"So, whose shoes are they?" Lillian asked. "Who might have had them on that morning?"

"He wouldn't tell me where he took them from," Burtt said. "Stopped me at that point and said he'd have to call his lawyer, if we were going to spend any more time together. I don't want to spook him too much, so I decided to drop it, for now. We'll get a list of the properties he manages and see what that turns up."

**

Lillian sat in the car, debating with herself. She had two more items to cross off on the list she'd brainstormed with Nevada: interview Marlon Tanaka, the tour guide, and talk to Barbara again.

She was feeling weary and about ninety percent of her wanted to just go back to her suite and her couch, brew a cup of tea, and chill out. But she gave herself a mental push: miles to go, and all that.

She wasn't sure where she'd find Marlon Tanaka but she decided his tour company was the best place to start. Her house was on the way to the Florida Floral Tour company, and she found herself driving down her street. It was almost as if the car pointed itself that way.

The house was still black from smoke and water damage. She felt her spirits sink as she looked at it and tried to remember it as it was.

She had to do something to cheer herself up.

Just then, her phone rang. *Donovan* on the call display. Definitely would cheer her up.

"Hi there, how are you?"

"Just great, Grandma, how are you?"

"Doing fine, Donovan. What's new?"

"Not much. Just working every day at the marina. Catching a few fish. How about you, are you catching anything?"

Lillian grinned. "Hah. No, but I'm still fishing."

"I saw your latest column, Grandma," Donovan said. "You're turning into quite the agitator."

"Dog world, it turns out, has lots of inspiration," she said.

"Grandma, I'm thinking I'd like to come over to visit with you for a couple of days," he said.

"But, Donovan, there's nowhere for you to stay, in this new place where I am," Lillian said. "The house isn't fixed yet."

"That's okay. I understand that. I'll stay in a hotel."

"Oh, no, Donovan—"

"It's okay, Grandma. I've done it before. I know how to do it." She could hear the smile in his voice.

Lillian felt torn. She would love to see him, but . . .

"Donovan, this might not be the best time for a visit. I'm really busy right now, with looking into this dog killing."

"I know, Grandma, but Mom is concerned about the people you're mixing in with."

"Donovan, I am just fine. I have Carl with me all the time, and I'm surrounded by new friends at this condo I've moved into. Tracey, you met her, and Kyra, Joyce, Doris and Dwayne, Sam. And they've all got big, ferocious dogs. I'm totally protected."

She had him laughing and she hoped that would be enough to keep him away. She realized she really didn't want him on Alamos Island and really didn't want the possibility that he would bump into Iris Kendall somehow. She didn't know what it was that she thought might happen, but she just knew she didn't want those two to meet.

Of course, one way to deal with that was head on. Tell Donovan about Iris, about his grandfather's other life, and about her decision to maintain the silence all these years. The thought of it made Lillian queasy.

But why? It was her secret to keep—well, hers and Marv's. She wanted to protect her family from the pain she'd had to go through, when she found out the truth about her husband. She knew she would gain their sympathy and their allegiance if she told his secrets. Even now, even if they were critical of her decision to maintain the silence over the years, they would understand her reasons, especially once they knew what he had done.

But none of that would erase her pain or change things that had happened in her life after she found out about him. It would be revenge, nothing more, and it wouldn't ease the pain.

Best to let those dogs lie.

Lillian was about to put the car into gear and head over to Tanaka Tours when she heard a tapping on her side window. Two of her neighbors stood beside the car. What were their names again?

Lillian rolled down her window. "Hi there! How are you?" She said as brightly as she could, trying to cover the memory gap she was having. It wasn't that big a lapse; she really hadn't known them very well. She'd spoken to them once or twice in the entire time she'd lived there.

"Hello, Lillian. How are things?" The woman had a friendly smile that blunted the standoffish message her huge sunglasses were giving.

"Just fine. And you?"

"All good here. We haven't had any excitement since that night at your house. There's been lots of activity around your place lately though. Looks like the repairs are just about to begin. Bob was just saying the other day that he hoped you were going to get started soon."

Bob! That was it. Bob Nicholson. And Kate.

"Well, Kate, it took the insurance adjusters a little while to do their jobs," Lillian said. "Have you ever had a fire? Is this an unusually long time, compared to your experience?"

"No, we've never had a fire," Bob said. "We're just looking forward to having the street back to normal."

"I hope it will be, too," Lillian said.

"We've had some people around, asking about you," Kate said.

This was weird. "Asking what?"

"Whether you've been gone long, when you'll be back. I mean, all anybody has to do is look at the house and they can see you're not living there."

"Did this person actually come to your house, knock on your door?"

Kate shook her head. "No, just spoke to us when we were walking by, with the dog."

"Young? Old? Business type? Military?" Why did it have to be like pulling teeth? Come on, Kate.

"Average-age guy, muscular build," Bob said. "Not anybody I've ever met or seen in the neighborhood. But he was walking a dog, so maybe he was here to go to the doggie park."

"A dog?' Lillian asked.

"A Rottweiler."

**

Lillian finally was able to extricate herself from the Nicholsons and her old street by saying that she had a doctor's appointment and had to go. As she drove toward the Tanaka Tours office, her mind was shouting questions.

What was Zhivago Picard doing, looking at her burned house and asking neighbors about her?

Why did she assume it was the dog trainer?

Maybe it was . . . somebody who worked for Arlo Serranno. Somebody who worked for the dog breeder. Or Ellison Mills.

Tanaka Tours was a tiny operation, housed in a small office in a strip mall on Tamiami Trail. After telling the receptionist that she knew Mr. Tanaka from the golf club and that she was looking for some help in booking a tour weekend for some friends who were arriving next week for a college reunion, she found herself sitting across a desk from him.

"Mr. Tanaka, we met a while ago at the Garden," Lillian began.

"Yes, of course. Mrs. Howe," he said, beaming. "I know who you are. I've been following your columns in the newspaper."

She decided the direct approach was the best. "Then, I saw you a few days later, in the Everglades. You were stowing your golf bag in your trunk and when I went over to speak to you, you took off. As if you were running from something. Or from me."

Marlon laughed. "You've got quite an imagination. Maybe you should be a writer. Oh, that's right, you are a journalist, aren't you? I wasn't running away from anything. I was just hurrying to get over to the golf club for a tee time. Do you golf? If you did, you'd understand."

It was plausible. Lillian hesitated, not sure what her next question should be.

"Look, I'm as upset as you are, about the idea that there's a dog killer on the loose," Marlon said. "I love my dogs. I love all dogs. And I love this town. We don't want it to become known as a place where dogs are murdered. I'm one hundred percent behind the police finding the guy, but I think we should let the police do their jobs."

He stood up in a signal that the conversation was over. "Now, if you don't mind, and if you don't have a tour to book for a group of at least a dozen, I'd like to get on with my day. Must be nice to be retired, yeah? What's on the rest of your schedule for today, Lillian? Maybe a visit to the

Botanical Gardens? Or maybe, a stroll over at the dog park, with your chocolate Lab?"

Lillian wasn't quite ready to leave. "Yes, that sounds like a nice idea. Do you use the dog park a lot, Marlon? With your Scotties?"

"No, I never go there," he said. "Too many big dogs there. I like to take the lads up and down my street. That stretches their legs and gives them plenty to look at."

"What part of town do you live in?"

While he described his neighborhood, his neighbors, and all of their dogs, Lillian took the opportunity to observe his office. His surroundings were as cluttered as his conversation. The shelves behind his desk had two books and about two dozen objects, ranging from sea shells to souvenir pennants to framed photos to a collection of dog show trophies. Stacks of brochures filled every empty inch of space on his desk and a credenza in the corner was home to magazines and file folders.

"Have you always lived in that neighborhood?"

It was enough to send him off, for another five minutes. No, he'd lived in five other places before settling there and had a lot to say about each.

Lillian nodded politely and made occasional eye contact, while she examined the items she could see behind him on the shelf. The framed photos were mostly tight close-ups of his dog family but just above his head, and to the right, she could see a group of people outdoors somewhere. They seemed to be standing under a banner of some kind, and two were shaking hands.

Once Marlon wound down on the descriptions of his various living arrangements over the years, Lillian stood up to leave.

"Thanks for your time, Marlon, and thanks for answering my questions."

"No problem."

"Just one more," she said, then pointed to the photograph on his shelf. "Do you mind me asking where that was taken?"

Marlon turned to look. "Oh, that's the Instinct Revival Facility. Have you heard of it? It's a dog training center where they're doing wonderful work. Getting dogs to live up to their full potential. So many of our dogs are just treated like lap dogs or pretend-babies and they could be working dogs."

"Yes, I have heard of it," she said. "Have you had your Scotties out to it? Teaching them to herd sheep or something?"

"No, no. But I have had them in a couple of the basic classes. But no, I have a different sort of interest in the IRF," Marlon said. "I'm one of the investors."

"Investors?"

"Yes, Zhivago Picard, the guy who started it, has expanded in a few different directions and this permanent facility is one of them."

"Mr. Picard is an associate of yours."

"Well, I guess you'd say we're partners," Marlon said. "I'm very proud to be involved with him and his work."

"One last thing, Marlon."

"Yes, of course." He beamed at her. He really did give off a very amiable vibe.

"When I saw you, across the parking lot in the Everglades, I thought I saw a dog crate in the back of your SUV. And my friend thought she saw a small, long-haired, reddish-colored dog—"

"My mother's dog," Marlon interrupted. "He needs to get out more than my mother does so I often take him along with me. Loves his car rides."

Lillian's mind was breaking the sound barrier, as she walked out of the office and down to her car. Marlon and Zhivago as partners—what did that mean? Was it just an exchange of money on a project of mutual interest? Did Marlon do things for Zhivago and vice versa? Had either one

been at the dog park in the early morning hours when Turtle
was taken there?

CHAPTER 20

LILLIAN COULD SEE THE HUMOR in her reaction to Marlon's suggestion that she was so underemployed and overindulged that she spent most of her day going from one recreational activity to another. She'd been mildly insulted, but at the same time, her mind was on finishing up this interview and getting home to pick up Carl so they could go to the beach. It was ironic, yes. But so what? Carl was delighted to see her when she opened the door to her condo. His joy knew no bounds when she went straight to the hook where his leash hung.

"Come on, Carl, we're going to the beach," she said.

Thunder clouds were gathering in the eastern sky but it looked as though they would hold off for at least the hour she wanted to spend clearing her mind with the fresh breeze at the beach. And, it was always possible they'd just dissolve and disappear into a bright blue sky, as often happened at this time of year.

Lillian parked near the trail, then went around the back of the car to let Carl out. He danced around like a crazy thing for a few moments, then calmed down and submitted to having his leash attached to his collar. They walked slowly toward the sand, Lillian taking care to avoid any uneven ground and Carl taking his responsibility to her seriously. But all the while, she could feel his well-contained excitement about being at the beach and as soon as they crossed the last strip of beach grass, she unsnapped his leash and let him go.

He bounded away from her toward the water line, where two terriers were dashing around, playing in the waves.

Lillian watched the three of them. Those two looked familiar.

"Hello, Mrs. Howe."

Iris Kendall looked like a magazine ad for a luxury resort on a Caribbean island. She wore a beautiful turquoise and coral dress, a wide white straw hat with a coral band, and bangles on both of her wrists. She was barefoot.

"Hello, Iris. It's nice to see you."

"It's a great beach, isn't it? We've been coming here every day, since I heard about it. The dogs love it here."

"So does Carl," Lillian said.

Iris took a second to check on them then turned back to Lillian. "Are you going for a walk? Do you mind if I walk along with you?"

"Not at all. I'd love the company."

"I'm sorry if that was upsetting for you the other day. About my grandfather." Iris said. "I didn't want to traumatize you. But I've kept it to myself for so long and I just couldn't hold it in any longer."

Lillian walked in silence for a while, debating with herself over how much to say. She liked this young woman and she'd like to set her mind at rest, but there were many more people than just the two of them to consider.

"That's alright, Iris," Lillian said. "I've been thinking about it since I saw you and everything is fine. I've known about it for so long now that I can hardly remember how I felt, when I first heard about it. It almost seems normal, you know? Although, not in the literal definition, of course. It's not normal, it was very abnormal. And hurtful. But it has no effect on my life now, and it can only upset me if I let it. I choose not to."

Now, it was Iris's turn to walk in silence. The first minute stretched into five, each woman lost in her own thoughts and memories.

"You're very wise," Iris eventually said. "I like that. I think I'll choose not to, too."

Lillian smiled at her. "I do have one request. I've never discussed it with my kids or my grandchildren and I don't know whether they've heard about it from anyone else. If your path ever does happen to cross any of theirs, would you keep this information to yourself? I still might tell them some day, in some way. I don't know. But I'd like to be the one to do that. It's my story to tell."

"But you know, it is my story too," Iris said. "It had an effect on me. It's part of my life, and it should be my choice how much I say about it, and who to." She looked up toward the water. Both of her dogs were watching her, maintaining a certain distance while they played, moving along the shore. She raised a hand to summon them and both instantly ran toward her, dropping to sit at her feet. Carl was close behind them. She grinned at them, then sent them off back to play.

"They're very well-trained," Lillian commented.

"They are, aren't they?" Iris said. "I thought it was really important, when I got them, to make sure they were taught something. I've met a lot of models who bring their dogs with them and they're just horrible little brats. I decided that if I was going to have a dog, it would be a good dog."

One of the Jack Russells ran to her feet and dropped a stick for her to throw. Iris obliged him. "I know it probably looks like they have me trained," she laughed. "But they know who's boss. I make sure of that."

"Did you learn that at the Instinct Revival place?" Lillian asked.

"No, I had them with another trainer. In New York," Iris said. "For months, when they were pups, and then for refreshers, all the time." She dropped the stick that her dog had brought back; it wasn't going to be a long game of 'fetch'.

They walked along without speaking for a quarter-mile or so. Iris seemed to have something on her mind; Lillian decided just to wait her out.

Finally, she spoke. "Even though I don't think you can tell me what I can or can't say about my own life, Mrs. Howe, I do understand how sensitive it is. You can count on me not to discuss it. Especially, if I ever meet your grandson."

"Thank you, Iris." Lillian said. "I appreciate it."

When they reached the end of the beach, they turned back toward the parking lot. The dogs had exhausted one another and wanted nothing more than to trot along at their heels. The clouds that Lillian had seen earlier that afternoon had spread out to fill in the entire sky. Just as they reached Iris's car, the rain began to fall.

"This is me!" Iris said, fumbling for her keys.

"I'm glad I bumped into you, Iris," Lillian said. "You take care now. Look me up sometime."

The young woman reached over to give Lillian a hug, loaded the dogs in, and drove away. Lillian watched her go for quite a while.

**

When Lillian checked her messages, she was surprised to find that Barbara Nugent had left a voice mail, asking her to come over her house for a few minutes. She was on deadline for a major project, she said, and her home office was a better place to work on it than the newspaper office. But she needed to see Lillian. Today.

Anytime this afternoon, she said.

There was no clue as to what this was about. Lillian had a distinct feeling of being summoned and she wasn't sure she liked it much, but perhaps that was just the vibe that Barbara gave off, after years of being in charge, no matter where she went.

Lillian pulled up to the callbox in the stone wall that surrounded Barbara and Gerald Nugent's property, then pushed the button. While she waited for a response, she

171

looked around. Very impressive. Lines of Royal palms traced the edges of the estate and a dozen varieties of colorful perennials enhanced the lawn. She caught sight of Carl in the rearview mirror. He was looking around with great curiosity.

The gate swung open and Lillian drove to the front door. Barbara was on the steps, waiting for her.

"Thank you for coming over, Lillian, on such short notice," she said. "I've had tea put out on the back patio by the pool. It's shady there, at this time of day."

She led the way through the house and Lillian had a passing impression of opulence, coupled with comfort. She would have no use for the grandeur but could live very well with the comfort, she thought. Especially since her own house was a disaster area.

"Hello, Lillian!" The voice was the deep, honeyed tone of a late-night radio announcer, but the man who owned it had the build of a jockey. Well, that was an exaggeration, Lillian scolded herself, but he was certainly a small, not a tall man. Gerald Nugent rose from a patio lounger chair, then extended a hand.

"I don't know that we've met before," Lillian said, taking his hand.

"Not formally, anyway. Not without a lot of other people around," Gerald said. "I wanted to tell you I've been enjoying your columns in the newspaper."

Lillian smiled. "Thank you. It was wonderful of Mrs. Nugent to see that older people needed a voice on the paper . . . and to give me the opportunity."

Gerald pulled out one of the wrought-iron chairs and helped Lillian seat herself. "The ones you've been doing lately, about the dogs, have been particularly compelling."

Barbara pulled out a chair for herself and sat down next to Lillian. "You know, I was opposed to printing that first one, but now that it's out there, and with the follow-up of the other two, I think it's worked out fine."

A housekeeper appeared at the patio door. "Shall I serve drinks now, Mrs. Nugent?"

Lillian spoke up. "I'm afraid I can't stay for tea, Barbara. Or drinks. I thought I was only stopping in for a few minutes, and I was just coming from the beach with my dog, Carl. He's in the car and I just can't leave him there long."

"Oh, bring him round here to sit with us!" Barbara said. "Of course, he shouldn't sit in a hot car, even for a few minutes. That way, we won't have to rush. We can have our drinks and get better acquainted."

"Bring him around the side," Gerald said.

Lillian did as she was told, and followed the housekeeper to the front of the house. She opened the car door for Carl, and followed the woman back to the patio, using a paved pathway through the side garden. Both Gerald and Barbara glanced at Carl but didn't greet him. In his usual quiet, confident way, he sniffed a few things, then lay down beneath Lillian's chair.

Gerald stood up. "Please excuse me, Lillian, but I have an appointment and I have to get going."

"Really, Gerald? Right now?" Barbara's voice was shrill.

Her husband rolled his eyes, but he sat back down.

"I understand if you have to go, Gerald," Lillian said. "It was nice to meet you. Let me say, thank you, too. For giving the green light for Riccardo to talk with me earlier this week."

"Not at all, I hope he was of some help."

"I asked you to come over, Lillian, for a chat about the future direction for your column," Barbara said.

"Of course," Lillian said. "What are your thoughts?"

"Are you planning on writing more about Barbara's dog?" Gerald asked.

Barbara inhaled sharply.

Lillian felt as though a confrontation was brewing. *Was it appropriate, that he ask her about future content in the newspaper?*

"I don't really know, Gerald. I guess it depends on whether I have new information. Or a new opinion," Lillian said. "Has there been anything coming from the offer of the reward?"

"Not so far," Barbara said. "Are you planning to write another column about Gerald's dog's kidnapping?"

"Well, I don't know."

"Because there were a few facts wrong in the last one," Gerald said.

Ah, now I get it. This is how rich people handle complaints to the newspaper.

"I'm sorry to hear that, Gerald. I'm sure Bobby Murrow would be happy to print a correction, if that's necessary." Lillian's cup of tea hadn't arrived yet but she was wishing she could find a way to leave. But Barbara still hadn't said anything about the reason for this visit.

"Wouldn't you say that if we say it's necessary that it's necessary?" Gerald asked. "And just between us, I think there are a few misconceptions about things that need clearing up."

He started to pace. "Yes, there is a friendly rivalry between Ellison and me, about our dogs, about showing them, but that's all it is. We prank each other back and forth, and that's all the deal was with Mr. Hyde turning up under his table."

"You're friends?" Lillian asked.

Gerald nodded. "And he's my doctor. I've been seeing him for the past couple of years."

Well.

This had Lillian back on her heels. She wanted to ask about a dozen questions, about Dr. Mills, about their views on Zhivago Picard, and about whether they'd invested in the place the way Marlon had. But Barbara was speaking.

"You'd better hurry, Gerald, or you're going to be late. Lillian and I have quite a bit to discuss, too, about her column."

"I still don't have an answer, Barbara. Will there be more columns? And . . . about what?"

"About what?" Lillian echoed. "About the same question I've been pursuing for a few weeks now. Why would anyone hurt a dog? It just makes me crazy angry, what was done to Turtle and I want to see justice done."

Gerald looked at her. "Absolutely. Yes, of course, Lillian." He seemed satisfied with her answer, turning to give Barbara a brief nod and then heading out the door.

It turned out that Barbara had prepared about a dozen story ideas that all fed her vision that Lillian's column become the 'go-to' for people over seventy-five in southwest Florida. Lillian took out her phone to make notes, which made Barbara very happy.

Later that afternoon when Lillian called Nevada to go over the latest developments, she was hung up on Barbara's interest in the column.

"Why would somebody in her position take so much interest in a column in a community newspaper?"

"Lots of people like that are essentially control freaks," Nevada said. "She's the owner but she also wants to be the one polishing the taps in the restroom."

"Maybe." Lillian wasn't convinced. "Anyway, she certainly is staying on top of the investigation into Turtle's death. She also knew about my conversations with Deputy Sheriff Burtt and she said she's been consulting with him regularly."

"She might be interested in your well-being," Nevada said. "What does the Deputy say about his suspects?"

"He hasn't said much of anything about that," Lillian said. "Just warns me to stay alert."

"Good advice," Nevada said. "Have you talked to everybody now?

"Everybody that I know of. Everybody except Marlon Tanaka has an alibi . . . although it's a bit murky because we're looking at two different time periods. The time when Turtle was poisoned and the time when he was clubbed and left at the park. And Marlon has no alibi—but no motive."

"In a way, nobody has a motive, not a direct one, anyway. Poor Turtle never did anything to anybody. But who had a motive to harm Barbara or Gerald? Any business enemies showing up? Anybody afraid of them?"

"We do have Arlo, the property manager," Lillian said. "Maybe they knew he had taken some of their things and maybe they'd threatened to expose him?"

"And we have Selena, the birder who hates dogs."

"Is terrified of them, you mean."

"Fear is what's behind a lot of crime. If we hear somebody was afraid and that's why they did a horrible thing, we tend to try to understand them, even forgive them. But they still did a horrible thing," Nevada said.

Lillian thought that over for a bit. She liked Selena and she didn't want to think she might be the person responsible for killing a dog.

"And what about her husband, the doctor?"

"Has an alibi," Lillian said.

"Hmm." Nevada paused. "Could it have been some lunatic passing by the park?"

"Yes, but then how did Turtle get from his pen to the park, to be poisoned and then beaten by this lunatic stranger?"

"Some lunatic passing by his house?"

Lillian sighed. "I really have no idea. But thanks for debriefing with me, Nevada."

"Any time, m'dear. How are you feeling about all this, by the way?"

"Just fine. Why?"

"I remember, from some of the more intense stories I covered, that you can get *infected*, almost, by the emotions of the people in the story and by the details. You don't realize it, at the time, but then all of a sudden, it can jump up and bite you. Or, it gets you days or weeks after you're finished with it.

"Sometimes, too," Nevada went on, "you've got people you're covering or people from your audience who are just as touched by it as you are, and they start doing their own thing, maybe coming at you. Just make sure you're taking time for yourself, Lillian, and staying aware."

"Thank you, Nevada."

"Where are you now?"

"At the dog park. It's about time for Carl to stretch his legs again. He's been sitting in the car or under a chair on the Nugents' patio for hours and it's his turn now. I'm going to give him a walk. I'll call you again soon."

Jasmine Park was busy at this time of day. Lillian often avoided the late afternoon hours, when all of the employed people got off work and headed for the dog park with their best friends that had been cooped up all day in a house or a backyard. Sometimes, the energy in the park at that time was frenetic, with under-exercised canines tearing around, from palm tree to palm tree. Some wanted to meet and some wanted to be left alone, and occasionally, one wanted to fight.

Most days, she found all this overpowering, and was grateful for the flexibility she had in scheduling her time. She could walk Carl at six a.m. and take a nap in the afternoon, or walk him at three, when other people still had two or three hours left to work. Carl needed some social time, though, and so every few weeks she tried to make sure that she got him over to the dog park when other dogs would be there.

Today, a pack of friendly Golden retrievers had taken over the big lawn, chasing tennis balls thrown by well-trained owners. Two Corgis scampered around, greeting as many other dogs as they could intercept. A Mastiff checked out the territory in a counterclockwise sweep, while a Chihuahua indulged his desire to dig in the dirt bed surrounding a pair of palms.

Carl calmly jumped down from Lillian's car, surveyed the scene, and waited for her signal that he could go. Then, he tore off toward the center of the lawn, slowing down once or twice to look over his shoulder to check that she was on her way, in the same direction.

Lillian walked over to her favorite bench, located in a spot with a wide view of the entire park and the water. Whoever had thought of putting a lake in this park had had a stroke of genius; the retrievers, the spaniels, and the German shepherds were in their glory, splashing around, particularly on a hot day. She settled in to watch, keeping an eye on Carl, who had found a friendly Poodle to play chase with.

It had been quite a day. Lillian ran over the events and the conversations in her mind, one by one. Deputy Sheriff Burtt. Arlo. Iris. Barbara. Gerald. Marlon. Nevada was right, once again; it did become rather exhausting, to focus so much on something so loaded with distress and with so many questions and secrets. She sighed, and then took a moment for a deep breath. Maybe what she needed was a long walk on the beach. But, wait—hadn't she just come from the beach? But Iris had been there, and they'd had a heavy talk about the past. It wasn't the same.

Maybe what she needed was a nap before dinner. She looked at her watch. She'd given Carl half an hour to run off his extra steam. He should be ready for his supper and a snooze, himself.

As she looked toward the lake, she saw a fit, middle-aged man. It took her a moment to place him; so often, when you saw someone out of his or her usual environment, or at least the environment you knew them in, it was difficult to recognize them elsewhere.

She stared at his striped shirt and scarf. *Zhivago Picard.*

This was twice in two weeks that she'd seen him at this park. Did he live somewhere in this neighborhood? She looked around; he didn't seem to be with any of the dogs.

Zhivago stopped a few feet from the lake and seemed to be looking for something on the ground. Then, he turned and began walking toward the parking lot.

Lillian decided that she needed to talk to him. She stood up and waved. "Zhivago!"

She was sure he heard her, but he gave no response, just kept on walking.

Lillian could see that she'd have to move quickly if she was going to catch him before he left. She looked around for her dog. "Carl!"

She scanned the park from north to south and from east to west. No sign of him. That didn't surprise her; he often romped around in the bushes, chasing some other hound or other.

"Carl!"

It usually didn't take more than two or three calls for him to come running up to her, his nose dirty from some exploration behind some tree or other.

But there was no sign of him.

Lillian stood up, then strolled around the park. It might be hard to pick him out, there were so many furry friends here today. But she was surprised he hadn't come when she'd called; that was unusual.

"Carl!"

An older man stood in front of the lake, his arms crossed, watching the swimmers. He heard Lillian's call and noticed her, looking for Carl.

"Is something wrong" he asked.

"I'm looking for Carl, my dog," Lillian explained.

"What breed is he?"

"Chocolate Lab."

The man nodded, then joined in. "Carl!"

In five minutes or so, half a dozen dog owners were joining in the call. Their dogs became curious and came over, and Lillian soon had a group of a dozen people and dogs, swirling around her, as they looked and called for Carl.

A sick feeling was starting to grow in her stomach. She saw the Poodle he'd been with earlier, but no sign of Carl. She wished the dog could talk, and tell her which direction he'd taken.

Then, the man called her. "Excuse me, ma'am? I think he's here."

Several people stood around a bush, squatting down to look beneath it.

"Somebody, call 911," someone said. "Or a vet."

Lillian hurried over. Just as she reached the edge of the group, a woman put out her arm to hold her back. "You might not want to look at this."

Lillian ignored her and pushed forward. There on the ground, under a bush almost out of sight, Carl lay, panting. When he saw Lillian, he tried to get up but he couldn't.

She took a closer look. A leash was looped around his back legs and each time he tried to move he tripped and fell back. After three tries, he lay still.

Beneath his head and left shoulder, the ground was dark. Lillian stepped forward to get a closer look.

There was blood.

CHAPTER 21

LILLIAN DROPPED TO HER KNEES and pulled Carl's head into her lap. The blood was still flowing from the cut on his neck and in an instant, it spread out into a stain on her shorts. She called his name but got no response. Oh, dear God, what had happened to him?

The sheriff's car was there in ten minutes.

Lillian felt strong hands grip her elbows and looked up to see Deputy Sheriff Burtt, staring into her eyes.

"Mrs. Howe! Come on. Get a grip. For Carl's sake."

Yes, for Carl. Lillian turned to Burtt and nodded.

"All right. I hear you. What do we do?"

"We have to get him to a vet, I think. Is there someone in particular—?"

"Doc Rosenthal. On Dickens Boulevard."

With the help of some of the dog owners, they tried to get Carl loaded into the back of the Deputy Sheriff's SUV. He whimpered in pain when they first moved him, but then he passed out. Lillian thought at first that he was gone, but the Deputy put two fingers against his chest and then turned to her.

"He's still with us. We have to get him over to the vet."

**

Lillian sat with Carl for eight hours that night. Her heart broke for him. He was barely past puppyhood and she wanted him to have many more years to come. She didn't want to lose him, lose his companionship and the joyful spirit he brought to her life.

She also felt that it would be a terrible shame if he paid for her choices. She wrote the columns she had written and she'd asked the questions. The guilt would be hers if he paid with his life for the choices she had made. It would be bad enough if that happened with another person, but if it had to do with an innocent animal that had no understanding of the issues and the stakes involved, her guilt would be boundless.

Doc Rosenthal sat with them until well past midnight.

"I've done everything that can be done, Mrs. Howe," he said.

"Please call me Lillian," she said, smiling at him. "After all we've been through, I think we're on a first-name basis."

He smiled back. "I'm going to go home and get some sleep. I think you should do the same."

"Will he pull through?"

Doc Rosenthal shook his head. "Too soon to tell. We'll know more tomorrow. Or maybe the next day."

"What was he hit with?"

"Could have been any large object. Baseball bat. Golf club. Piece of lumber. Brick."

"What did the leash around his back legs do?"

"Nothing, really. I don't know what it was there for, to be honest."

Lillian stared at Carl's closed eyes. "I think it might have been a message to me. When Barbara Nugent's dog, Turtle, was found dead, he had a black belt tied around his hind legs."

The vet looked at her for a moment. "You think this attack on Carl is revenge?"

"Or a warning," she said.

Doc shook his head. "The world is full of a lot of screwy people. I'm going now. I'm practically asleep on my feet. I've stitched him up but we might have to do surgery for him tomorrow. We'll see. You could stay, but I wouldn't want you to be alone."

"I'll stay with her and Carl," a man's voice said.

Lillian turned to see Donovan standing in the doorway. "How did you know we were here?" she said. "Is it all over the news, what happened?"

Donovan shook his head. "Tracey called me."

"Who called her?"

"I did," Doc Rosenthal said. "'You both bring your dogs here. Tracey referred you to me when you first moved here, don't you remember? I didn't see you on your phone, connecting with anybody, and I thought she'd be the best person to spread it around."

"To spread what around?"

"That you needed help." The vet picked up his bag. "I'll be back in a few hours. Call me if there's any change."

Lillian and Donovan watched him go, then Lillian settled herself in beside Carl's cage, a finger through the slats to rest on one of his front paws.

"He's going to be all right, Grandma, I'm sure of it," Donovan said.

She smiled at him, as she always did. "I'm sure you're right," she said.

"Any thoughts on what happened to him?"

Lillian shook her head. "I just took my eyes off him for a moment and then we found him like this."

"Doc Rosenthal hinted at someone taking their feelings about you out on your dog. Do you buy that?"

"I hope it's not true," she said. "It's hard to believe that anybody would care that much about something written in a newspaper column that they'd attack a dog because of it."

"Not that hard to believe if you read the news online," Donovan said. "There are many . . . let's call them . . . 'passionate' people in this country."

"Maybe it was random," she suggested.

"It's possible," Donovan said.

Lillian watched Carl sink lower and lower. It wasn't right, that he should suffer for her choices. And yet, despite her guilt, she resisted blaming herself for this. She was not the one who had battered a dog! Someone else was responsible for this and that person needed to be held accountable.

But who was it? If Lillian had to bet, this moment, she would point her finger at Zhivago Picard.

But could a dog trainer, a man who'd chosen dogs as his constant companions and his life's work, be the one responsible for an attack on an innocent animal—perhaps on two, maybe more? Lillian had read about cases where nurses had killed newborns in their care and mothers had injured their children; couldn't it be possible that a dog trainer like Zhivago might be the one she was looking for? She could think of a half dozen possible motives or psychological drivers, but that didn't matter, at this point. She had no evidence, just a couple of signals.

She needed to pursue them before they flickered out.

CHAPTER 22

WHEN DOC ROSENTHAL RETURNED a few hours later, there was no change in Carl's condition. Donovan had fallen asleep in a chair, while Lillian paced the office, from the front door to the street, past the receptionist's desk to the examination rooms, to the back where Carl lay. She knew she'd probably slept a few minutes, around two a.m., when she'd dropped into a chair herself and tried to get comfortable enough to get some rest. It hadn't worked very well and her muscles ached, particularly in her neck.

But it was rest enough for what she had to do, today. This had gone on long enough; in fact, she felt angry with herself for letting it go on this long. She was going to smoke this killer out and her first move would be to her computer, to use the weapon that she had: her newspaper column. She would send an email to Bobby, letting him know that she had something that had to go today.

Lillian's first call when she got back to her condo was to Tracey.

"Hi! How is Carl?" Tracey asked.

"We won't know until later today what else needs to be done. He's sleeping; Doc drugged him up."

"Oh, Lillian, I'm so sorry. Is there anything I can do?"

"Yes, there is. I want to go out to the dog training place to see Zhivago Picard and I don't want to go alone. Do you think we could get a few people together?"

Tracey was on it. "People like Dwayne and Sam."

"Yes, and I was thinking Kyra, too. She's known him a while. Maybe he'd be more likely to speak with me if she's there."

"Let's meet in the lobby in half an hour," Tracey said. "Unless you think you might need to get some rest before we go?"

"Half an hour is good."

Lillian went into the kitchen and pulled a muffin out of a tin. She couldn't remember the last time she'd eaten. From the corner beside the stove, Carl's dog bed sent her a silent message and she felt a wave of sadness go over her. The poor guy—she wished there was a way to turn back the clock on yesterday. If only she'd kept her eyes on him every minute!

She stooped to pick up his favorite stuffy toy, a fuzzy, floppy-eared puppy he'd had since she first brought him home. She'd take it with her in case there was time to drop it off at the vet's office before they drove out to Zhivago's place.

Lillian was almost out the door when her phone buzzed. She grabbed for it, hoping that the display would show the vet's name. Deputy Sheriff Burtt was there, instead.

"Mrs. Howe? How is your dog this morning?"

Lillian almost choked up. "We don't know if he'll make it," she said. "We were with him at the vet all last night."

"Where are you now?"

"I'm at home. With my grandson, and a few friends." She hesitated. Something was telling her to share her plans with him. But she felt foolish. She had no proof of anything and she had no plans to make accusations or anything like that. She was just going to take a drive with a few other dog owners out to a dog training facility to chat with the head trainer about some local events affecting some of the dogs in their world. That's all.

"Well, you rest assured that we're doing everything we can to find out who's responsible for this," the Deputy

Sheriff was saying, when she tuned back in. "If you remember anything else about yesterday at the park, or about any of these things that are going on, you let me know, alright?"

"I certainly will, Deputy Burtt. Thank you."

"Thank you, ma'am. And let me say, thank you for your columns, too. Thank you for helping us send the message that animal cruelty will not be tolerated in this county," Burtt said. "Do you have any plans to publish any more?"

"I definitely do," Lillian said. "In fact, I've got one coming out in today's paper."

"I'll keep an eye out for that," he said. "Bye now."

Lillian had completely ignored the newspaper when she came home and opened the door this morning. She went back to the doorstep and picked it up. A banner across the front page urged readers to find Lillian Howe's latest in the next section on the front, and there it was, above the fold.

Why Would Anyone Hurt a Dog?
by Lillian Howe

> The recent dog killing on Alamos Island has received much attention but no results.

> You have to wonder what the dogs think. We give them very little—just their food, water and a warm place to lie down at night.

> In return, they give us undying love and wholehearted attention. They hang on every word we say and every move we make, and they put us first, ahead of any other creature or thing they might bond with in their short lifetimes.

Do they look at us and wonder why we're not protecting them? As I write this, I'm looking at my own best friend, Carl, a beautiful chocolate Lab, who was attacked in a public park yesterday.

What would I do to protect him?

Does he trust me to protect him?

Is that trust well-placed?

Even though the scum that killed Turtle hasn't been identified yet and even though the creep that attacked my dog is still out there, walking around, make no mistake. He or she or they *will* be found and *will* be punished. We're coming for you.

-30-

**

In the lobby, Sam, Dwayne, Kyra, and Tracey were waiting, just a few feet from the door. They all looked grim and there were no jolly smiles or greetings.

"Thank you for coming out," Lillian said. "This is my grandson, Donovan, everybody. Has Tracey told you what this is about?"

"That you need our help," Sam said. "That's about it."

"I thought you'd be able to explain it best," Tracey said. "And I guess, I really have no idea what you have in mind."

Lillian nodded. "We're going out to the Instinct Revival Facility to have a talk with Zhivago Picard. I don't know for sure that he's done anything or knows anything about what happened to Barbara Nugent's dog, but I want to talk to him again. He was at the dog park last night when Carl was attacked. Since dogs are his business, he'd certainly know what would be poison to a dog and how to get him to eat it."

"Motive?" Sam asked.

"I've heard that he has money problems and he wanted the Nugents to invest in his place. They said no."

"He asked me for money, too," Kyra said. She looked white as the walls and Lillian put out a hand to steady her.

"Does he have any criminal history?" Sam asked.

"I don't know," Lillian said. "I hadn't thought of that."

"Well, whoever he is and whatever he is, we'll find out about him." San looked determined and Dwayne had pulled himself straight to stand what looked to Lillian like several inches above six feet.

Donovan had said nothing, just looked back and forth, from one to another. Finally, he said "I'll bring the car around to the front to pick you up."

"Let's take two cars," Sam said.

The drive out to the Instinct Revival Facility seemed to take twice as long as Lillian's previous trips. She took advantage of the time to phone Doc Rosenthal's office to ask for an update on Carl's condition. No change. Still hadn't regained consciousness.

Lillian stared out of the window while Donovan drove her car, thinking about Carl. What would she do without him, if she didn't get him back? She gave herself a shake. She just refused to think about that. He would heal and be back on his feet and in their home, in no time. That was all there was to that.

Finally! She saw the turn off the highway onto the sideroad that led to Zhivago's place. Now that they were almost there, her feelings were mixed.

On one hand, she wanted to get there and get in front of him as quickly as possible. But on the other, she didn't know yet what questions she was going to ask him.

She just wanted the answers.

CHAPTER 23

WHEN THEY DROVE INTO THE YARD, Zhivago was nowhere to be seen, but the sound of barking made it obvious there were many dogs around. The noise was coming from many directions, behind doors and fences in all of the kennels and buildings. All of the dog runs and pens close to the driveway were empty, but none of the dogs was running loose.

Donovan parked Lillian's Karmann Ghia and Sam pulled in beside him. They stepped out of the cars, some more slowly than others. Lillian could feel her joints continuing to protest after her long night spent trying to sleep in Doc Rosenthal's armchair.

"Any idea where Picard might be?" Sam asked.

Lillian shook her head

"My guess would be his office, then."

"Let's go."

"My feeling is that we should all stick together," Kyra said. Lillian could hear the fear in her voice. Why fear? It was broad daylight; this man was the one she was planning to hire to train her own dog. She'd said that several of her friends had left their treasured pets with him. Why would there be the least bit of fear about encountering him without as many people as possible around her?

But, whatever. Lillian was just so appreciative that they'd come along with her on this … this—what? If she called it an adventure, it seemed as though she were trivializing it. If she called it a journey, it felt too cerebral and too hypothetical. This was all very real.

The six of them walked into the main reception area but there was no one there. Odd, for a Wednesday morning, in the midst of business hours. Lillian spotted a call button on the front desk and pushed it. No reply for about two minutes, and then a woman's voice said,

"Yes, may I help you?"

"We're here to see Mr. Picard," Donovan said.

"Do you have an appointment?"

"No, do we need one?"

A long pause. "It's not absolutely necessary. Please excuse me, I am in one of the outer kennels, doing the morning duties. Usually, we have an assistant but she called in sick today. Zhivago had to go into town on an errand and I'm here on my own. I'll be up to the front to greet you shortly."

Each of the six of them took advantage of the unsupervised time to check out Zhivago's operation in their own way. Kyra went straight to the bookcases lining two walls with full-color, hardcover books about various dog breeds. She pulled down two and checked the inside covers for inscriptions before turning to Dwayne and commenting, "Gifts from happy clients."

Dwayne was in the midst of a walk around the entire perimeter of the room, looking in every corner and through each window. He stopped near Sam and pointed out the tiny video cameras, set into two upper corners of the room.

Sam took up a position in front of each of them, in turn, and seemed to be assessing how much of the room would be covered by that camera.

The rest of the front office looked like every other combination dog grooming salon and pet store Lillian had ever seen. Displays of toys, collars, leashes, bandannas, doggie clothing, and treats lined one wall, surrounding a fire extinguisher and a retro phone, hanging on the wall. Apparently, Zhivago had thought of the possibility that a hurricane could knock out cell coverage and he might need to get in touch with a vet.

Tracey had gone behind the counter to look over the computer. "I've got the daily calendar here on the screen," she said. "Nothing scheduled for today."

Donovan had taken up a position to stand watch by the door. Lillian found herself drawn to the door that led to Zhivago's inner office.

It was two offices, actually. One area held his desk, a heavy, Victorian affair, made of rosewood with pearl inlay and brass fittings. It had numerous drawers and if she got enough time, she would go through each one of them.

The second area had a boardroom table, surrounded by eight chairs. She thought it might have been a dining room table, in another life. A large whiteboard dominated one wall. Lillian studied it for a few minutes, then stepped out of the room to call in the others.

Donovan held his post by the door.

"Look at this," Sam said.

The five of them stood, side by side, looking over this lengthy list of dogs Lillian assumed were currently under care or training at the IRF. The owner's name was listed in the next column, then two dates: one that must have been the date training began, since it was a date already past, and a future date: perhaps the projected completion?

Lillian picked out the ones she knew. *Mr. Hyde/Gerald. Ice Cream/Kyra. Flash/Iris. Macduff/Arlo. Coral/Barbara*

Sam and Donovan looked through piles of folders on a side table. Lillian began to help them, then noticed a closed door at the back of the room. "I wonder where this leads."

Kyra followed her to the door. Lillian half-expected to find it locked, but it opened into a room that Zhivago had set up as an apartment.

"He lives here?" Kyra said. "But I've seen him around the Aragonese."

Lillian shrugged. "Maybe he decided he needed a place to stay over here from time to time. Let's take a look."

The room had the atmosphere of an English country house. Hunter green walls embraced dark cherrywood furniture and a burgundy Persian carpet hugged the floor. It seemed rather odd, in the midst of the Florida tropics, and Lillian could hear the air conditioner earning its keep. A trophy wall displayed framed certificates for 'Best in Show', 'Preferred National Agility Champion', 'K9 Detection Dog Champion', and 'Sheepdog Champion'. A bookcase beside the bed gave pride of place to a collection of dog figurines of various sizes, made of ceramic, porcelain, wood, copper, even stainless steel.

Lillian took a closer look. They were all Rottweilers.

She looked around the corners and the ceiling of the room for more video camera lenses and when she didn't spot any, she moved closer to the bed, which was covered in a plaid comforter that didn't work with the English pub décor at all. On the night table, he kept two stacks of novels, each paperback with a bookmark inserted partway through. She picked up the top one and then looked at the others. All were espionage thrillers.

Something white between the stacks caught her eye and she reached out for it. It was the lid of a medication bottle. The bottle was three-quarters full of white pills and the label on it read: Lisinopril. One tablet each day. Prescriber: Dr. E. Mills.

A noise from the outer room made her jump.

"Someone's coming!" Tracey hissed from the other side of the apartment door.

Lillian put the bottle back in what she hoped was the exact spot where she'd found it. She and Kyra hustled back into the meeting room and closed the door. They were almost back to the front office when a woman's voice challenged them.

"What are you doing back there? Who are you?"

The young girl couldn't have been more than sixteen, although Lillian knew that her accuracy in guessing ages these days was hit-or-miss. She had a clipboard in one hand and a key ring in another.

Lillian decided to try the authoritative approach. "We are clients. Who are you? Are you new?"

"Well, yes I am." She seemed quite confused. "This is my second day."

"Where is Zhivago?" demanded Sam, understanding instantly and following Lillian's lead.

"He won't be in today," she said. "I'm Madison. I'm in charge of feeding the dogs and getting some of them out for some exercise." She waited, expecting an equal exchange of information.

Lillian wasn't giving it. "Please tell Mr. Picard we stopped by." She threw her head back and walked straight toward the outer door.

It was pulled open just as she got to it.

"Why don't you tell him yourself?"

CHAPTER 24

ZHIVAGO'S HAIR LOOKED as though he'd just got out of bed but otherwise, he was as pulled together and well-groomed as it was possible to be. In all the times that Lillian had seen him, even though he worked outdoors with big dogs throughout the day, he looked as if he might have just come from his job at a high-end men's clothing store.

He had her on the back foot, but only for a moment. She knew she had to get her balance back and hold her own. "Mr. Picard! What a pleasant coincidence!"

She said nothing more, although he seemed to be expecting something. "Madison, that's all I'll need you to do today," he said, eventually. "Please leave your notes over there so I can go over them."

She looked down at her clipboard. "Not much to tell you. Coral had a restless night. The bloodhound from Gainesville is a bit aggressive this morning. One of the Rotties—Zeus—was off his food for some reason this morning. The others are all fine."

"All right, Madison, that's good. That's enough," he said, taking the clipboard from her. "See you tomorrow."

When he held open the door for Madison to leave, for some reason Lillian felt moved to follow her out.

"Whoa, wait a moment, I thought you wanted to see me?" Zhivago said.

"I did," Lillian said. "But maybe we could talk outside? It's a gorgeous day. I actually wouldn't mind seeing a bit more of your property, Zhivago, and the operation you have going here."

He seemed a bit suspicious, but mostly ready to show the place off. "I'd be delighted to give you the tour," he said.

He led the way through the door, looking back to see Lillian and her five helpers following. She was happy to get outside and away from the video cameras. Madison was in the parking area in front of the office, just about to get into her tiny electric car.

"Madison!" Zhivago called to her. "I've changed my mind. Could you stay for another half hour? Mrs. Howe and her friends are here to take a look at the Facility and the group is quite large, for me to take around by myself."

"Yes, of course," she said.

"Madison does all my tours for prospective investors," Zhivago said. "Start with the kennels right by the office, Madison. Let them have a look at the puppies, before they all go back to sleep after breakfast. I'll take Mrs. Howe around to show her the agility training ring."

Did he not think Lillian would enjoy puppies? She wasn't sure what this was about but she decided to watch it play out.

"Delightful, Zhivago, thanks so much. And thanks for a tour, on such short notice," she said, giving Tracey a smile, Sam a nod, and Donovan a firmer nod, at the sight of his budding objection. Donovan wouldn't want her going off with the dog trainer alone, but she knew she'd be more likely to get Zhivago to open up and answer questions that way.

She and Zhivago set off toward the far kennels, and after a moment's hesitation, Donovan and the others followed Madison into the kennel nearest the office building.

The agility training was at the far edge of the property. It was a bit of a hike for her in the heat, but she had on good walking shoes and wasn't having any trouble with it. When they came to a fenced area that enclosed hurdles, ladders, and cones, she walked over to the fence and leaned on the top rail.

"I am surprised to find you here," she said, for want of a better opening remark.

"I'll bet you are." Somehow, he didn't seem as friendly as before.

"This is quite a setup," she said, continuing to try to find a rapport. "My Carl would have a blast here."

Zhivago fixed her with a severe look. "Let's get to the point, okay? Why are you here?"

"Just wanted to look around," Lillian said.

"But why?"

"I'm looking for some training for my Lab and I wanted to see what you have here."

He looked at her and said nothing.

Despite her determination not to, Lillian started to feel flustered. "I also heard from my friend, Kyra, that you're looking for investors for the Instinct Revival Facility. I do some investing and I might be interested."

Again, he said nothing.

Thankfully, her phone buzzed with a text and she pulled it out of her bag. It was Donovan.

Tracey had a call from the front desk at the condo. Someone's broken in to her place. They're going to head back right away.

Lillian got to work, tapping the keys with her forefinger.

That's terrible!

Yeah, not the best news. Are you wanting to stay much longer?

No, I think I'm ready to go.

I'll wait for you by the car.

"Something going on?" Zhivago asked her.

She looked up from her phone. "Yes. Trouble at home. We're all going to have to leave and get back to town."

Zhivago put a hand on her elbow. "I want you to understand, Mrs. Howe. I've put my life's savings and all of my knowledge into this place. It was my dream ever since I was a kid and I'm only getting started with it. Yes, I need money, but things are coming along. My reputation is everything and I can't have you going around, hinting to people that I might be less than what they think. I had nothing to do with Mrs. Nugent's dog's death. Why would I?"

He was growing more agitated by the minute. Lillian stared, pointedly, at his hand on her arm and he dropped it.

She heard the sound of dogs barking in the distance and a bird singing, not far away. For a long moment, it was a standoff between her and Zhivago. Then, he gave a snort of something that might have been anger and might have been self-control.

"I have some things to do, Mrs. Howe," he said and stomped off in the direction of the house.

The fence rail was a handy thing to use to steady herself. She hadn't stopped to think, on the way into this, about what she would do if he lost his temper. Lillian stood there for a few minutes longer, then walked back toward the yard and the main building.

But when she got there, it seemed deserted. Her car was gone. Every vehicle was gone.

"Donovan?" she called.

No answer.

This was very strange. Donovan's body language when she'd gone off for her walk with Zhivago had been very tense. Why would he leave before she was back?

Lillian walked up to the front door. It was locked. She checked the doors to two of the closest kennels. Also locked. Inside, one of the dogs heard her rattling the door handle and set up a blaze of barking. What sounded like thirty other dogs joined in. Sound was coming from every one of the eight kennel buildings that stood in two rows, leading toward the agility training ring and several other open pens.

Lillian started to walk down the driveway between the kennels. As she approached each building, the barking became more intense. It didn't taper off after she had passed by. At one building, a window had been propped open and she went to it to check it out. Would she be able to see inside? She made herself as tall as she could but she just couldn't get up high enough to see anything.

It was eerie, how empty the place seemed to be. Empty of humans, that is. From the sound of things, there were plenty of dogs.

"Donovan!" She tried calling again a few times, but there was no response.

"Mr. Picard! Zhivago!" Still, no answer.

At the far end of the property, just near the agility circuit she'd seen with Zhivago, she saw a pile of something under a tarp that looked like farm equipment. Maybe a small tractor, used in maintaining a garden? Or maybe a ride-on lawnmower? Lillian walked toward it, noticing, as she approached, a smell that didn't belong there. Not the smell of dogs, not the smell of dog kennels that needed cleaning. Actually, the whole place seemed very fresh and outdoorsy, given that thirty dogs were eating, sleeping, and living within the space.

It was an acrid smell, a strong smell. It seemed to come along with a wave of something else, moving through the air toward her.

It was heat. Lillian got within ten feet of the pile and felt a surge of hot air assault her face. Her senses had suddenly become acute: the sharp smell; the feeling of heat against her face; and, now that she was aware, a crackling, ominous sound.

She reached forward, carefully, toward the edge of the canvas tarp. It was too hot. She just couldn't get any closer to it. Slowly, she extended her right foot toward it and tried to kick it aside. What *was* under there? And what was going on?

It took three kicks before the canvas moved. Just a few inches, though. Oh, what she wouldn't give to have Carl with her right now—on a leash, his long body extended toward this pile of something, with his teeth able to grab hold of the edge of the tarp and pull it away.

Lillian felt the temperature rising all around her. If she didn't move the canvas and see what was under there soon, she would have to back away. Her moment was now.

She kicked at the corner once more, but nothing moved. She realized she would have to lie down. She might not have Carl's head, mouth, and teeth, but she did have arms.

Lillian lowered herself to the ground, as far away from the pile as she could get while still being able to reach out and grab a corner with her hands. She flattened her stomach against the dirt, reached out to grab hold, then yanked the canvas tarp away from the smelly pile.

It was her car, smoldering. Someone had set it on fire.

CHAPTER 25

FOR A LONG MOMENT, Lillian was paralyzed, not believing what she was seeing. Her car. The car that she'd bought with Keith's bequest and traveled in across the continent, from northwest to southeast corners. The car she'd used for nearly eight years to explore nooks and crannies of her adopted state. It was much more than having one of her possessions damaged. She felt as though she'd been violated.

Lillian rolled to her side and as far away from the smoking vehicle as she could. Now what should she do? Would that glow and those embers turn into something bigger? Would it spread? Were the nearby buildings in danger, too?

Lillian looked around for someone to call, but there was no one. No one but the wildly barking dogs. Dear God, what if the fire spread and they were all locked inside?

She jogged back toward the main building, not sure what she could do. The doors there were locked and there was no one nearby to call.

"Donovan! Zhivago! Tracey!"

She hadn't seen any of them in a very long time, but somehow it comforted her to call out the names.

She walked around, looking at the windows, hoping for inspiration. She *had* to get inside.

Around the back, beside a small vegetable patch, she saw a rake. That would do it. Lillian carried it back around to the front of the building. The window to the right of the door smashed easily and she thrust her hand through to reach the doorknob, the way she'd seen them do in the movies.

Her memory tickled with a thought about something in that main office that she needed, something that would be useful. Hah! There it was. The fire extinguisher she'd seen on the wall behind the display of collars, treats, and leashes.

Lillian pulled it down from the wall and ran with it, out into the yard. It seemed to take forever to get to the far end of the property where her car stood, smoldering and shooting off sparks.

She held out the nozzle and pointed it toward her car, spraying wherever she could see flames. This was not like anything she'd ever seen in the movies, where you saw one 'whoosh', and the flames disappeared. Each time she sprayed one spot and turned it charred and dead, another sprang to life, with new sparks or red glow or small flame. It seemed to take hours, and the entire time, she worried about the fire extinguisher running out of foam. At least, she'd had the good luck that it was operational and not empty. That might have happened.

Lillian took a deep breath and then immediately regretted it. The stench from the smoldering rubber and metal was almost overpowering. There seemed to be cinders of something in the air that she'd inhaled. Nose running, eyes smarting, she pulled her blouse up to rub her face.

Her first urge, as soon as the adrenalin ebbed, was to feel sorry for herself. This really sucked! She almost wanted to cry. What was she going to do now? Nobody around, and now, no car. Lillian hated being without her own car. Ever since she was a teenager, at sixteen when she got her license and her father let her borrow his car, she'd always tried to make sure she used her own transportation, even on dates. 'Meet me at the restaurant', she'd say, or. 'I'll get to the party on my own'. It was her way of having a 'back door', a way out.

People had teased her about it over the years and when she tried to advise her own teenagers about it, they'd jeered. The situation hadn't been helped by Marv suggesting that getting other people to pick you up or drive you home was the clever way to go (not to mention, the economical, as they'd be paying for the gas). She'd tried to make her point but he was very touchy about her 'undermining' him, as he called it, so she gave up before it got confrontational and decided to be philosophical about it. The kids would form their own opinions.

If she were in a debate with one of them about it today, she'd have to concede that having your own transportation didn't always work, and this was a perfect example. Lillian looked around the part of the yard that she could see; just completely deserted.

But, she wasn't alone, not really. She had dogs. They were still barking nonstop and although they were in the kennels, it was certainly obvious that she wasn't alone. But in the absence of any snow and a dogsled, that wasn't going to help her much.

It would be a long walk back to Alamos.

Lillian leaned against the fence and looked out toward the horizon. She could find her way back to the road, she was sure, but after that, which way would get her home?

Wait—her phone would know! Her amazing, so precious, thank-God-for-it phone. Her computer in her pocket, complete with GPS and maps. Why hadn't she thought of it before?

Come to think of it—she didn't have to walk! She had a phone in her pocket. Lillian fished it out and tapped the screen. The battery was low, but it still worked.

The sound of the dogs barking, constant in the background, suddenly became louder. The overall audio landscape up to now was a mixture of about ten percent deep barks and a whole lot of yapping, all muffled by the aluminum siding of the kennels. But this new sound was not only louder, it was one hundred percent deeper.

Lillian looked in the direction that it seemed to be coming from, and about thirty yards off, she saw four Rottweilers pounding toward her.

Were they the same ones that had stalked her at the Dog Show? Who cared, and why stop to try to figure that out now?

Lillian shoved her phone back in her pocket and took off, running as fast as she could.

She hadn't done much running in the past twenty years, believing that regular yoga classes, line dancing, and lots of walking was the exercise a woman in her age group should do.

She hadn't planned on needing to outrun a dog.

But she had to give it her best shot—what else could she do?

The main building looked as if it were about a mile away but Lillian set off as fast as she could, heading for the driveway between the two lines of kennels. The paths behind the buildings were narrow and fenced along the property line. She could just imagine how horrible it would be to be pinned against that fence by an aggressive Rottweiler.

Her phone rang but she didn't want to break stride or risk slowing down, to answer it. No doubt, by now, Tracey and the others at the condo were wondering where she was or what had happened in her conversation with Zhivago. Maybe Donovan had made his way back to town, somehow, and had set up an alarm. Maybe people were hunting for her.

She could also see a few possibilities if she couldn't get to the main building fast enough. The kennel about halfway along the driveway had an old-fashioned storm shelter built right beside its door; she could try that if the dogs were gaining on her.

Think, Lillian. Don't let the panic get to you.

The distance to the main building was shrinking and she started to allow herself to hope she'd make it. Her thigh muscles burned and her lungs hurt as she gasped for more air. She passed the storm shed and kept going.

When she reached the end of the driveway, Lillian desperately scanned the yard for another car parked in front of the training facility door. Maybe someone bringing their dog for a class? Maybe Sam, come back to look for her? Maybe Madison, the kennel cleaner/dog feeder? Maybe even Zhivago? At this point, she' rather take him on than these dogs.

But there was no vehicle there. Lillian hauled herself up the steps to the door beside the window she'd broken earlier. She could hear the dog barking coming closer and closer.

Lillian rushed into the house and slammed the door behind her. The furious dogs thundered up the steps and hurled themselves at the door. It rattled and she prayed that it would hold.

She could see them just beyond the window, flinging their heads from side to side, spittle and foam shooting off in all directions. It would be just a matter of time before they figured out that they could probably leap through that broken window—either figured it out or worked themselves up into such a frenzy that they came crashing through it.

Lillian sank to the floor, her back against the door, and allowed herself the luxury of melting into tears. Great, gulping sobs overcame her and she could not have stopped crying if she tried. When she started investigating Turtle's death, she thought she was helping with a puzzle: find out what horrible person had killed a harmless dog. She hadn't expected to put herself into a situation like this.

Where was everybody? Why wasn't someone coming to help her? Why on earth would Donovan have left if he thought she was still here?

Lillian pulled the phone from her pocket to call 911.

The battery was dead.

She waited, for what seemed like hours. She had to get out of there eventually; she needed a restroom and a meal. She listened to the sound of the barking diminish – maybe they were getting tired too? If they did, and either fell asleep or wandered off, she could find her way to the main road and flag somebody down. Maybe even hitchhike, the way they'd done as kids in the 50s.

The dogs *were* getting tired. She heard the barking drop off until there were just a few sounds every few minutes. Then, it stopped.

Everything was silent now. Lillian peered out of the window; no dogs were to be seen. She gingerly opened the door and looked around. A large, black and brown body came rushing at her and the big dog jumped, its paws toward her shoulders and its head toward her arm.

She felt the teeth sink in and then she felt nothing more.

CHAPTER 26

THE LARGE, ROUND, ANALOG CLOCK on the wall reminded her of the clocks from her schoolroom days. The sound of the ticking was the only one in the room. Two-thirty.

Where was she?

Lillian started to roll over but the movement was interrupted by tubes that ran from her body to a machine beside her head.

A hospital bed.

Carefully, she raised herself up onto her elbows to take a look around. The blinds were down on the only window in the room, but between the lower edge and the windowsill she could see a dark night with some sort of artificial light coming in. A streetlight, perhaps?

A door in the corner probably closed off a bathroom. Aside from the bed, the monitoring machines and a tray table on wheels, there wasn't much else in the room, except for a chair in the far corner.

She ached all over and her right arm was dressed in a medical bandage. Her vision was blurry.

Lillian lay back and tried to get her eyes to focus. Gradually, as she stared at the clock, the four hands merged into two. She breathed deeply and concentrated on relaxing her body, from feet to crown of her head.

While all of this made her feel better, what she was really after was her memory. What had happened? Why was she in this bed in a hospital?

She looked toward the door to the hallway. Was anyone around that she could ask? She thought she heard a radio playing softly but otherwise, there was no sound.

A call button! Hospital beds always had a call button somewhere. Lillian groped around and found the cord.

A few minutes later a nurse arrived, carrying a small paper container with pills in it and a glass of water. "So, we're awake now, are we, Mrs. Howe?"

"Yes, thank you. And thank you for the water. I am really thirsty."

"How do you feel, otherwise?" the nurse asked after she gave Lillian the pills and the water.

"A bit beaten up. What happened?"

"I wasn't here when you were brought in but your chart says that you were knocked down and bitten by a dog."

Lillian closed her eyes. Yes, she did remember something about that. A massive, black monster of a dog had chased her down, cornered her, and sunk its teeth into her. Someone had sent it and no one had come to save her.

"The other nurses told me a young woman came in to work at the dog place and found you. She was able to lift you into her car and brought you in. You've been sleeping since they did the stitches when you first got here."

Lillian motioned with her left arm. "He bit me here?"

The nurse nodded. "You didn't lose much blood though, and it all cleaned up nicely."

"Just one bite?"

"Yes. I guess we don't know why he stopped biting, but we can be thankful that he did." The nurse reached behind Lillian's head and straightened her pillow. "Are you comfortable? Is there anything else I can do for you right now?"

Lillian shook her head. "Nothing. Thank you." She didn't tell the nurse that what she'd really like was to get over the feeling of being deep in a tunnel, all alone. "Was it really necessary that I had to stay here? My own bed would be better."

"I think they just wanted to make sure you were really all right before sending you off home," the nurse said. "Observation, you know. Very important when there's a fall with a woman your age. You'll want to sleep some more now, and then in the morning, after the doctor sees you, you'll probably be going home."

Over the next half hour, Lillian's memory squeezed out details of the previous day. The dog bite was bad but what was even worse was coming up so dry on finding out whether Zhivago Picard was the one responsible for Turtle's death. She looked toward the window. Someone out there, probably Zhivago, had poisoned and beaten a beautiful animal. Had attacked her precious Carl. Had set dogs on her.

Lillian wasn't someone who felt fear often in her daily life, and even with the events of the past few weeks, she had been so focused on following the trail that she hadn't had time to be scared.

Usually, she was comfortable in her own skin. Her mind was so busy that she rarely spent much time looking at herself as someone else might. But now, at three o'clock in the morning, she 'saw' a shrunken, tiny woman, lying in a room through which sick people came and went, with a massive bandage on her arm where a crazed, ferocious dog had bitten her.

But, in spite of her self-pity and her feelings of being old and alone, memories of details of yesterday came back to her. She recalled running across that yard. She had outrun a dog! Not just one dog, but four dogs. They were chasing her, desperate to catch her, and she had escaped them.

**

When she awoke again, Donovan sat in the chair in the far corner.

"Hey, Grandma," he said softly.

"Donovan." She smiled weakly. "Have you been there long?"

"An hour or so. You've been sleeping really soundly. How are you feeling?"

"Much better," she said. "Ready to go home. Who is taking care of Carl?"

"He's still at the vet's. Doc says he's much better but wanted to keep him a bit longer."

"Did you hear about what happened to me?"

He nodded. "I did."

"I think it's the dog trainer we're after," she said.

"Things sure seem to be pointing in that direction. How did those dogs get out?"

"I don't know," Lillian said, " but I think the same person responsible for that is the person responsible for torching my car."

"Your car! Grandma, what the hell?"

"I know, Donovan, I know. It's completely crazy, isn't. it? But before we go on another minute . . . where did you go? What happened to you?"

"You know, I really don't know. I was looking around a bit and I found a big building that was a storage shed. For dog chow and stuff like that. Then all of a sudden somebody rushed me from behind, put a hood over my head, and pulled my phone out of my pocket. They shoved me to the floor and I was trapped in there. I piled up some crates so I could get near a window and climbed out."

Donovan got up to pace around the room. "I'm so sorry, Grandma. There was nobody around, anywhere and I thought you'd gone with the rest of them. So, I walked up to the road and hitchhiked back. I called Sam and Tracey as soon as I could and when they said you were here in the hospital, I came right over."

She smiled at him. "It's good to have you here."

He couldn't smile back. "I'm so sorry. If I'd known you were still there, that someone was destroying your car and setting dogs on you—"

"It's alright, dear. You didn't know and you couldn't have known," Lillian said. "Please don't beat yourself up. You look exhausted."

He stopped his pacing and came over to the bed, laying a hand on the top of her head. "I'll be here till morning. Then, Tracey's coming in and I'll go get some sleep."

"Thank you, Donovan," she murmured sleepily. The drugs were taking over again.

CHAPTER 27

LILLIAN WOKE FROM A DEEP SLEEP that was filled with disturbing dreams.

"Hey, Grandma."

There he was, sitting in that uncomfortable chair. What had she done, to deserve such a dear boy—correct that, *young man*—helping her, in her life?

No matter how often she corrected herself, and forced herself to recognize that he was a man now, he would always, somewhere on her radar, be eight years old. And adorable.

"How are you feeling?"

She shifted around in the bed. Not nearly so stiff and not so much pain. She touched her right arm cautiously. It immediately let her know that it would like to be left alone for a while.

"I'm doing fine. Looking forward to getting home," she said. "Have you heard anything about Carl?"

"Great timing," a voice said from the doorway. Doc Rosenthal stood there, with Carl, on a leash and looking quite bewildered by the unfamiliar surroundings.

Then, he picked up Lillian's scent and he changed, instantly. The tail wagged and the head went up, as he looked around.

"Carl." She couldn't help but smile at his beautiful, chocolate brown face.

The vet let up on the leash and Carl trotted over toward the bed. Lillian reached down to pet him. "I'm so glad he's all right," she said to Doc Rosenthal. "Thank you for putting him back on his feet."

"My pleasure."

"And for bringing him over."

"I thought he might cheer you up, after your horrendous experience," Doc Rosenthal said. "But, I think you're looking like you've got yourself back in balance all on your own."

"She's amazing," Donovan said. "Most women your age would still be in a state of shock," he said to Lillian.

She smiled reassuringly at him. "I'm fine. Just eager to get home."

"And everyone there is eager to have you back," Donovan said. "I've heard from every one of them, and Sam has called four times."

"He's called me a few times, too." The man in uniform tapped at the door frame. "May I come in?"

"Certainly, Deputy Burtt," Lillian said.

"I know you're leaving shortly, and that your grandson is going to take you back to your place, but I'd just like to ask a few questions before you go." He had a notepad and pen in his hand.

"Yes, of course. Doctor, thanks again for bringing Carl over."

Doc smiled and tipped an imaginary hat at her, then handed Carl's leash to Donovan before leaving.

"Grandma, we'll wait for you in the lobby. The nurse told me at the floor station that the doctor has signed off on the paperwork for you to leave."

"Thanks, Donovan. I won't keep you waiting long. Deputy, what is it you want to ask me?"

"I'd like you to tell me what you can remember about yesterday. Every detail," the deputy said, after Donovan had gone. "I wish I could leave you alone and let you recover for a few days or a week. But the sooner you try to remember, the better."

"I agree, Deputy Burtt," she said. "I don't need a week to recover. I want to get on top of this as quickly as possible."

He looked at her with amusement. "Fair to say, you're not intimidated by all this?"

"Fair to say, I'm ticked off," Lillian replied. "Pissed off, as the young people would say."

"But you wouldn't say that?"

She laughed. "I have sixty years of training, not to use bad words, plus I spent about a dozen, training others not to use them. Every time I try to swear, a voice echoes through my brain, criticizing and scolding me. So, I say I'm quoting somebody else. 'As the young people would say'. It's not me. No, I'm not saying that. It's the young people."

He was laughing, too. "Who do you think you're fooling? And why do you need to answer to anybody?"

"It was a different generation, what can I say?" Lillian pulled herself to sit upright in the bed. "I'm getting out of here just as soon as we're done talking, so let's get on with it. I want to get my boy home to his own bed." She motioned toward Carl, who lay beside the heart monitor, relaxed but alert.

"All right. Let's start with why you went there."

"I've interviewed every one of the suspects in Turtle's murder. Do we call it murder or homicide, if it has to do with a dog, by the way?"

"I don't think so," the deputy said. "Killing falls under the whole category of animal cruelty."

"Whatever they call it, I think we know you can't go around killing dogs that belong to other people. Or your own. You own them but they have rights. It's not like a car or a coat—you own it, you do what you want with it. A dog might belong to you, but you can't do whatever you want with it."

The deputy nodded. "Varies from place to place, though. I remember a case in Michigan, where shooting a dog was allowed, because it was self-defense."

"Well, I don't think we have that situation here, since we know that Turtle was poisoned. I can't imagine somebody throwing pills at a charging dog, in self-defense. And he was battered after his death, so there was no issue of self-defense." Lillian looked around her tray table for a bottle of water.

Burtt waited while she drank. "Okay, so you went to this Instinct Recovery Facility—"

"Instinct Revival."

"Yeah, that. You wanted to interview the owner, Zhivago Picard. Who went with you?"

"My friends from my condo building. Sam, Tracey Simmons, Kyra, and Dwayne. And my grandson, Donovan."

"The one who's coming back to give you a ride home."

She smiled. "That's him."

"Okay. Now, details. Anything you can think of. What happened when you first got there. What were the kennels like? Any signs of anybody around? What did Picard say and do? What was his attitude?"

Lillian recounted the experience while he took notes. Just saying some of the words that had been running through her mind seemed to clarify things for her. Clarified, and raised new questions.

She had wandered off, in her thinking, when he pulled her back on the path with a question. "Why do you think Zhivago Picard came to see me yesterday afternoon, then?"

"What? He came to see you? When?"

"It was about two o'clock. Probably right about the time you were making the acquaintance of those Rottweilers."

"And shortly after he'd finished talking with me," Lillian said. "He must have gone right from our interview to his car, to your office."

"Must have been something in your conversation that made him feel he had to do that."

"What did he say?"

"He didn't directly address the possibility that he was under suspicion of anything. Just said he was concerned about the recent incidents of dog assault—Turtle, your Carl—and some dog thefts that he'd heard about. Wanted to make sure the Sheriff's office was aware of his place and the work he does there. Said he was increasing security but he wanted us to be on guard, too, in case he became of the target of whoever was behind these dog crimes."

"Hmm." Lillian felt a little overwhelmed by the barrage of information. Her arm ached. Maybe she wasn't quite as spry as she thought, and perhaps she would need some time to bounce back from her experience yesterday.

Geez, she hated that word 'spry'.

"Mrs. Howe?" She tuned back in to the deputy's voice. "What can you tell me about the dog attack?"

"They were Rottweilers," she said. "Absolutely huge. They seemed to be completely insane, barking and growling."

Lillian went silent for a few moments, as she recalled the way they ran at her, full tilt, their heads down like lances. She didn't know whether they meant to bash her, like rams in battle, or use their teeth on her. She'd had no lance of her own and all she could do was hope that she could make it to the door of the main IRF building.

"I outran them and got inside Picard's office. I waited for the longest time and they seemed to all go away. I thought it was safe to open the door . . . and there was one, still there, and it jumped on me and bit me. It was almost as if he deked me out on purpose. Do you think dogs can try to trick you, like that?"

Burtt shook his head. "I think they go pretty much on instinct, rather than mind games. But who knows? I'm no dog expert."

"Neither am I. But I do know I can't look at what I see around Carl and extend that out to all dogs."

"No, they have just as many different personalities as people do," Burtt agreed. "So, here we are."

Lillian looked around the hospital room. "Here we are."

"The timing seems to be that Picard was at my office at the exact time your car was being torched and the dogs were trying to run you down."

She smiled. "Approximately exact. I'm sorry but I wasn't checking my watch."

"Tell me more about the dogs."

"The Rottweilers?"

He nodded.

"Well, as I said, four of them."

"All about the same size?"

"Yes, same size. Same coloring, same markings."

"You're sure you weren't seeing double? Or quadruple?"

"Ha. A comedian cop."

Burtt laughed. "Okay, four dogs. Or, maybe you were just magnifying the danger, in your mind?"

"You mean, like ooh, I was so scared, it must have been four, not one. No, wait, I'll bet it was ten . . . or fifteen dogs! Yes, that's what it was, I was attacked by fifteen dogs!"

"It happens, in eyewitness accounts. You'd be surprised how much difference there often is, when two or three people were all at the same event, seeing the same thing. Time passing—that's another thing that messes with recall."

"Well, it wasn't fifteen dogs, it was four," Lillian said.

"Were they all identical or was there anything about any one of them that was different? Could one have been slightly bigger than the others? Maybe a white or other-colored patch somewhere that you noticed? Maybe ears bigger or smaller? Nose flatter? Eyes a different color?"

"You know, I wasn't facing them. Most of the time, I was on the run," she said.

But she was thinking. There was something. Much as she didn't want to, anymore, she re-visualized the moment that she heard them, that she turned and saw them, and that she peeked out the office window to look at them. What *was* it?

Suddenly, she looked at Burtt and her gaze turned outward again, coming back into focus.

"Deputy Burtt, I'm ready to get out of here."

**

All the rest of the morning, Lillian went over the facts in her mind. When Donovan came to pick her up and take her home, she barely spoke. He probably assumed she was tired, from the scare at the IRF and the lack of sleep at the hospital. That was fine; she didn't feel like making conversation anyway. She was just too wound up about her idea.

Once he saw her home and settled, Donovan went off to buy groceries and pet food for Carl. Lillian immediately reached for her phone and tapped the speed-dial number for Deputy Burtt. It was important to get everyone gathered, and quickly; the Nugents' house would probably be a good location.

"Deputy Burtt? Lillian Howe."

She could almost hear his smile over the phone. "Mrs. Howe, everybody has call display these days. I know it's you." He sounded almost affectionate.

"All right, sorry." *Why do I say sorry? Nothing to apologize for.*

"What's up, Mrs. Howe? Did you get home from the hospital all right?"

"Yes, I'm here, and Carl is, too. We're just relaxing in front of the TV. Everything is all right, except for one thing. I can't find my purse."

"Your purse? We have a purse snatching now, too?"

She laughed. "It was kind of chaotic when we were leaving the hospital. I didn't think of it. And of course, I was out of it, when I went in last night so I didn't notice where it was put."

"Maybe the young woman from the dog training place didn't bring it with you."

"That's possible," Lillian said. "I'll ring her later and ask her. Anyway, I was watching a program, chewing over what we know so far about Turtle's killing, and I had a thought. Our conversation this morning has been on my mind constantly and I think I have it."

"A thought? Or a solution?"

Lillian smiled. "*The* solution. I've talked to everybody who might know something but I want to talk to them all again. Together."

"All right," Burtt said. "Let's bring them all together. When?"

"This afternoon," she said.

"Oh! Okay, soon. I'm assuming that's Picard, Mills—"

"And his wife, Selena Birkenshaw."

"Serranno? Tanaka?" Burtt asked.

"Yes, and Riccardo Lopez."

"I'll take care of that," Burtt said. "Anything else?"

"I'll be bringing Carl along," Lillian said. "Make sure Barbara and Gerald know that. I'll get Donovan to drive me over, but I won't ask him to come in."

"Okay. Are you going to tell me who it was?"

"You know, I'd like to spool that out in front of you and everybody else," Lillian said. "And I could use a few more hours just to ponder the whole thing. Make sure I'm right."

"Well, that doesn't make me feel too confident, hearing that," Deputy Burtt said. "I really think I need to know ahead of time, before we put all these people through this, take up their time."

"All right," Lillian said. "How about if you pick me up and drive me over there, and I'll tell you on the way?"

"Sounds like a plan," Burtt said. "I'll get back to you to confirm and I'll see you in a couple of hours."

CHAPTER 28

WHEN LILLIAN PULLED INTO Barbara and Gerald's circular driveway, she felt her fear level decline a bit, on seeing Deputy Sheriff Burtt's car by the door. Half a dozen other vehicles were parked around the Nugent's private road. She recognized Zhivago's van and Marlon Tanaka's SUV, and she assumed the others belonged to the people she'd suggested that the deputy invite to this get-together.

Hah! "Invite". That was a polite way to put it.

When she rang the bell, the deputy was the one to open it. "Hey, Miss Lillian," he said. "Ready to get started?"

It was a long walk from the front door to the living room. Almost every seat near the gas fireplace at the other end of the room from the floor-to-ceiling aquarium was occupied. Lillian hadn't seen this room when she visited, and if she was impressed then, by the luxury of the back patio and the pool deck, she would have been even more blown away by this space.

She looked around for Gerald's Pomeranian, but there was no sign of any dogs. The deputy showed her to an armchair and all eyes turned to her.

"Thank you, Deputy Sheriff Burtt. Where shall we start?" She turned her gaze toward them and took silent inventory. Zhivago Picard. Marlon Tanaka. Arlo Serranno, standing at the far end of the room, near the aquarium. Ellison Mills. Selena Birkenshaw. Gerald Nugent. Barbara Nugent. Riccardo Lopez.

"Maybe we could start with why the police are bringing you in on this and why you're in my living room, taking over?" Gerald said. It was framed as a question but it didn't feel like one.

Lillian felt the best thing to do was ignore him. "Selena, let's start with you. You hate dogs and you've made no secret of it. Even if your reason is a good one, or one we might feel sympathy for, that you have this irrational, overpowering fear of dogs, it still puts you high on the list of possible suspects. And a lens cap was found outside my house. You use binoculars and a camera."

Selena looked like she was going into a state of shock. Ellison leaned closer to her on the couch. Lillian could sense that Gerald was having difficulty controlling his temper.

"I don't understand why we're listening to this!" He turned to Deputy Burtt. "Shouldn't you be the one speaking to us? You led me to believe that you have some new evidence about the killing of my wife's dog and now, here we are, listening to this senior citizen play detective. With all of these other people in the room! My living room!"

He rose from his chair, then Deputy Burtt went over to stand beside him.

"Sir, I'll have to ask you to calm down," the deputy said. "As you know from your wife's own newspaper, Ms. Howe is not just 'some senior citizen'. She's the reason we have a solution to this case and I'm going to let her be the one to explain it to you." He nodded to Lillian. "Please go on, Ms. Howe."

Lillian nodded in return. "But you have an airtight alibi, Selena," she said. "You were in a yoga class and forty other people can verify that.

"I thought for a while that it might have been you that morning. I saw a gray Bentley at the park and when I found out that your husband had one, I thought you might have borrowed it. But after I checked out your story at the yoga studio, it was time to consider something else."

"Turtle was poisoned and then attacked with something like a golf club. Something that takes a major role in your life," she said to Marlon Tanaka. "In fact, you carry clubs with you, in the trunk of your car. I saw them."

"Circumstantial," Marlon said.

Lillian ignored him. "It was also very strange, the way you ran away from me, that day I saw you in the Everglades."

Marlon stared at her. "That had nothing to do with you. Or the dog. I had called in sick at the last minute, said I couldn't take a tour group out, one that I'd committed to. I decided I wanted to golf that day instead."

Lillian raised an eyebrow. "I see. I also couldn't figure out why you would want to go after a dog, even a valuable dog like Turtle. I couldn't turn up any motive—there didn't seem to be any connection between you and the Nugents. I had all sorts of theories: maybe you were trying to blackmail Barbara about something and she wasn't caving in? Maybe you were trying a brutal way to scare her into putting something you wanted in the newspaper? Maybe you wanted one or the other of them to acquire your little tour company?"

"This is outrageous!" Lillian expected Marlon to continue to protest, but it was Gerald who leaped to his feet.

"Sit down, Mr. Nugent," the deputy sheriff said.

"Thank you, Deputy Burtt." Lillian was hitting her stride. "Even if I had discovered a motive, I still couldn't answer the questions about opportunity, Marlon. Jasmine Park is a public place and there might have been a way for you to sneak up on Turtle and club him, but he'd been poisoned hours before. When and how would you have been able to give him the poison? And nobody saw you anywhere near the park at six that morning."

The slight sneer on Marlon's face had disappeared and he was listening to Lillian with total attention.

So were all of the other people in the room. Selena had moved even closer to Ellison on the couch and he had taken her hand. Gerald rose from his chair and began pacing the open space between the couch and the west wall.

Barbara fixed her gaze on Lillian's face, while Zhivago, slouched back into another couch, put his hands behind his head and stared at the ceiling.

"Arlo." Lillian looked over toward the aquarium at the far end of the room where the property manager stood, almost as if he felt he didn't really belong in a room like this. Or perhaps he just wanted to distance himself from the whole discussion. "Arlo, you definitely were seen at the park at six a.m. You live right next door and you came over to talk to me and find out what was going on. You and I found Turtle's body together. Then, the police found footprints there that came from a pair of Dr. Mills's shoes."

"Your shoes!" Selena turned sideways on the couch to face her husband.

"I guess I didn't tell you about that."

Lillian continued. "But it turned out that Arlo had stolen the shoes—"

"Borrowed!" Arlo's shout from the back of the room turned every head toward him.

"From one of the vacation rental properties that you were managing, Arlo," Lillian said.

"Are you kidding me?" Selena said.

"Indeed," Lillian said. "What's that saying? The more I know about people, the more I like my dog. Or your birds."

"So, is Arlo Serranno the one who killed my wife's dog?" Gerald stopped, mid-pace, to direct his question to Deputy Burtt.

Lillian didn't let him take over. She had to continue, slowly and carefully, on the steps she'd laid out, to take them through her thinking. "When I found out that you were a part of the dog show community around here, Arlo, I wondered whether you'd crossed paths with Barbara in some way that made you want to kill her dog," Lillian continued. "It was just a little too coincidental, that you happened to be awake so early and looking out your window to the park that morning."

Arlo walked toward the group around the fireplace and stopped in front of Lillian's chair.

"I disagree, Mrs. Howe," he said. "I was just there. Sometimes, things are just what they seem."

Lillian decided to ignore his interruption. "When you turned up at the dog show, I was even more suspicious that you had some kind of beef with either Mr. Nugent, or Mrs. Nugent, or both. I thought maybe you'd kidnapped his dog, too, but then it turned up under Ellison's dog's table."

"How about you take a seat, Mr. Serranno?" Deputy Burtt indicated an empty chair to his right. It was clear it was a rhetorical question.

Lillian looked from face to face. "It wasn't logical that Ellison had kidnapped Gerald's dog, even if it did turn up under his table. Somebody put it there."

"Are you suggesting I kidnapped that dog?" Arlo's voice was low and slow.

"Not at all, Arlo. I think it was someone even less likely than you." Lillian turned in her seat toward Barbara Nugent. "Why did you kidnap Mr. Hyde?"

Barbara stood up, in a stately, regal way. Not going to take this sitting down, apparently. "Why are you making such an outrageous allegation?"

Lillian rose from her armchair and met Barbara's gaze, straight on. "I think you are the one who took your husband's dog and hid him."

Barbara stared at Lillian and the two women waged a silent war for dominance. Then, Barbara's chin dropped a few inches. She reached for the arms of the chair behind her and lowered herself into it. "Alright. I took him, and hid him at the newspaper office. I knew I couldn't keep him there long, though."

"So, you asked Marlon to keep him for a few days then deliver him to the dog show," Lillian said. "When I saw him that day in the Everglades with a dog crate in the back, that was Mr. Hyde, in that crate."

"And why did you let him be found under the table at the dog show?" Deputy Burtt had his small notepad out.

"Look, we're not here to talk about me taking my husband's dog for a few days and putting him into Ellison's care for a few hours," Barbara said, "Why don't we just move along?"

"You didn't 'put him into my care'!" The doctor's face was red. "You stashed him under my bench at a dog show and made it look as if I'd stolen him or hid him away to keep him out of competition!"

Lillian stayed focused on Barbara. "I think we all want to know why you made an effort to frame Dr. Mills," she said.

Barbara looked at her as if she couldn't believe anyone, especially someone she employed, would be so disrespectful and brazen. "I did not make an effort to frame Dr. Mills."

Lillian stood up and walked over to stand in front of the fireplace. She spoke to the deputy sheriff. "Dr. Mills breeds and shows Pomeranians and Collies. Mrs. Nugent has recently acquired a Collie puppy from champion stock and she's set her sights on the Westminster Dog Show. First, she has to rise to the top in her own area with this new puppy and she's identified Dr. Mills as her competition.

Lillian turned to Barbara. "You wanted to distract and confuse Ellison, and the entire dog community."

"So, both of them, both Barbara and Gerald Nugent, see Dr. Mills as their main rival," Deputy Burtt said, his pen going double speed on his notebook.

Lillian nodded. "Both Dr. Mills and Gerald Nugent drive a gray Bentley, the type of car that I saw at Jasmine Park that morning. That annoyed you at first, didn't it?" she said, addressing Gerald. "You wanted to drive a unique car. But later on, you started to see some advantages."

He turned and glared at her. His expression was so fierce and so threatening that Lillian faltered for a moment.

"Go on, Ms. Howe," Deputy Sheriff Burtt said.

Ellison Mills was next under her microscope and Lillian turned toward him. "I saw a gray Bentley that morning. You drive a gray Bentley. Turtle was brutally clubbed with a golf iron. You play a lot of golf. I found a bottle of prescription medication at the scene, with your name on it as the prescriber. You have no alibi for that Wednesday morning."

"You know, most people don't go through life making sure they have alibis every day, in case they're accused of something!" Ellison's face was flushed a deep red now and Lillian wondered whether he was in need of some of his own health care advice.

"Indeed," Lillian said. "But most people don't obsess over breeding champion show dogs and most people don't make it their business to keep files on every other owner of a dog that might be competition for their dogs. You had no interest in Barbara Nugent or her Saluki. It was only Gerald and his Pomeranian that you had on your radar. But when you heard she was buying a pick-of-the-litter Collie pup with the intention of turning him into a champion like Turtle, I thought you might be trying to find a way to stop her."

She walked around the room, mainly to try to keep her thoughts in order and not forget any details. The other benefit was that every person in the room kept their gaze on her. Where was she going and what would she say next?

"But I just didn't feel that was enough of a motive, Ellison. And I had no solid evidence. The medication bottle? There are probably thousands of them out there, with your name on them." Lillian stopped at the grandfather clock in the corner and put one hand behind herself, as inconspicuously as possible, to touch the warm wood and use it as support.

"When the police analyzed the footprint of your fancy running shoe, I thought maybe that was some sort of proof that you killed the dog, Ellison. Then, we heard about

Arlo's light fingers in your personal cupboard at your vacation rental. There was nothing to tie you to the scene.

"We couldn't tell whose medication it was because the lake water had ruined the part of the label with the patient's name and the numerical code. But I had a feeling I knew whose it might be."

Lillian walked to a spot in front of Zhivago Picard. "Why are you taking high blood pressure medication, Zhivago?"

The dog trainer shrugged. "It is a problem I have had since I was a teenager. Occasionally, it rises up again, particularly when I am very busy and the stress is very strong."

Lillian held up the pill bottle she'd been holding since they all entered the room. "Is this your medication?"

He shook his head without looking at it. "I have my bottle at home," he said. "I never have more than one."

She nodded. "I saw only one, when I looked in your apartment at the Instinct Revival Facility, and the police found only one, when they searched your place," she said.

"With a warrant, of course," Deputy Burtt added.

"Most people would think it would be impossible for a dog trainer to be a dog killer," Lillian said. "I didn't think of you as a possible suspect, although when I saw you, the day I was touring my condo building with my friend Tracey and with Mr. Serranno, I was curious about your reason for being there.

"You seemed to have a stellar reputation among your clients, the people whose dogs you trained and boarded. The morning that Turtle was found, you were at an agility competition with your Rottweilers, and dozens of people saw you.

"But you might have had somebody else do the deed for you. Maybe the alibi was a deliberate setup. Turtle was poisoned and that was some time before his body was discovered. You were over at the Nugents' home shortly before Turtle turned up dead. Maybe you slipped him a bunch of pills then."

She leaned against the back of a couch and stared into Zhivago's eyes. "You weren't there to talk to Barbara about training her new Collie pup, were you? You were there to talk to them about an investment, and the discussion didn't go well, from your point of view, did it?"

Zhivago stayed locked on her eyes. "What makes you say that?"

"Am I wrong?"

He didn't answer and Lillian just waited, listening to the ticking of the old clock across the room. She half-expected Gerald to leap in and try to take over again, but he didn't speak.

Zhivago suddenly seemed to give up. "No, you're not wrong. I talked to them, like I talked to a lot of my clients about investing. Didn't get far. And it was damn hard to keep it confidential. I was trying to handle it all in a sophisticated, careful way, but it wasn't easy. I'm going to continue asking, though," he said. "Dogs are my life and that training facility is something the world needs. I would never batter a dog." He spoke as if he were making a solemn promise.

Lillian smiled at him. "I know now, Zhivago, what you were doing. And why it looked as though you had the secret I was trying to uncover. It turned out that you had a secret, but a different one."

When Lillian had rehearsed this meeting in her mind, it had taken far less time than this. She was beginning to feel fatigued and for a moment, she considered just pointing a finger and saying a name. But she felt she owed it to them all to walk them through it.

"It was Turtle's blood, in the end, that got us to the answer," she said. "Turtle's blood was analyzed, and the police were looking for any place that traces of it might turn up. There was plenty at the vet's office and on the blankets used to transport him there. There were spatters on the ground all around the spot where he was found."

Barbara turned her head and briefly closed her eyes.

"There was none at the IRF," Lillian said. "None in Zhivago's vehicle or Madison's jeep, none in any of the vehicles belonging to anyone associated with the place. The police are very appreciative of how cooperative everyone was, by the way."

"Nobody had any idea why we were being asked to allow our vehicles to be inspected," Marlon said.

"It was done very quickly and very quietly. Well done, " Lillian said, with a nod to the deputy. "There was another place that law enforcement decided to investigate. The police also got a warrant and searched Riccardo's apartment," she went on. "Oh, and by the way, that apartment? It's in a building right beside the newspaper office. I heard from Bobby Murrow at the paper one day that something fell from an upper floor of that building, but by the time they went to take a look for whatever it was, it was gone.

Lillian turned all of her focus on Riccardo. "I think it was a golf club or bat or something that you used to hit the dog."

Riccardo slumped. "Baseball bat," he muttered.

"And somebody moved it from the lawn to a dumpster somewhere?"

"My cousin."

Lillian nodded. "And with this search warrant, the police found one of your socks with spatters of Turtle's blood on it."

Riccardo's shoulders slumped even further. He seemed upset but Lillian couldn't tell whether it was because he felt bad about Turtle or because he felt bad for himself.

His state of mind was escalating to frantic. "I took the dog to the park but I didn't kill him!"

"I know, Riccardo," Lillian said. "Turtle was poisoned with a blood-pressure pill—maybe more than one.

Probably tucked into a meatball or something else he loved to eat. You just drove him to the place where he was found." She stared at the man and felt her stomach turn over in disgust. "And caved his head in with that baseball bat."

Lillian went back to the arm chair where she'd started. All of a sudden, she felt weak at the knees and had to sit down. "One more thing, Riccardo. Do you know anything about my house burning?"

Riccardo seemed to shrink another two or three inches. "That was Mr. Nugent's idea, too," he said.

"But you were the one who brought the rags and the gasoline?" Lillian said. "You were the one who watched with binoculars until you saw me go out?"

Riccardo nodded

"You dropped a lens cap on your way out." Lillian said. "And left an innocent dog in the house. Did you actually look at him, locked inside, before you did it?"

Riccardo said nothing.

"But none of it was your idea, you claim," Lillian persisted. "Are you saying Mr. Nugent told you to commit arson?"

"Stop!" Gerald exploded. "Stop talking! Deputy, I insist that we stop all this and you let me get my lawyer over here."

Burtt ignored him. Everyone else in the room leaned forward in their seats, mesmerized by Riccardo. Everyone but Barbara.

"I want to tell them," Riccardo shouted back at Gerald.. "That's the way it was."

"And was it you, calling to fool my friends at the dog training facility about a problem back at home?"

Riccardo nodded.

"And you, my car on fire?"

"Yes," he said. "And it was me, who let the Rottweilers out at the dog training place. Not Mr. Zhivago."

"And at the dog show?" Deputy Burtt asked.

Riccardo nodded once more.

"But you knew that," the deputy said to Lillian.

She nodded. "That's what turned the final corner for me. When you grilled me on whether any of the four Rottweilers was any different from any of the others, I remembered. One had a red bandanna, tied around his neck, when they first started running at me. By the time they chased me down to the office door, it had fallen off."

"Rottweilers chased you down?" Selena looked horrified.

Lillian nodded. "And the pack that followed me through the parking lot at the dog show had one with a red bandanna, too.

"For a while, I thought it was all Zhivago Picard, trying to distract me and everybody from Turtle's death," Lillian went on. "Then, I thought it was somebody who didn't like my writing in the newspaper and who was trying to scare me into shutting up.

"Then, I saw the Rottweiler's red bandanna. The same as one I'd seen on Riccardo."

Riccardo stared at her as if he'd never seen anything like her before.

"But why would Riccardo Lopez hurt dogs?" Lillian wondered. "Or try to scare an oldish woman out in the middle of nowhere?"

Lillian walked across the room to confront Gerald. "Maybe it was to earn his wages. Maybe he was just an employee, used by somebody else, like a weapon. Was it that, Mr. Nugent? Was it to shut me up and muzzle the newspaper? Or was it to hurt one more innocent bystander in your wife's life?"

She stared at Gerald for several long moments. The rest of the room was silent; everyone was probably in shock.

"One thing I don't understand, though," she said. "Why did Riccardo batter him with a baseball bat after he was already dead?"

"That was something Mr. Nugent asked for." Riccardo spoke up from the other side of the room. "He told me to put the dog in the car and take it somewhere that it wouldn't matter if it got messy. He told me to hit him around the head a few times, really hard. I think he wanted him to look really horrible. For Mrs. Nugent."

Lillian glared at Gerald. He lifted his chin, defiantly. She turned back to Riccardo. "Why would he want to make it horrible for Mrs. Nugent?"

Riccardo stared at his shoes. "They didn't get along."

"That might be understating it," Lillian said. "It was your bottle of blood pressure pills, wasn't it, Gerald? You killed Barbara's dog to hurt her. You used Turtle. You used an innocent animal in your sickening conflict with your wife."

Every person in the room hung on her words. "You fed the dog the poison, Gerald, and then you had your assistant drive the body to Jasmine Park and dump it there. With its head clubbed in and a black belt tied around its legs, just to make it look weird. Maybe like some sort of ritual. You had him do it soon after six in the morning because you knew that it would be a while before some early morning walkers and dogs would stumble on Turtle.

"Riccardo refused to take Turtle in his car so you had him use yours. You sat in the car like a coward and watched while he dragged the dog's body over to the bushes, out of easy sight. You saw me walk by with Carl and you turned on the headlights to frighten us away.

Gerald scowled at her for so long that she thought he was done saying anything. Then, it was as if all filters came off.

"She provoked it," he said. "Our marriage was hell on earth and I had to put up with her every single day of it. I had to do something to save my sanity and getting rid of that miserable dog did the trick."

Lillian glared back. "You should have restrained yourself, even if she did provoke you. You should have forgiven her, whatever it was."

"I can't even tell you, that's how bad it was. I couldn't forgive her for it, not then, not ever."

"But it's poisoned you, Gerald. It poisoned you and it led you to do something as horrible as killing a defenseless animal." Lillian wouldn't give so much as an inch, no matter how fiercely he looked at her. If she gave even a bit of ground, she wouldn't be able to finish this. "You can forgive something somebody does without condoning their actions. You can and you should. That's what saves your sanity."

Gerald seemed to have gone into some kind of trance, as the weight of years of resentment showed on his face. "She sold my 1965 Caravelle," he said. "Right from under my nose, or my feet, or whatever. I went to see it one day at the marina where I keep it docked and it was gone. I'd been away for three weeks; I came back and it was gone. Doing some spring cleaning, she said. Getting the books in order. Removing a non-performing asset. I couldn't believe it."

Barbara got to her feet but she didn't move toward him. "That was fifteen years ago."

"It feels like yesterday," Gerald said. "I loved that boat."

"You have three others, Gerald!"

"It's a collection, Barbara. Each one is unique." Gerald's face was bright red and he was breathing hard. "And by the way, it's worth five and a half million dollars today!"

"Sometimes you just have to let it go," Lillian said.

"I can't!" Gerald exploded. "I couldn't buy that boat back now, even if I wanted to. Most of my money is tied up in that stupid newspaper."

Lillian could feel Barbara's hackles rise. "It is not a stupid newspaper."

"All newspapers are stupid. It's a medium whose time is past. It's like a cave painting. Or a blacksmith shop!"

Interesting as this was, Lillian wanted to get on with finishing this meeting. She looked around for Deputy Sheriff Burtt, and noticed he was no longer in the room.

"It's all on you, Barbara. You sold my boat. You tried to run my life, and you never listened."

"So, you had my dog killed?" Barbara said. "You didn't want to come after me and you wouldn't consider divorce, so you targeted an animal? An animal that I cared about."

"Let's move on, shall we?" Lillian said, even though she had no idea where to go next.

"Yes, let's," Deputy Burtt said as he walked back into the living room. He carried a white bag in his left hand. Lillian's purse.

"I went to check out Mr. Lopez's car and this turned up. Is it familiar, Mrs. Howe?"

She reached out for it. "It's mine."

He handed it to her, then held up the item in his right hand. A red bandanna.

Deputy Burtt went over to stand in front of Gerald. "Mr. Nugent, I'd like you to come with me. I can spare you the handcuffs and the rest of the drill for now—we'll do that in the car or at the station, if you're going to cooperate."

"Uh-uh," he said to Riccardo who was edging toward the door. "Don't make another move until I say so. You're coming with me, too."

Gerald Nugent suddenly slumped. He knew when he was defeated.

Barbara was a statue. She sat back down on the couch, her back ninety-degree-angle-straight, breathing deeply. It was the only time Lillian had seen her so silent and so still.

It was time to reveal the last fact. Barbara's role in all this.

"You knew all along," Lillian said to Barbara.

Lillian heard Selena's intake of breath. *Yes, who wouldn't be shocked?*

—————

"You guessed that he'd administered some of his high blood pressure medication to Turtle. You accused him and he admitted it to you. Then you let us all run around, trying to figure out what had happened, when you knew all along. That was why you were so opposed to having the paper cover it or letting me file columns about it. You were covering up the truth about your own husband's actions."

This was one element that Lillian wasn't quite sure was a fact. Her intuition had suggested to her, some days or even weeks ago, that this might be the case but she just wasn't sure. It was a secret that Barbara—or Gerald—could keep if they wanted to.

It was also the sort of secret that would fester.

Lillian wasn't sure whether they'd ever know what Barbara knew and when she knew it. But then, the newspaper publisher burst. "It's not that I didn't care about Turtle, I did. Very much. I didn't condone Gerald's actions, and I wanted him to pay for what he did. That's why I took Mr. Hyde and hid him away."

"Why didn't you call the police?"

Barbara sagged. "Well, he is my husband. My training about loyalty goes back a long way. Even though we didn't get along anymore, and he was doing things to hurt me on a daily basis, I still felt I had to be loyal."

"Well, he certainly didn't feel he had to be loyal to you," Lillian said. "Your marriage had broken down so far that he killed your dog. Did you know how he felt about you selling the boat?"

"No," Barbara said. "I mean, I knew at the time. but I thought he'd got over it, long ago."

"Some people never learn that holding onto a grudge is no way to live a life," Lillian said. "When was the last time you saw Turtle?"

It was Tuesday evening." Barbara almost seemed to be in a trance. "We were arguing about something . . . something about money . . . and I said I wanted to take Turtle to competition at the National Dog Show. He thought I should take care of that on my own, out of the newspaper part of the pot, and I thought it was a trivial thing to be discussing. I'm sure he probably did, too, deep down, but he was jealous of Turtle's success and he wanted to do as well, with Mr. Hyde, as I was doing with Turtle. He is just a very competitive man, to his core."

Barbara was starting to choke up. Lillian opened her bag and pulled out a tissue for her. "And then what?" she said.

"And then, suddenly, Turtle was retching. I guess it was Gerald's medication, that he put it into his supper, somehow. I thought it was just something he'd eaten or that maybe he'd caught some kind of virus. It seemed quite serious. Gerald called Riccardo and they bundled the dog up into a blanket, said they were taking him to the Emergency Animal Clinic.

"That was the last time I saw him."

Barbara was in tears by this point and everyone else in the room seemed stunned. Lillian didn't know about the rest of them, but she was just exhausted. She watched as Deputy Sheriff Burtt escorted Gerald and Riccardo out of the room, then one by one, each of the others followed. No one spoke, but she noticed that Selena and Ellison were still holding hands.

Only she and Barbara were left in the room.

"Barbara—" Lillian began.

But there was nothing left to say. She walked out and didn't look back.

CHAPTER 29

LILLIAN WALKED THROUGH the front door of her apartment. She hadn't expected ever to feel at home here, and she still flinched at the sight of the kitchen décor. But she also felt grateful: grateful for the citrus scent that she'd noticed on the first day; the bird calls she could hear, faintly, through the bedroom window that she'd left partly open; the peaceful sense that somehow came with the way the couches and chairs were arranged in the living room.

Carl, his puppy stuffy in his mouth, bounded past her to find his bed in the kitchen and drop it there. He raced back to her and stood as close as he could to her knee, as if trying to hug her with his entire body. Lillian smiled down at him, taking a moment to be grateful for his survival.

"Are you going to be all right here on your own, Lillian?" Tracey carried the overnight bag in and put it on a chair. "I could unpack for you, if you'd like."

"No, that's fine. I'll do it and bring you back your bag later," Lillian said. "I think I want to find things to do to keep me busy."

"You could come over to my place and help me tidy up." A man's voice from the hallway drew her attention to the doorway. Sam stood there, a bouquet of chrysanthemums in one hand and a rawhide chew toy in the other. Carl instantly rewarded him with a wagging tail and a huge smile. Sam handed over the bone and Carl disappeared into the living room with it.

"Carl says thank you." Lillian held out her hands for the flowers. "And so do I. I'll put these in some water, while

I think about whether I want to clean up someone else's place."

"If you're looking for things to do, you're welcome to help me put up my Halloween decorations," Kyra said.

Lillian looked past Sam and Tracey to see Kyra, Joyce, Dwayne, and Doris standing in the hallway just outside her door. "Well, hello, all of you."

"We won't stay long. You're probably exhausted," Kyra said.

"I am very tired," Lillian admitted. "But it's nice to see you all. I'm still feeling foolish about dragging you into all this and putting you in danger that day at the dog training place. If I'd had any idea what was going on—"

"If we'd had any idea, we never would have left you there on your own." Sam said.

Doris reached around Kyra to hand Lillian a casserole dish. "We've been cooking for you, since we thought you might not feel like coming down to the dining room just yet. This is one; we'll have a few others to bring along later."

"Thank you, Doris," Lillian said. "That is really thoughtful. Please, come in, everybody. Let me put this in the fridge and then let's sit down in the living room."

Donovan took this opening to get on his way. "Grandma, I can see you'll have lots of company, now that you're back home, so I think I'll head back to Miami."

"Please give Hailey my love," Lillian said.

"I will, and we'll get back to visit you soon," Donovan said, giving her a kiss and a hug.

Doris, Dwayne, Sam, Kyra, and Tracey followed Lillian into her suite. Joyce stood back, looking at Lillian, and tilting her head from side to side as if she were trying to figure something out.

"Come in, Joyce, there's plenty of room," Lillian said. "Maybe I should put on some tea."

"You'll do no such thing," Tracey said. "You don't need to be the hostess for us, when you just got back from being in the hospital."

"Yes, and we should be going, too," Kyra said. "We don't need to stay for tea or for a longer visit. Lillian, I want to drop off my casserole, too, but I'll do it later today."

Joyce seemed to wake up from some sort of fog. "Yes, I'll do the same. She looked deeply into Lillian's eyes. "Do you ever go by 'Lil'?"

Lillian laughed. "Not for years."

"Or Lily?"

They stared at each other for a long moment. Lillian hadn't socialized all that much over the years but she knew that feeling when she clicked with somebody and when there was potential for friendship.

Two somebodies in this room, she thought, looking at Sam, who was over near the kitchen door, bending down to scratch Carl's ears.

A few minutes later, she was on her own again, after they all left. Two more loose threads she wanted to tie off: phone calls to Nevada and Chelan.

She thought it was more likely that Chelan would have her little kid down for an afternoon nap later on, and so she decided to delay on that call, and phone Nevada first.

"Hi, Lillian, thanks so much for calling." Nevada sounded as though she was breathing hard.

"Is this an okay time?"

"Yes, it's fine. I'm just out for a fast walk in the park" Nevada said. "Trying to keep these middle-aged joints in the game."

"I understand," Lillian said. "I just wanted to call to say 'thank you' for all your help, and for listening to me when I was trying to figure things out."

"Any time, you know that. How are things going?"

"We got the guy."

"And it was the dog trainer?"

"No, it turned out that the connections and the circumstances didn't add up to guilt, after all," Lillian said. "It was Gerald Nugent."

"Barbara Nugent's husband!"

"Soon-to-be ex, I'd bet," Lillian said. "He wanted her dog dead in revenge for all the marital grievances he had against her. and she wanted his dog . . . well, if not dead, certainly gone. That's why Mr. Hyde was kidnapped."

"What happens next?"

"The authorities haven't made that clear yet," Lillian said.

"I hope they throw the book at them. Make the point that nobody can use their pets as fodder in some sort of relationship battle."

After Lillian hung up, she sat for a few minutes, contemplating Nevada's last remark. So well put.

She was fast asleep when Chelan phoned.

"Hey, Lillian, I just wanted to check on you."

"I'm doing fine, dear. It's very nice of you to call."

"I heard from Nevada that everything is wrapped up down there and that you got the bad guys. I'm really glad to hear that."

"Thank you. We're all relieved to finally know the full story of what happened."

"I'm also calling to let you know some news. I'm moving. To the United States, like you did. Drew's been offered a job in Palo Alto, California, with one of the big tech companies, working on artificial intelligence, and we're going to try on life over there."

"Congratulations, Chelan."

"Thanks. It's a new adventure. The little one still keeps me really busy and I don't feel ready to go back to full-time, out-of-the-home-work so it won't matter if I can't find anything else for me to do right away. And it's an exciting place to go to. They say, 2016 will be the year of the app."

The year of the what?

"There is one question I still have," Chelan continued. "About my friend, Iris. Do you think she knew anything about it? She was spending a lot of time around Zhivago Picard and the club that the Nugents belonged to. And she was acting strangely, when I was there. I mean, I know we haven't been as close as we once were, but after she invited me down she had barely any time for me."

"I think she had a lot on her mind," Lillian said.

"I know you talked with her a few times," Chelan said. "Did she let you in on what was going on with her?"

"She did," Lillian said. "But a lot of it was told in confidence, so I'm sorry, but I just can't go into it in any depth."

"Just one question," Chelan said. "Did it have anything to do with why you were living in your car, back in Canada?"

Lillian hesitated. This was moving a bit faster than was easy for her. "No, I'd have to say, when you get right down to it, no. I was in my car because I chose that."

"Why would anybody choose that?"

"Freedom," Lillian said. "Personal freedom."

Chelan was silent for a few moments. "No, I'm sorry, but I don't get that."

There might come a day when the time was right to share her whole story with a young friend like Chelan. But not now, not before she'd even decided what or how she'd discuss this with her own family.

Sleeping dogs.

That evening, as she poured Carl's dinner into his dish and stirred the sauce for her pasta, she let her mind wander back to her past, to her homeless days, to Marv and her family, to her teaching days, and her radio reporting days before that. She didn't often let herself do that. She'd found over the years that it hurt too much and it just wasn't good for her mental health. But, once in a while, almost like a day of indulgence or a night of self-pity, she loosened her discipline and just let her mind go where it wanted. Like a horse with too much pent-up energy—let it run itself out and wind down all that drive, so that she could have calm, once again.

It also defeated the itch to reveal all the details to people who perhaps did not have the capacity to live with it, as she had.

When she let go like that, it was the tiny detail that came to her mind. She recalled the sight of the open water and the boats near Key West, the feeling of the bright Florida sunshine on her face. She went back seven years and remembered the stale smell inside the car where she was living. Another twenty years and she heard the happy voices of her children, as they ran back and forth on a soccer field, then Marv's angry words, knocking down the house of cards they'd built. Thirty years, and she could taste the calamari and the baklava on the Greek island where she'd disappeared for a while. Another ten years, and she was standing in the radio studio at four in the morning again.

Lillian stared through her kitchen window to the palm tree just outside, then let her gaze go vague. She saw the tiny tables crowded into the coffee house on Yonge Street, smelled the haunting cigarettes, and listened to the acoustic guitars. She recognized everyone—and she recognized no one. They were dogs in siesta, dead to the world and to her mind.

Let them rest and let the drama end.

Carl whined at the door and she snapped out of it. It was time to get him out for his exercise and time for her to get her head back into the 21st century.

CHAPTER 30

LILLIAN BUSTLED AROUND THE KITCHEN of the party room, checking the platters of hors d'oeuvres and the drinks glasses. She had no idea how many people would show up, but she was ready for anything.

For a week now, she'd been feeling nothing but gratitude for the help that everyone had given her. The people at the newspaper, the people in the condo building, the people at Doc Rosenthal's office and at the dog park— Chelan was right. It was better to face the world with all those friends alongside.

And Donovan was right. Being retired was a concept from the past.

So, she'd booked the condo party room and invited everyone who'd helped her since the day her house burned.

The hallway door opened and she turned to find Sam standing there, a bottle of something in his hand.

"Last time I saw that hand, there were flowers in it," Lillian said, with a smile and an outstretched one of her own, to take the bottle.

"That's what I was taught," he said. "Never show up at a party empty-handed. Is there anything I can do to help you get ready?"

Lillian was about to brush him off with the usual automatic response, and then she remembered the air conditioning. The system had been running poorly since she'd come in, and the room felt too warm.

"Would you mind taking a look at the temperature thing-ey?" she asked. "I don't think the AC is working properly."

"The temperature thing-ey?"

"Oh, you know what I mean," she said with a smile.

He clearly did, and went off to the hallway to take a look at the thermostat.

The door opened again.

"Tracey, hi!"

"Hi, yourself. I thought I'd get here first. Give you a little help, getting ready."

"Thanks, but you can't. Sam Gavigan is already here."

Tracey raised an eyebrow. "Aha! Good for him . . . and for you. Where should I put these?" She didn't wait for an answer but carried her two charcuterie boards into the kitchen.

Over the next half hour, Lillian had a steady stream of arrivals. Doris and Dwayne, still squabbling, with Joyce beside them, looking amused. Bobby Murrow, dressed in his best Hawaiian shirt. Angela and Carrie from the newspaper, looking a little uncomfortable but curious about who else might be at this party. Lillian was actually a little surprised that they'd decided to attend, but maybe it was far too early to assess relationships.

"Excuse me?"

She turned to see a man in a delivery-guy uniform, with a florist's label on one pocket, holding a tall plant in an adobe pot.

"I'm looking for a Lillian Howe?"

"That's me," Lillian said. "What a gorgeous plant."

The man held up the pot and turned it in various directions. It had a long stalk and a flower with purple and orange blossoms.

"It's called a bird-of-paradise," the man said. "Yeah, it's very pretty."

"Stands for freedom," Kyra said. She'd just pulled open the door behind the florist delivery man. He flinched a bit at the sight of Ice Cream on the leash beside her.

"It's okay, he's friendly," she said. "I thought since this is a party celebrating the defeat of a dog killer, it might be okay to bring along our dogs." This was directed to Lillian, who nodded enthusiastically.

"Yes, of course, and so handy that it's on the main floor and it's easy to take them out, if we need to. Yes, thanks for bringing Ice Cream, Kyra. I might just slip upstairs to get Carl, after a while."

She took the plant from the delivery man. "Thanks very much."

"Stunning flower," Sam said. "Air conditioning's back to normal. Can I take that from you and put it over there on a table?"

Lillian handed the bird-of-paradise to him and smiled as he went. She turned back to see the delivery man on his way out and Tracey, back from the kitchen. "Nice guy," she commented.

Lillian was pretty sure she was talking about Sam. "Yes, he is."

"Did he send you the flower?"

"My guess is that it came from my grandson."

"Any more news about the Nugents?" Tracey asked.

"I've been wondering the same thing myself," Bobby said as he approached, beer in hand.

"The deputy sheriff rang me up this morning and told me Gerald is going to be charged with animal cruelty. Riccardo is up on arson charges and possibly something else, if they make a solid connection between my car problem and me ending up in the hospital."

"What about Barbara?"

"Again, same question," Bobby said. "What happens to Barbara has a lot of impact on us at the newspaper."

"Again, Burtt said they're still thinking everything over. Technically, I'm guessing she didn't really do anything to be charged for. She stole her husband's dog, temporarily. Then put him back in a place he'd be sure to be found."

"Gerald would probably argue that she provoked him into doing what he did."

"He'd be wrong," Lillian said. "I happen to believe we're all responsible for our own choices and actions. She can provoke all day, if she wants. He still shouldn't take action . . . other than leaving, maybe. But killing Turtle? No amount of provocation justified that."

After they had all insisted on helping her to clean up and then gone home, Lillian sat outside on one of the benches in the flower garden with Carl curled up at her feet.

"You like it here, don't you, boy?" she asked. "Well, I do, too. Maybe we'll stay."

WHAT'S NEXT FOR THE MEDIA WOMEN?

Lillian Howe takes her column *Oldish in South Florida* to a Miami newspaper

Nevada Leacock digs into book world in New York

and

Chelan Montgomery follows a trail of corruption to uncover a crime on social media, in Book Four of the Media Mysteries series.

COMING SOON—Spring 2022

Kangaroo Court

Why is a social media influencer trying to ruin the reputations of a famous athlete and a struggling politician?

If you enjoyed *Sleeping Dogs Lie,* please leave a rating and a review. It really does help other readers find Gail's books.

We'd love to have you join our newsletter group. You can sign up at the WindWord Group publisher website here or at Gail's website here . We'll send you a short story and updates when there are new books, special pricing, or giveaways.

ABOUT THE AUTHOR

Gail Hulnick is a former journalist and broadcaster. She is the host of the podcast *Brainwave*, based in south Florida, where she lives and works with her husband. The award-winning author of six novels, five travel memoirs, and a collection of short stories, she is currently working on Book 4 of the Media Mysteries series.